Then Begins a Jou

by

Philip W Lawrence

Books by PW Lawrence

Looking on Darkness   Book 1 Detective Toni Webb

The Blind do See   Book 2 Detective Toni Webb

Then Begins a Journey   Book 3 Detective Toni Webb

No Quiet Find   Book 4 Detective Toni Webb
(Due out 2020)

The Eight   The life of an English boy
(Book in process don't hold
your breath lots to do)

With thanks to my family and friends for their comments and the time they gave to read my work.

To Sanjay Gupta who inspired me to write, although I did not realize how much time it took, not the writing, that came fairly quickly, but in my personal editing and the constant adjustments needed to make everything fit together, which it never really does.

I like spell-checking software; my dyslexic fingers never match my thought's, or it is the other way around?

To my lovely Margaret who allowed me the space and time, when time is now so precious.

All the locations in this story are based on real places I know. The characters and plot in this tale however are fictional; any similarity to real persons or events is purely coincidental.

I still do not believe in coincidences.

Then Begins a Journey

For my children
Daisy Paul and Jason

Weary with toil, I haste me to my bed,
The dear repose for limbs with travel tired;
But then begins a journey in my head,
To work my mind, when body's work's expired:
For then my thoughts, from far where I abide,
Intend a zealous pilgrimage to thee,
And keep my drooping eyelids open wide,
Looking on darkness which the blind do see:
Save that my soul's imaginary sight
Presents thy shadow to my sightless view
Which like a jewel hung in ghastly night
Makes black night beauteous, and her old face new.
Lo thus by day my limbs, by night my mind
For the, and for myself, no quiet find.

Shakespeare's Sonnet Number 27

Prologue

He was cold and a little out of breath it was very dark, no matter how he strained he could see nothing. He instinctively knew there was nothing wrong with his eyes, it was just very black. He was lying on his back, his hands by his sides felt the softness of the material on which he was laying. He sat up and turned over to be on his knees. His head spinning with the motion made him pause for a moment delaying his intention to stand. He leaned back sitting on his heels waiting for some slither of light to tell him where he might be and for his head to clear. His lips were so dry they almost stuck together, he would like to drink but had no idea how.

He felt very strange knowing it was not normal to be like this, perhaps it was a dream, but it did not seem that way, he was not worried which felt wrong. He reached out with his hands and spun to the left and right trying to contact something to guide him in this perpetual darkness, to his right his fingers brushed a chilled metallic like surface, he slowly stood with his hands in contact with this wall of iron. Once standing he could feel the softness give a little under his stockinged feet. Where were his trainers? He moved hand over hand along the cold, hard sheet of metal, step by step feeling his way with outstretched fingers, he came to the edge of the thin mattress in three short strides and to a corner in two more. He turned and followed the wall three more steps to the next corner. A seat of some kind blocked his path along the wall, it seemed familiar. He continued round the rest of the tiny room back to the mattress. The walls were smooth with no breaks or signs of a door. He reached up and could just touch a ceiling on tiptoes. The room was three steps wide and five long.

He couldn't understand why he was not in a panic; being locked in a small dark box of a room, with no idea how he got there, was not scaring him in the least. Kenneth was not a timid boy however this abnormal frightening situation should have stimulated some emotion, but he felt nothing. He moved around the room again, more slowly and carefully, he discovered the seat had a lid, he lifted it and the sudden smell of his stale urine shook his mind back in time, inducing the memory of its use; he had been here a while but for how long he could not remember. He recalled   there had been a light from above, why was it not working now?

He continued to feel his way round finding a very fine crack at one end of this steel cell; he traced the line with his fingers, making him aware of an opening of some kind. He knew it was there he had a vison of his stepping through the small gap. His tiny fists hammered on this semblance of a door, without any real conviction, just to see if anything would happen; nothing did. He kicked something with his unshod foot, he bent down to find a plastic cup on its side, familiar but empty. A vague thought he had been here for many days; or even weeks persisted; the passage of time eluded him. Fleeting flashes of memory impinged on his fragile mind; the bed in a van, a cheese sandwich, sweet lemonade, needles full of blood and cold-water showers went as quickly as they came.

His breath was coming in short bursts now and his thirst was ever more demanding, tiredness overtook him as he returned to the mattress and sat leaning against the cool wall trying to remember what had happened. Breathing was becoming difficult, both arms raised involuntarily his hands began to flap like a fledgling testing its feathers for the first time. He lay on his side nauseous and dizzy, drifting into an unnatural sleep.

Mummy was making him lunch, what was taking her so long, he wanted to eat quickly then go back out to play again before it was time for bed.

He woke with a start from coughing, his throat was so dry, lips swollen and cracked; his tongue clung to the roof of his mouth, he pulled at it with his fingers so it stuck out over his lower teeth. Now gasping in lungs-full of stale air, each breath triggering the demand for more and more, he was panting like an overheated dog, his whole body felt drained he could hardly move. The pain across his chest grew like an ever tightening band as his eyes began to see a feint glow in the distance, had someone opened the door and let in this welcome sensation, this light of salvation. He could not see anyone and the glimmer began to fade as the pain overwhelmed his whole being. He cried without tears.

His arms and legs began shaking out of control, convulsions gripped his whole body for a few moments then ceased abruptly; all was calm. He felt relaxed now the pain had gone, he didn't need to breathe anymore, no more of this foul and poisoned air entered his already carbon dioxide saturated lungs.

Mummy was at the door calling him to come to her, he could see her smiling face shrouded in a halo of white light shining through the black.

"I am here Mummy; wait for me I'm coming home".
Kenneth stepped into the light.

Chapter 1

The boys were running with a joy in their steps, nearly there, can't wait. The sunny Autumn start promised them a warm rain free day to come. They were both thinking the same, straining to attain their imminent arrival at the show. They had taken the train from Basingstoke to Reading West, the sports stadium their destination. The ground being some way from the station, they had allowed a half hour extra to walk there before it opened, but impatience stimulated them to run.

The vintage car show had been in their sights for weeks, now the long-anticipated Saturday had finally come. The entrance was awash with people waiting for the gates to open, there were no orderly queues, so the boys slowed to a walk looking for a way to wheedle their way near the front. Most of the crowd were men or boys, with just one or two girls on their own and a few girlfriends or wives, who had been persuaded to come along, hanging tightly onto the arms of their partners, fearful they may become separated in the crush.

"This way Jerry".

Michael grabbed his friend's arm and led him to the far edge of the huddle against the heavy wire fence.

"We can work our way along here and get closer to the front".

Jerry followed his pal as he always did, Michael was the leader of this inseparable pair. There was still ten minutes before the gates were due to open. They clutched their entrance tickets in their hands, the ones Michael's Dad had bought for them online some time before; this meant they would not have to queue up to get in. They squeezed along the fence a few steps at a time moving ever nearer to the gate. One or two objections from others as impatient to enter as our boys, the words of admonishment were ignored by Michael, Jerry following on, his head down, not wishing to offend or lose touch.

They managed to get within thirty feet of the gates before the dense throng, now tightly packed, halted their progress. Once the gates opened the compressed group rapidly expanded into a wide-open area of the ground's approach, with nearly everyone moving towards the ticket office in a mobile unit just inside the entrance, leaving the boys free from the crush. They ran by this queue and the adjacent fast food van, up the steps to the short queue at the turnstiles, the pre-purchased tickets allowing them to enter through into the foyer of the stadium complex with little delay. The indelible stamp on their back of their hands assuring them of a re-entry if they came out to use the mobile catering and extra toilet facilities which were situated outside the main area of the show.

A multitude of stalls were packed inside selling every conceivable spare and add-on for all the wonderful cars of yesteryear. They would come back to mull over these later, but immediately headed out through the wide-open doors onto the concourse itself. They were in heaven, dozens of cars were laid out before them, all grouped together by make and model. They stopped, looking from left to right trying to spot the areas where their favourites were allocated. Jerry nudged Michael in the ribs to gain his attention as he stood open mouthed scanning left and right undecided which way to go.

"Come on Mike lets go down".

"Okay Jerry, I was just looking for the Jags, I want to see them first".

"We can work our way along, we'll come across them soon enough".

Jerry didn't have the need to see any car in particular he liked them all, although his favourite was the MGA. He knew Mike loved the old E type Jaguars and the XJS with their massive V twelve engines and would want to seek them out a soon as possible.

Jerry was more patient than Michael so allowed his friend to rush him along the lines of cars looking for the Jaguar stand. Rewards a plenty greeted their hungry eyes as they hurried through the paraded old cars restored by their competitive owners to levels of finish like new and beyond. The organizer had the cars laid out in alphabetical order the stand they sought was roughly in the middle so came across it almost straight away. The Jaguar site was not a disappointment to Michael with a full range of models, a few XKs, XJs of all types and four E types to die for and a very rare D type.

The star for him was the red and black XJS with its bonnet open revealing a V12 masterpiece that shone like a jewel. The proud owner was very wary at first when Mike stuck his head under the bonnet, a little too close for his liking, but Mike's tirade of queries and obvious knowledge of the mark soon alleviated the owner's trepidation as he fired question after question about the history and the work undertaken to get it to its current pristine condition. Jerry wandered off a little looking at the other Jaguar models nearby knowing his friend would be occupied for some time.

"Just going to look round a bit Mike, wait here for me I'll be back in ten minutes or so".

Mike showed a thumbs up of acknowledgement and a wave as Jerry moved off. Jerry found the MG stand almost next to the Jaguars just Lagonda and Morris in between; he immediately looked out for the MGA. There was only one amongst a large number of MGBs and some of the earlier TCs and the like. The red body of this little beauty was more orange than the bold deeper red of the Jag that Mike was drooling over. The soft top was down so Jerry could see inside with its red piped rust brown leather seats and chromed instruments nestled discreetly in the pale wood dash.

"Want to sit inside lad"?

A big man with a bald head came up behind Jerry as he was peering at the wood and leather headed gear lever, set in its chrome plated gate. He turned quickly surprised at the offer.

"Can I"?

"Of course, jump in".

The man leant across Jerry and opened the driver's door; Jerry hesitated, checking his trainers for mud and dirt, he slipped them off.

"Go on I won't bite and don't worry, there is a bag for your shoes in the back. The mats are covered in plastic anyway and can be cleaned if they get a little dirty".

The hesitation was momentary and seconds later Jerry popped his shoes in the Tesco bag he was offered and found himself in the seat with his hand clutching the hand-made wood and alloy steering wheel, his stockinged feet resting on the pedals. The man climbed in beside him. He checked the gear was in neutral and the hand brake was on. He inserted and turned the ignition key then pressed the starter button. The engine sprang into life with a mild backfire followed by a continuous purr. Jerry's heart jumped a few beats.

"Wow"!

"Don't touch the gear lever just dab the throttle a bit with your right foot".

Jerry did as he was told in a bit of a dream state, as soon as he hit the throttle the purr became a roar which he felt deep in his stomach, the body of the car rocked as the sudden torque wrestled with the rubber engine mounts. He dabbed his foot again with the same effect. He could have sat there all day doing this, but the man reached across and switched off the ignition.

"There how was that then young man"?

"Fantastic Mister, magic. Thanks".

"Good, okay, now out you get, or I'll have a queue soon".

"Can I look under the bonnet please"?

"Not now lad, I will be driving round the track soon for the presentation parade and want to keep the engine bay pristine ready for the inspection. There's a prize for the best car. Come back after and you can have a good look then, I might even take you for a real spin".

"Thanks again mister, I'll come back later. I'll watch out for you on the track, I hope you win".

Jerry squeezed his trainers back on without undoing the laces and almost ran back to the Jaguar stand straining to tell Mike what had just happened. He wasn't there; the red and black XJS had gone too. Jerry looked round but couldn't see the car anywhere, perhaps it had gone to be part of the parade and Mike had followed. He wasn't tall enough to see beyond the cars in his immediate vicinity and as the show had filled considerably there were now many bodies blocking his view and path. Jerry moved back to the steps of the foyer and climbed up to get a better view. At the top he turned and was just able to see the area where the parading cars were beginning to file out onto the track. A man was announcing the event over the public address system. He strained to see if his friend was down by the fence overlooking the cars as they moved out. The announcer began to describe the first car.

"A fine Alvis of 1956....".

The announcer went on, but Jerry did not listen, he had spotted the Jag in line waiting to come out and was on his way down the steps certain Mike would be nearby. He would give him an earful for going off like that.

He reached the temporary tape and pole fence right opposite where the Jaguar was just moving into line, but there was no sign of Mike. He ducked under the tape and moved up to the window of the Jaguar and tapped on the glass. The man inside shooed him away, but Jerry insisted by tapping even harder.

"What the hell do you want? Move away its dangerous".

"Please mister have you seen my friend he was with you when we first came, you were answering all his questions, you must have seen where he went"?

"Sorry young man I have to move now, I do remember him though a real expert he said he would come back after the parade, but I have no idea where your friend went".

The man turned away, the car began to move off and the window closed forcing Jerry to step away. He ducked back under the fence and made his way back to the Jaguar stand just in case he had missed him perhaps looking over one of the E types. He weaved his way through all the cars, Mike was nowhere to be seen at the Jaguar stand.

Jerry moved back to the MG stand in case Mike had gone to look for him there. The man with the MGA was still in the parade, a few people were looking at the other models on display but no sign of Mike, he was at a loss Jerry wondered where his friend could have gone, the toilet maybe, he would go back to the Jaguar stand and wait.

He was annoyed Mike had gone off and left him; he felt in his pocket for the sandwiches his Mum had given him. She had packed them along with an apple and a plastic water bottle in a bag. He didn't want to be lumbered with the bag so had wedged the pack into the pocket of his jacket; he'd already shared the apple and the water with Mike disposing of the empty bottle and bag on the train journey. Cheese and pickle, no surprise, his Mum was very predictable, he leaned against the rail of a section of a permanent fence adjacent to the stand and munched away at his lunch even though it was way too early. He ate half the sandwich, stuffing the remainder back in his pocket for later.

His anger slowly changed to concern, every minute that passed Jerry became more and more anxious; there was nowhere to sit, his legs were beginning to ache from standing in one place all the time. After an hour the red and black XJS returned to its position. Jerry moved over to the man to ask again if he had seen Mike.

"Sorry young fellow, I left him here when I went to the parade, I haven't seen him since. He has probably wandered off and forgotten the time, I suggest you go to the announcer's or security office they may be able to put out a call for him to meet you there".

Jerry thanked him and decided to go back to the MG stand once more. The MGA had returned, Jerry went over to ask if he had seen Mike.

"Hello there, nice to see you again, want to have a look inside the engine bay eh"?

"Thank you, sir, but not now I have lost my friend Michael and don't know what to do, you haven't seen him have you perhaps looking for me"?

'Well no, I have only just got back what does he look like"?

Jerry described Mike short black hair same height as him, jeans, striped blue and white trainers, white T shirt and a short blue hoodie jacket. Jerry was dressed almost the same, except his jacket was a dark brown.

"I don't recall anyone like that, why don't you go to the security office they may be able to help, if he turns up, I will send him there. Come back when you have found him if you can".

Jerry decided to follow this advice even though he knew Mike would not just wander off without him. The announcer's office was right at the top of the main stand with a glass window giving a complete view of the whole show, although too far away to be able to identify any individual from the crowd. Jerry knocked on the door and explained his predicament. The man behind the microphone would not normally get involved but sensed Jerry's desperation so agreed to help.

"This is a security announcement, would Michael Soper please come to the security office where his friend Jerry will be waiting for him, thank you".

The man repeated the announcement and said he would do it again in ten minutes, telling Jerry to go down to security and wait as he was sure Mike would hear the call and go there right away.

The security office was close to the entrance where two men in yellow jackets, with a security emblem on the back, were sitting.

Jerry went and knocked on the glass door, the one nearest rose and opened the door.

"What can I do for you young man"?

"I want to wait for my friend he has got lost".

"Ah, the announcement eh"?

"Yes sir".

"Come in sit there, I expect your mate won't be too long".

Ten minutes went by, nothing, a few minutes later the announcer repeated the message. Another ten minutes and still no response from Mike. The security man then questioned Jerry more closely about how they had become separated finally asking for a description of Mike. Using his radio, he spoke giving a description of Mike requesting those officers around the grounds with receivers keep a look out for this missing boy. He then switched channels and spoke to the announcer.

Another announcement for Mike to come to the office or report to any security officer in the yellow jackets was made and repeated five minutes later.

Still no response. Jerry wanted to call home, but Mike had the mobile and most of their money. Jerry only had his return train ticket half a sandwich and two pounds his Mum had given him, intended for an extra drink at lunch, the time for which had come and gone.

''Please Sir can I use your phone, I want to call my Mum''?

"Of course, but give it another ten minutes before you call, you don't want to worry her unduly just in case your mate is on his way here now. Want a drink?"

Jerry nodded; the officer threw him a can of coke; not a drink his Mum let him have but he was dry as a bone so accepted thankfully. He was glad to wait a little longer as he didn't want to get his pal in trouble, for he knew his Mum would call Mr. Soper which would be big trouble for Mike. Another ten minutes went by, Jerry scanned the concourse his now tearful eyes training for a glimpse of Mikes blue jacket.

"Where are you Mike"?

Jerry yelled across the heads of the crowd.

NOTHING.

Chapter 2

It was very quiet the mist shrouded the park's grass verges hiding the Autumn leaves carpeting the ground under the trees. The stillness had left the gold and brown remnants of the Summer accumulating where they dropped yet to be scattered by the wild wintery winds soon to come. The boy looked like he was waking from a sleep, sheltering under the branches, propped against the main trunk of the old oak. His legs were lightly covered by the few leaves that had fallen during the night, his arms by his side palms on the ground as if preparing to push himself up. His head was bent forward eyes open staring unseeing at his stockinged feet. His skin was white and tight as parchment paper; very cold.

Doctor Debbie Taylor looked at this lad with sadness in her heart. A child of twelve or thirteen should never end their lives so early, let alone by the hand of another. She could not rule out natural causes, but the body looked wrong, she was sure he had died elsewhere and been posed against this old oak, for a reason she could not yet fathom.

She took photos from all angles before moving him. His limbs were loose, rigour was long passed, an unresolved question in her mind. There were no obvious signs of trauma anywhere visible. She lifted him forward and opened his blue jacket and lifted his T-shirt, the back was clear of wounds, no damage marks of any kind. His arms and hands were clean just a black ink smudge on the back of his right hand some faded indistinct writing, even the palms resting on the ground had picked up very little debris. His feet were clean; just a few small soil particles had stuck to his socks.

The body sheet had been laid out next to him, she rolled him away from the tree onto the plastic, one of the SOCOs bagged his outer clothes as she took them off, revealing an undamaged torso, removing his jeans revealed his legs the same. Blood had settled in his back and buttocks indicating he had been on his back for a period immediately after his death. She noted no shoes or underpants on or near the body. There was only a screwed-up handkerchief in one jeans pocket, a five-pound note and a few small coins, all less than ten pounds, however nothing to identify him. No idea of how he may have died came to her mind at this time; it would need an autopsy to reveal the cause.

She probed the liver, temperature just a single degree above a cold ten degree ambient, so he had been dead some considerable time, could even be longer than a day. More reason to think he did not die here. He was not here at eight last night when the park closed, the keeper was certain as he had passed this very spot on his way out of the park at that time. The same keeper had found him when he opened the gates at seven this morning. Someone had carried him to the park after dark and laid his body against the tree. A lot of trouble carrying and posing the body, there must be a reason for disposing of him here.

Detective Inspector Jonny Musgrove was talking to the park keeper, glancing occasionally at pathologist Debbie Taylor and the forensic guys as they went about their work.

"You know officer this is the second one, two years ago the man on the seat and now this young fellow, in all my years nothing like it before. This has been a quiet place you know just kiddies and their mums on the swings, the early morning dog walkers and the old folks who come and sit when it's sunny".

"I'm sorry you had to see this Mr. Baker, but I believe you discovered the body".

"Yes, he was here when I opened up, I come in through the lower gate at seven and walk by this tree every morning, the same on the way out every evening, he certainly wasn't there last night. I thought he was just asleep, he seemed to move when I came towards him, I thought he was going to get up, well it seemed like it. I asked him what he was doing but of course he didn't answer".

"Did you touch him"?

"Oh no Sir, as I got closer, I saw he was not moving and his eyes were open staring like, I felt he was dead".

"What made you think that"?

"I just did, you know, look at his eyes, no light in them. I phoned you lot and waited like before".

"Did you see anyone or anything unusual on your way in this morning"?

"No, it was just an ordinary day, Jimmy was waiting at the gate with Felicity as always, we came in together, he went around the lower path, and I came up the hill towards my tool shed when I saw him sitting there".

"Who is Jimmy and Felicity"?

"He comes every morning to walk her you see, he lives over by the lower gate, I don't know the number it's the house with the dark red door. He may not be back yet; he usually goes out by the top gate and into town. Bloody hell, he won't be able to get out, I forgot I haven't been up to unlock that gate yet; I must go and unlock it and the other one by the car park".

He started to move away but Jonny took his arm.

"Please don't do that sir I need to keep the park closed for the time being, my officers will man the bottom gate; where will Jimmy go when he finds the top gate closed and by the way what is his sir name"?

"Sorry I only know him as Jimmy. He will probably go to my hut first and then back this way by the top path. He should have been here by now though, so perhaps he went back the way he came and left by the bottom gate before you got here, I didn't notice him, sorry".

Thank you, Mr. Baker, go to your hut for now and if you see Jimmy please tell him to come here, I will look for you there to let you know if and when you can open the park".

Jonny noticed the pathologist appeared to have finished so he moved over towards the scene and waited outside the tape for her to come to him.

"Doctor Taylor what do you have for me"?

"Hello detective Musgrove, not too much, no cause of death or anything to identify him at the moment, a white boy aged about twelve, been dead at least twenty hours probably more, difficult to say exactly rigor has passed but in a young boy with small muscle mass it may not necessarily have been severe, no signs of trauma, I need the autopsy to confirm time and cause of death. I don't think he died here though, his body was lying flat on his back for a while after he died and was moved some time later and staged in his current position. No sign of his shoes or underwear nearby, they are not on the body. I can't say at the moment if he was wearing underpants at the time or before his demise; unusual for a young boy not to do so. His missing shoes are a mystery too. Scene of crime officers have finished here so come and see before we move him".

Jonny ducked under the tape and looked down on the face of a young child now lying on the plastic sheet awaiting transportation. He shuddered with the thought he would soon be informing a mother with the tragic news of this shocking event. He had been able, over time, to detach his mind from fearing the dead but being the deliverer of the news to a family of their loved one's demise he still found terrifying. A twisted knot would tighten in his stomach waiting for the fleeting moment of disbelief to pass before the wail of grief would be thrown at him like a wave from hell. The cliché of words he uttered would never dispel the void he had opened in their hearts. Each time he was the unwelcome messenger carrying the unwanted news, he died a little inside.

He shook of his morbid reverie deciding to call DCI Toni Webb; 'she would want to know about this'.

"Jonny here Ma'am, I thought you should know we have the body of a boy about twelve years old found in the park south of town. No obvious cause of death but still suspicious as the pathologist thinks the body has been moved from where he originally died. No ID as yet, I'll get Constable Busion to check on missing persons. There were no witnesses as such, just the park keeper who found the body and a dog walker I still have to find and interview, I'll also collect any CCTV footage, Mel is organizing the door to door on both sides of the park I'll be back soon as I finish up here".

"Thanks for letting me know, to save you a call I'll tell Compton to carry out the missing person search. You'll be SIO for this one, Jonny; I'll have a couple of extra uniforms stay on, you will need them I would think. Let me know if you need more when you get back".

Jonny Musgrove walked down the sloping pathway to the lower gate to try and find the dog walker. The uniforms would be here soon who would carry out the usual door to door, but he wanted to speak to 'Jimmy' whilst his memory was fresh. The red door was obvious as the only one anywhere near the gate, he knocked and waited, no answer; he turned to leave when an elderly man came hurrying along the road towards him, his small dog's legs scurrying in an effort to keep up with his master.

"Hang on young man I'm coming".

"Jimmy"?

"Yes that's me Jim Sage; what's going on in the park; you a copper eh"?

"Yes Sir I'm Detective Inspector Musgrove". Showing his warrant card. "I need to ask you a few questions if you don't mind".

"Oh dear, I knew something was up when I found the top gate shut and Mr Baker was nowhere to be seen. Wait a second I'll open the door".

He fiddled with his keys pushed through the door letting the dog off his lead all in one practiced movement. The dog ran down the hallway into the open plan kitchen.

"Felicity likes a drink after our walks, creatures of habit aren't we all. Come in come in please".

"Thank you sir".

Jonny followed Sage into a modernised spacious open living space who offered him a chair at the dining table by the front window.

"Can I get you a drink, tea coffee "?

Jonny gained the impression that James Sage was looking for a bit of company other than Felicity, so accepted his offer as he might be more forthcoming if he was not rushed.

"That's kind, a black coffee two sugars would be fine thank you".

The kitchen was almost part of the living area separated only by a long low work unit. Whoever was in the kitchen could remain part of whatever was going on elsewhere. Designed to suit a young person's lifestyle rather than for this elderly man. He could see Sage busy with the makings, so looked out the window noting that he had a good view of the park gate, 'maybe he saw or heard something, we'll soon know'. Jimmy set two cups on the table and sat opposite Jonny.

"Well fire away"!

"I understand you entered the park with the keeper first thing, where did you go"?

"Just the usual, Baker goes to the left and I go right, habit like I said; anyway I got to the top gate in slow time she likes to sniff around and have a pee, anyway when I got to the top gate it was shut. I usually see Cyril, Mr Baker, that is, up there by the row of benches; he picks up the litter blown in overnight, funny thing it always seem to accumulate under those seats. When he wasn't there I went to his hut, not there either, so I went back to the top again then went down the way I came in out the bottom gate turned left to give Felicity a bit of a run, not our usual route, we normally go out the top gate and into town; anyway I was on my way back to speak to Cyril when I saw you at my door, and there you have it".

"Did you see anyone new or anything unusual"?

"No, the lady who was waiting to come in at the top is always there I don't know her name though, I didn't see anyone else, the park is quiet at that time".

"What about the evening before when you were home"?

"Yes, I don't go out in the dark, well not often, I watched TV till eleven then I went to bed".

"Did you hear or see anything different"?

"Come to think of it I was reading in bed when I heard a car pull up, I thought it was outside my house, when I looked it was a small white van on the other side. There was a man looked like he was dumping rubbish over the fence, I was going to take his number but I couldn't see it in the dark and I wasn't going to go out and confront him either not at that time of night. I went back to bed. About ten minutes later I heard him drive away. I was going to tell Cyril in the morning but forgot all about it till you asked me".

"What time was this"?

"I don't really know, well after twelve I would think; I read most nights for an hour or so before I go to sleep".

"Would you recognise the man if you saw him again"?

"Oh no, I only saw his back, it was too dark to see much, no street lighting along this bit of road".

"Thank you for your help Jimmy. Here is my card give me a call if you remember anything else. By the way some uniformed constables will be canvassing the street later today, they won't know I've been so may call on you again".

"That's alright, you still haven't told me what has happened".

"I'm sorry to say Mr. Baker found the body of a young boy in the park this morning".

"Oh my, who is he, how did he die, was he murdered"?

"We don't know at this stage, there are no visible injuries; I'm sorry Jimmy I can't tell you anything more".

"It could have been the man I saw last night; am I glad I didn't go out he may have killed me too".

"Mr. Sage please don't get carried away I'm sure the man you saw probably had nothing to do with it, most likely the boy is a runaway who simply died of exposure, that happens much more often than you would think. Violent death is very rare. In any case I would like you to keep this to yourself, you don't want to upset your neighbours unnecessarily".

Jonny left hoping his white lie would quell the spread of panic from rumours that a child murderer was on the loose would generate. He was almost certain the man Jimmy Sage saw had indeed dumped the body of this child, pity there was no chance of him identifying the man or his van.

Constable Compton Busion laid a printout copy of the missing person report on DCI Toni Webb's desk at the same time as her verbal one.

"A twelve-year-old boy went missing Saturday afternoon, Ma'am, from a car show in Reading, he lives in Hook. His parents reported him missing the same evening his name is Michael Soper. The Reading Police took the report. He's the only one who fits".

"Thank you, Compton, give a copy to DI Musgrove when he comes in, you'd better open a murder file too by the look of it, oh and ask him to come and see me".

"Yes Ma'am".

The report had little information, a description of what he was wearing and a photograph of questionable quality. There was no physical description not even the colour of his hair or eyes. What were the Reading officers thinking they must have taken more information than was in this file, most likely the officer who interviewed the parents had no opportunity to write it up yet; she would ask Compton to get an update. A suspicious death was bad enough, but that of a child moved Toni in more ways than one. Having miscarried a baby many years before she knew the pain of losing a child. Her physical problem left her in a childless marriage which ended in divorce. The news reminded her of the hurt, not just for the victim, but for the family life will never be the same again. Child death more often than not caused a breakup of the parents, acute psychological damage to siblings with few who ever recovered enough to have a normal life.

Toni vowed whoever was responsible for this young boy's death, would be pursued to the end; then begins a journey, a journey for justice.

Chapter 3

The squad room was full, and very noisy, even some officers from traffic were there, news travelled fast in this small town nick. Two detectives from Reading were standing next to Detective Chief Inspector Toni Webb. Everyone at the station wanted to see this perpetrator brought down.

Toni clapped her hands together; two loud snaps caught everyone's attention and reduced the noise level to a potent buzz.

"Quiet there, come to order please".

Her louder than normal voice brought the room to a hush ready for Toni to open the meeting.

"Nice to see so many officers present, I would usually say some of you shouldn't really be here and you probably have something better to do, but this time I don't feel it is appropriate. The more minds brought to bear on this case the better. There are no secrets here no demarcation of tasks, anyone of you could see or hear something or have an idea that will help solve this crime".

She turned and stepped back allowing the two Reading policemen centre stage.

"Let me introduce DS Perry Lake and PC Mark Jacobs from Reading; welcome to Basingstoke and thank you for coming".

The visiting officers each raised their arm in turn at Toni's introduction; she then continued.

"The boy Michael Soper, a local lad from Hook, went missing from a car show at Reading sports arena. The Reading police were called in by the security guards at the show when his friend Jerry Franks lost touch with him in unusual circumstances. I'll leave DS Lake to report".

"Thank you, Ma'am we hope we can help. We were called to the sports ground by their head security officer who feared a young boy had been abducted. Michael Soper and his friend Jerry Franks had been separated and although Jerry had arranged to meet his friend at the Jaguar stand, he was nowhere to be found. Jerry asked security for help. Announcements were made with no response.

They were not too worried at this stage, but all the security personnel were asked to look out for him. They discovered a pair of trainers, which Jerry identified as belonging to Michael, on the ground next to a vacant space where one of the Jaguar cars had been parked earlier. At that point we were called in".

Toni now stepped forward and spoke.

"Young Jerry, in the meantime had called his mother who in turn contacted Michael's parents. Mr. Soper then set off in his car to Reading along with Mrs. Franks. At that stage we at Basingstoke had not been called in as the original missing person report had been filed at Reading. Please go on".

Toni nodded at PC Jacobs to continue. Jacobs moved to the front and referred to his notebook, looking a little nervous he began.

"I was called to the show ground at fourteen hundred on Saturday fourth October to investigate a possible missing person. I spoke to the boy Jerry Franks who explained the last time he saw Michael he was talking to a car exhibitor about his car, a red Jaguar XJS. Jerry asked Michael to wait for him as he was going to look at the MG stand for a few minutes. When he got back his friend was gone and so was the Jaguar. I checked with the organizer and interviewed the Jaguar owner, a Mr. Henry Brody, he had spoken to the boy about his car for a short while and then moved his car away from the stand to the join the parade leaving Michael at the stand. He said he had not seen him again however he did have contact with Jerry a little later who came looking for his friend at the parade and again back at the stand.

Jerry said he wasn't gone long, ten or fifteen minutes at the most. He searched the stand and the parade area and the MG stand and finally went to security for their help. It was only when they found his shoes that they were really concerned and called us in. The six security guards, myself and my partner Constable Weir did a sweep search of the grounds and other areas of the complex with no result, I came to the conclusion Michael had left the site. I then reported to the station I feared Michael had either been forcibly abducted or coerced to leave. Detective Sergeant Lake arrived at fifteen fifty-seven to take over the investigation".

"Thank you, Constable". Toni again indicated for the Sergeant to continue.

"My arrival coincided with that of Mr. Soper and Mrs. Franks, I questioned Jerry in depth with his mother present but only came to the same conclusion as Constable Jacobs, because of the shoes it was unlikely he had left the ground on foot. Jerry explained to me some owners loved to show off their cars and often allowed you to sit in them, it was a recognized common courtesy to remove your footwear when doing so.

I obtained a list of the exhibitors from the organizers and went to the Jaguar stand. There was one car missing, a 1966 dark green Jaguar XJ6 registration number MYX 188D entered by a Joel Jones. I questioned the other owners in the immediate vicinity, one remembered the car, notably because he had a similar model, but never saw the driver. He did notice the car was missing but assumed it had gone to the parade. The organizer informed me this car had not been selected for the parade so had no reason to move.

The CCTV coverage is poor in the grounds where the cars were on display as it is directed at the doorways and gates. We picked up the car leaving the grounds at twelve eighteen, but the image is too far away to identify anyone in the vehicle. The driver stopped at the gate and spoke to a security guard who then let him out. I interviewed the guard at the gate who remembers the car leaving but has little recollection of the conversation or of the driver, he doesn't remember any passenger. We checked the car to find the number is in fact false, it belonged to a 1966 VW beetle that had long since been scrapped. The number was never re-issued.

Further CCTV showed the car travelling over the M4 motorway bridge at Reading heading south. After that no further contact. I questioned the owners at the MG stand but could gain no more information than we had already.

I returned to the station with both parents and Jerry Franks to take formal statements and get a detailed description and a photo of Michael. Mr. Soper refused the offer of a Family Liaison Officer and left with Mrs. Franks and her son. He has phoned me twice since then for news, I reassured him we were doing everything we could, we were up last night trawling the CCTV of every camera for a fifty-mile radius with no result. Really, we had very little to go on, one minute he was there, next he was gone. Your search of our missing persons database triggered us to contact you".

"Thank you, Sergeant, our first task is to find that car…".

Toni's mobile rang she looked to turn it off but saw it was from Detective Sergeant Mel Frazer.

"What is it Mel?"

"I'm with Mr. and Mrs. Soper Ma'am at Richmond. I brought them here to identify the body, we got it wrong it wasn't him the dead boy is not their son, they don't know this lad".

"What! It looked like him from their photo".

"I know, I know I thought so too same clothes and all, but although very similar he is definitely not Michael. We were led astray by him going missing at the right time, fitting the brief description and crap photo we had. No other local missing persons were reported".

"Then who the hell is he? Look Mel deal with the Sopers as best you can and insist Family Liaison get involved this time, they will be pretty upset. I want you back here".

She didn't want to say anything in front of the assembled officers but the lack of description in DS Lake's report had caused a serious error in identification she would have a word with him after to find out why.

"Now listen up, there has been a major development. We have made a mistake assuming the deceased was Michael Soper. The boy's body had been sent to Richmond for autopsy where Mr. and Mrs. Soper were taken by Detective Sergeant Frazer to officially identify him. It is not their son Michael; a relief for them for the moment but a massive trauma expecting to see their dead child, nevertheless an error which should not have happened. Since this was not their son they will be wondering where the hell he is? The short lived relief will again become anguish.

This goes to show we must avoid making assumptions, this one led to a family thinking their son was dead, not good. The two missing boys could be connected in some way, but it may be two separate incidents which is how we will treat it. DI Musgrove you will continue to be SIO for the dead boy, I will take on looking for the missing Michael Soper. Jonny get to it, all the usual checks we'll meet here midday tomorrow or call me if anything significant turns up to link the two and I'll do the same. One dead, one missing let's try and resolve this quickly everyone".

Toni turned to the two Reading policemen.

"Officers, this is still officially your missing person case but seeing as how the boy lives here, I would like to take over, I'll contact your Superintendent to confirm of course and thank you again for you input. I'll personally keep you in the picture".

"I'm sure that will be fine Ma'am, if anything else turns up we'll let you know".

Following thanks and the shake of hands the two made to leave.

"Before you go Sergeant can I have a word in my office it will only take a moment".

She walked out of the squad room the two Reading officers followed, once in her office Toni closed the door.

"Sorry to bring this up but I'd rather do it here than make it official. The cockup with this boy's ID has been brought about through a lack of information in your incident report Sergeant. I just heard you say that you interviewed the parents and obtained a detailed description of the boy, why was it not in the report"?

Sergeant Lake was shocked and couldn't understand what this was about; he opened his briefcase and pulled out his file.

"This is the case file Ma'am if you look you will find the detailed description is there, I have no idea what has happened".

Toni looked through the file and true enough the details were there. She opened her file to reveal the cut down version.

"It is obvious the transcription of your report that goes into the general files has been watered down, this should never happen, indeed must not happen; I have no choice I will need to take this further".

Sergeant Lake said nothing he knew she was right; he realised that something was seriously wrong at their end, he was about to apologise and say he would investigate what had happened when Constable Jacobs interceded.

"Ma'am, I think I know what has happened here".

"Well speak up who do you think is responsible for this mess".

"We all write our reports from our notebooks sometimes it is not always word for word as the notebooks are often hurriedly written so we tidy them up on our computers".

"I know all that I was a beat copper once you know, I hope you're not saying Sergeant Lake omitted to include everything".

"No, not a chance he is very thorough, it's just the station uses a civilian agency to transcribe our reports and all types of paperwork concerning a case onto the main frame manually. The officers' PCs are stand alone and incompatible with the older main frame computers. The civilian staff are not always as diligent as they should be; also there is no supervision, or post transcription checks. If an operator has only inserted part of a report when five o'clock comes around it can get closed. There is no guarantee that the same operator will be there the next day so sometimes it never gets finished. Officers tend to use print outs of their own original entries in the case files, unless they compared these to that of the main frame they would never know the difference. When other forces access the system for a report it comes from the main frame, not the officers original file".

"We have the same civilian help here but have an officer supervise and monitor their work. This appears to be a failure due to untrained outsourcing; lack of funding for modern IT rears its ugly head once again. I will bring it up at the next ACC meeting, but not specific to this incident. Thank you Constable for your timely input. I will let your Super know how helpful you have been, sorry to have kept you".

"I will find out exactly what happened when I get back and do my best to sort it, I don't have much authority but my DI will help I'm sure".

"Do your best, that's all you can, goodbye Sergeant Lane; Constable Jacobs".

Cooperation was not always forthcoming, particularly with high profile cases, but seeing as how it is now just a missing person case and not a murder, they would be more likely to let them take over. If it had been a murder they would not have let it go easily if at all.

The case of the dead boy was different, his body was found in Basingstoke, it had nothing to do with the Reading police, he hadn't been to the car show. 'Or had he' the thought suddenly sent a shiver down DCI Toni's spine.

Chapter 4

"Compton, check on missing persons for me please, look further afield this time someone somewhere must have reported a young boy as missing, call me when you have something, I'll be in my office".

Jonny Musgrove wanted answers quickly; his team were now on a different track, prematurely and wrongly thinking the lad was Michael Soper; left them with an unknown deceased boy; they needed to find out who he was as soon as possible. Constable Compton Busion was the ideal officer for that task she was the best at searching through the maze of data bases available to the police, if the youngster was reported anywhere she would find him.

The Reading Super agreed to transfer the Missing Person file over to Basingstoke, he had just said his goodbyes to Toni and disconnected; she never mentioned the problem he had with the failure of civilians in transposing their files accurately, stirring up the crap would achieve nothing until she had someone of high rank on her side.

She stood at her desk holding the silent phone to her ear knowing instinctively she had taken on much more than a simple missing persons case and was now contemplating her next move. With Jonny and his team fully immersed in the murder, she was about to become involved on the ground again and needed some help to back her pending quest. June Owen, Keith Krane, and Peter Andrews were detective constables she had worked with before. The station had plenty of good uniformed officers but were short of trained detectives. DI Harrold Davis was the only other experienced detective officer at Basingstoke however he was currently dealing with a fraud case along with Keith and Peter. June was working with DI Jonny Musgrove and DS Melanie Frazer who were a good team she would not break up. She decided Peter Andrews would help her as she needed his detective skills. Harrold could use a uniform officer if he needed to replace him. She made the call to Harrold who didn't want to lose Peter but understood her need for help and reluctantly agreed 'as if he had any choice' was his thought at the time. The fraud case was almost done, just closing stages of the investigation tidying up the evidence for the CPS so he could spare Peter Andrews easily enough. He had hoped to have had a bite at one of these new cases and resented Toni taking on the role he felt should have been his. Being the newcomer, he had not yet grasped the mindset of his senior officer and was unaware of the high regard in which she was held. He bit his tongue when speaking with her but let it be known elsewhere of his misgivings.

Toni Webb now Detective Chief Inspector had reached this position from a difficult start in life, the tragedy of a lost baby and a broken marriage. Born Antonia Abakoba in Nigeria; her once affluent parents were from the mid-west who had been at starvation point during the Biafra war. At the first opportunity the Abakoba family Joseph, Maru, Dan and the baby Toni had emigrated to England living in London initially.

Clever and hard working her parents provided young Dan and later Toni the finest education they could afford. The family eventually moved to Southampton where Toni, met and married Larry Webb. Toni fell pregnant soon after but miscarried at month five. With her loss came an unacceptable void, filled by becoming a part time community police officer near her home. After some full-time years in the force proper she rose from being a beat copper to the rank of Detective Constable on through Detective Sergeant and eventually Detective Inspector four years before her transfer to Basingstoke and subsequent divorce. Her mathematics degree and she suspected her ethnic background, had put her on the fast track and through some difficult cases had now achieved her goal.

She wasn't sure she was doing the right thing by becoming too involved but did not know DI Davis well enough to trust him with this, she would bide her time and take it slow at first, maybe take her friend Debbie Taylor's earlier advice and step back a little; maybe give Jonny Musgrove free reign. By making him Senior Investigating Officer for the current case was a step in the right direction and would test her ability to hold back from interfering.

Compton Busion had been scanning the data bases of southern counties for missing persons who could be their dead lad.

"Sir, you have to look at this. Four cases of young people missing".

Constable Busion had called Jonny who was in his office going through the somewhat thin murder file. He came down to her station at once, keen to see what she had found.

"What have you got Compton?"

"Look here. A report from Esher in Surrey a boy John Digby aged twelve, went missing one week ago, another from Hove in Sussex a boy twelve three weeks ago and a girl the same age from Brighton on the same day and finally from Kent, a boy of thirteen Kenneth Swift disappeared four weeks earlier. I looked in Wiltshire too but nothing there".

Jonny was looking over her shoulder at the screen, straining to read the small print detailing the MP reports. 'I must get some glasses', he thought to himself, not for the first time recently, however there just never seemed time.

"Can you print these out for me Compton, and do we have any photos".

"Sure can Sir, but these four being about the same age struck me as likely candidates. There are other children missing but much older, only one other a three year old, but it seems that one is a family custody dispute. I'll spread the net wider if you like".

"Okay but let us have a look at these first".

Jonny took the sheets from the printer and took them to his office.

The first report was for a boy aged twelve John Digby who left home in Esher Saturday on the twenty seventh September with his friend Charlie Briggs before nine am. They were going to the racetrack at Esher, a fifteen minute walk from home, the annual Kit Car Show was their destination. Alarm bells were ringing loud and clear in Jonny's head. He read on quickly.

The boys became separated. Charlie searched but gave up and went around the show on his own expecting to either meet up with John later or he would see him when he got home. He went home at about five, and on to John's house, they lived in the same road, but he hadn't returned. No one was worried as it was still early. At about seven, when John had not come home, Mr. Digby drove to the show ground to find it had closed at six and only a few people were left packing up. He then called the local police.

Jonny stopped reading at that point and checked the photo of John it was not the boy from the park. The investigation being carried out by Surrey police was marked as open and ongoing. The car show business worried him though he would come back to this one later.

He picked up the next report. This was for a boy and his girlfriend who had run away together. He scanned on quickly to find they had been found three days later in Eastbourne and were returned home. He did not bother with the details but moved on to the next report.

Kenneth Swift went missing from his home in Old Basing on Saturday 6th September, his mother made the report when he did not come home after visiting a vintage car race meeting at Brands Hatch. There it was again, cars, another coincidence, no way. He searched for the photo of Kenneth and there he was, the young lad now lying in the morgue was staring back at him. In his line of work informing loved ones of the death of their relatives or friends was hard to deal with, but where dead children were involved he found emotional detachment near impossible. He hoped Toni would handle this one.

The parents had driven to Brands Hatch in search of their son and had called the Kent police. The report showed they thought he was a runaway, an open and ongoing investigation. Jonny wondered why Basingstoke police had not been contacted or at least informed of the missing child.

Jonny knocked on Toni's door.

"You should see this Ma'am; I think the cases are linked". He handed Toni a rundown of the missing person reports.

"Look at the dates, all missing on a Saturday, all three boys lost at shows to do with old cars and now this lad Kenneth lying dead on one of Debbie's slabs. He went missing on the sixth September, the information was filed in Kent because that is where the boy was reported missing but his home is near to us, and we knew nothing about it; now he turns up dead here one month later a couple of miles from his home. It's got to be one guy doing this the abductions are all so alike".

"Calm down Jonny I feel you may be right, but we mustn't go off half-cocked or we may miss something, the similarities are there, I give you that much, we should not ignore them but I want to continue with separate investigations, we are more likely to find evidence to support the link if we follow separate enquiries for now. Ask Compton to expand the search to other Counties, if we do have serial events this may not be the first time, also to look into suspicious deaths that might be related as well as missing persons".

"Yes Ma'am, but I still feel they are linked".

"So do I, Inspector, but let's follow our agreed procedure eh. First we need to inform the family and have them carry out a formal Identification preferably before the autopsy, I can do that if you like?"

His hoped for wish had been granted, her offer to help was there for the taking. No matter how much he wanted to offload this task he couldn't accept. It was his responsibility as SIO, he had to be the one who must help the parents over the next few dreadful hours. He put on a brave face and hoped his voice did not give away his true feelings.

"It's alright Ma'am I'll do it, I need to interview them anyway, I'll call Doctor Taylor to hold off the autopsy until after the parents have been, I'll take them this afternoon if I can then the autopsy can go on tomorrow as planned. Mel is due to cover it I'll let her know the outcome before she leaves".

Toni had a niggling feeling again; wanting to get involved in every aspect of a case had to be controlled; she knew she should leave it to Jonny to deal with the boy's possible murder. Her task was to get on with looking for Michael, but these reports were giving her pause. Even though Jonny had delegated viewing the autopsy of the deceased to DS Melanie Frazer, she decided tomorrow to watch the procedure on the lad they now thought to be Kenneth Swift. She'd send Jonny a text to let him know she was going to Richmond but would hint it was for some other reason, no need to upset him by seeming to interfere in his case so soon.

Chapter 5

Melanie's car was already in the Richmond car park when Toni arrived. Mel probably wasn't expecting her unless Jonny had mentioned it after Toni had sent him her text; unlikely as she had delayed sending it till late this morning to avoid any questions from her DI.

She walked up the short flight of steps to find Melanie along with a young uniformed constable in the lobby.

"Chief Inspector Ma'am, what brings you here?"

Melanie always felt at ease with Toni, her upfront almost impertinent question was just her way of expressing her surprise not really expecting an answer, or a rebuke for being so nosey. Toni understood what was going on and ignored the question.

"Good morning Sergeant Fraser, and who is this young man?"

"Err….. Constable Brian Johnson, Ma'am. The Inspector thought it would be good experience for him to attend an autopsy".

The constable blushed and nodded apparently tongue tied. Toni looked him in the eye and smiled.

"Take it easy young fellow I don't bite, it's a good idea don't you think?"

"Yes Ma'am". The constable found his voice and stepped back to allow Toni and Mel to enter the building.

"You are here for the autopsy of Kenneth Swift; I presume the parents have confirmed it is their son; who is the pathologist?"

"Yes, Ma'am the boy's dad came here yesterday afternoon with the Inspector. I think Dr. Hart is on this one".

"That's good as I need to see Doctor Taylor, I may look in on my way out to see how you are getting on".

Toni left them and walked along the corridor to Doctor Taylor's office, at least this excuse made her feel she was not intruding too much. She knocked on Debbie Taylor's door its clear glass enabling Toni to see Debbie look up and gesture for her to come in.

"Hello, Toni what brings you here?"

"A bit of subterfuge I'm afraid, I want to be at the sharp end of the boy Swift's autopsy results but do not want to seem to be interfering with Jonny Musgrove's murder investigation. I'm using a visit to you as my excuse for being here".

"Murder investigation? Without the results of an autopsy?"

"Well, suspicious death then".

"Coffee?"

"Love one. Thanks".

Debbie famously kept a coffee pot at the back of her office on the go all day, not just for personal use but for her numerous visitors.

"Just a little milk ta, no sugar, I'm cutting down so expect I will be having it black soon. I assumed murder because of the way he was posed and the fact he appears to have been placed against a tree in the park after dying somewhere else. He has been missing for a month, so I wonder who kept him hidden for so long before killing him and putting him in the park like that. We've just discovered some other boys are missing under similar circumstances to Kenneth Swift and Michael Soper".

"You think they are linked"?

"Yes I do but Jonny and I are conducting separate investigations for the time being".

"Ah….. now I see, he is lead on the Swift case and you on the missing Soper boy. Tut-tut you mustn't become a mother hen; I told you once before; give him some space Toni or Jonny will be upset".

"I know, I know, but it goes against all my instincts. If they are linked then this murder of a young boy and maybe something more sinister is happening, I just can't let it go".

"You won't have to; you and Jonny make a great team. Why not make him SIO for the whole thing, letting him know you are there as back up? It will give you a reason to have an active input without undermining his authority, he'd be pleased to have someone to bounce his ideas off".

"A wise head on young shoulders is one of your many attributes eh?"

"Not so young now, but think on what I have said, you and Jonny will work it out".

"How are things with you here, now this place has grown to be the major pathology centre in the South"?

"It is good, now we have better facilities but there is never enough time or staff. It comes in waves some days so busy we are here for hours others quiet so we can catch up".

"I know you were a heart surgeon once; it has always puzzled me, so if you don't mind me asking, why a surgeon who can save lives chose to work with the dead"?

"I am not sure if I know the answer, it just happened; I have never thought about it specifically. Forensic pathology was a not path I have deliberately chosen you know. I kind of drifted into it, except, I do recall I had a case once of a young man who arrived at my clinic dead from a heart attack with no apparent cause. He never smoked or drank exercised regularly and was in fine form except he died. I couldn't just let it go I had to know why. I attended the autopsy which eventually found out it was caused by an allergic reaction to an insect bite; I really enjoyed the investigative process; I had more joy looking for that solution than I did performing a bypass operation only prolonging a life for a short while. The insect had bitten the man; the inquisitive bug had bitten me so I went back to school to learn more.

I carried on with Cardiac surgery for some time not intending to change, but became sick of too many patients dying, a conveyor belt of patch up and misery. Nearly all had abused their bodies for too many years coming to me so late I could do nothing for them. The people who die for unknown reasons or at the hands of others needed answers too as do their families, so here I am. Are you going to view the autopsy?"

"Well you certainly have found your niche. I did intend to get involved in the case when I came here, but now I will just pop in and say hello to Penny and leave it to Mel. I'll find out the results soon enough when she comes back to the station".

"A sensible decision, the cause of death should resolve the question of whether it is murder or not. You didn't drink your coffee"?

She took another sip with a grimace and curled up her nose.

"I've cut out the milk but I'm still finding it hard without sugar".

"Persevere my friend you will grow to love it as it should be, strong and dark, just like yourself. See you soon, I hope. Bye Toni".

"I expect so, Cheerio Debbie, take care".

Toni left the office and moved to the corridor leading to the viewing gallery of the autopsy suite. She didn't feel strong but was certainly dark in her thoughts about the dead and missing boys. Her two officers were halfway along the mezzanine floor overlooking one of the central areas. She moved quietly forward as Melanie looked up and acknowledged her approach with a raised hand. Toni whispered, so as not to disturb the process.

"I'm not stopping just popped in to give my regards to Penny Hart".

She leaned over towards the glass partition, Penny was verbally recording her autopsy actions and findings which were relayed via the speakers to the viewing room. She stopped and recognised Toni's presence with a nod of her head. Toni saluted in response, said goodbye to Mel, and left somewhat reluctantly. Melanie was surprised to see her go as she expected the boss to stay and take over, wondering if perhaps she really has delegated this SIO position to Jonny, if so it's a first time for sure.

Mel turned her attention back to the job in hand, Constable Brian Johnson was watching and coping with the procedure so far, at least up here the smell and proximity to the body, normally causing newcomers to retch, was more remote. Doctor Hart was making the Y incision, Mel looked at young Brian and saw him wince, but he didn't take his eyes off the process. Penny Hart continued with her reporting of every action and conclusion, but nothing had come to light yet that showed the cause of death.

The significance of the pooling of blood in the back and buttocks showed he had lain on his back for some time after death confirming he had been moved post-mortem, having been found at the park in a sitting position. The major organs were removed and weighed; this process saw young Brian look away as he turned a shade whiter.

"Are you okay, you can leave if you wish, the toilet is just at the end of this passage".

"I'm all right Sir, sorry, I mean Ma'am it just caught me off guard a bit, I'll be fine in a minute".

"Just remember if you feel sick don't wait go to the loo at once and not so much of the Ma'am call me Sergeant, right".

He nodded and returned to the viewing window still a little queasy but not wishing to miss anything. The usual process of examining the organs produced nothing until the lungs were opened.

"Aha! Here we have something, some damage to the alveoli and signs of oxygen depletion, I believe this boy asphyxiated, some signs of acidosis too".

She cut a sample from the lung and placed it in a glass phial, writing on the attached label. She then moved back to the body and examined the neck in close detail she then opened the throat to reveal the oesophagus and airway passage.

"No sign of blockage or restriction".

She moved her attention to the eyes, using a magnifying glass, revealing tiny signs of petechiae.

"Probably not strangled. Could have had a pillow or plastic bag over the face restricting air flow but the lack of heavy petechial haemorrhage in the eyes suggests not, although children present differently in this respect so not conclusive. The signs of acidosis are a worry, very unusual; correction, not unusual I mean rare, only normally seen in diving and industrial confined space accidents. I will know more when we get the blood results and test this lung sample. Both arms have been subjected to having had needles inserted into veins, possible injections but more likely blood samples being taken".

The autopsy continued for another half hour with no other significant findings except there were some changes to the heart confirming asphyxia. Mel had no idea yet if the boy had died from an accidental or deliberate cause. The fact he had been missing for some time and the posing of the body in the park suggested some serious criminal action. He had died about twenty hours before being placed in the park, so some time on Friday evening between six and two am Saturday, give or take a couple of hours.

Doctor Hart promised to send her report through to Basingstoke as soon as all test results were back. Mel thanked her and left, with more questions than answers.

"How was that Brian?"

"Good, sergeant, very good in fact, I glad I came but also glad we were up in the gallery, I don't think I would have been able to hold it in if we had been down there and close to what she was doing".

"You get used to it, but not immune, this is a modern facility, in the old days you were standing right on top of the action, I was sick the first couple of times, so you did well. What about the results?"

"It seems we did not really have any yet, we still don't know if he died by a deliberate act or by accident".

"Not quite inconclusive, he was suffocated, not a normal way to die, especially for a young person, so the boss will still pursue this as a murder, and we do have an approximate time of death, a lot more than when we arrived don't you think?"

"I thought she would tell us exactly how he had died and how the killer had done it".

"That is now our job young man".

"By the way Sergeant, what is this 'particle hemerage'?"

She laughed a little to herself at Brian's pronunciation but glad of his interest. She spelled it out for him.

"It's called 'Petechial Haemorrhage' and appears as small spots or star like blood clots in the whites of the eye, under the eye lids or on the cheeks, it occurs when victims are strangled or deprived of oxygen, you will find out about that, and a lot more besides, if you want to become a detective and study for your sergeant's exams. You can look it up when you get back if you like. There are books on the subject at the station just ask the desk sergeant he will tell you where to find them. Sometimes a lack of something we might normally expect to find is also useful for building up a picture of what may have happened, the pathologist is just one small part of the investigation. Come on Brian let's get back, DI Musgrove will want to know what we have".

Chapter 6

Much as she wanted to know the results of the autopsy Toni waited in her office for Jonny to come to her. She was on her fourth unsweetened coffee of the day, since having cut out the milk and sugar she had become a bit tense. Not knowing if Mel was back yet or even if she had spoken to Jonny, stretched her resolve to remain in her office to breaking point. Unable to wait any longer doing nothing she decided to go down and speak with Compton to see if there was any new information concerning the abduction of Michael.

Constable Busion was at her desk as usual, she was almost a permanent fixture.

"Anything yet Compton"?

"There are more missing kids when I checked in other nearby Counties, no details yet, let you have them later. Trying to get a handle on the Jaguar but there are still over four hundred in circulation, not just as show cars but many are in daily use. There are various similar models too which brings the count up to near a thousand. Most are in the south but will exclude those registered at addresses over two hundred miles away. I will break them down into three basic types and colours it may be green now but whoever it belongs to may have changed the colour without registering the change. The false plate was for 1966 but our car could be anything from 1960 to 1969 or later if a slightly different model. I should have a short list by close of play, but it won't be that small".

"Well it is a start, let me know when you are done".

She strolled slowly out of Compton's office heavily in thought, moving up to the almost deserted squad room. She saw Peter Andrews at his desk.

"Ha, Peter how are you getting on with DI Davis?"

"Fine Ma'am, he is very thorough, by the book if you know what I mean, he has a way of finding out stuff I would easily miss, I am learning a lot though".

"Comes from years in the fraud squad I suppose. Anyway, I was thinking of pulling you off and have you join me as number two in the search for the missing Michael Soper, but I have changed my mind".

"Oh, the DI did mention it, he was none too happy I was going, so he will be glad".

That was an understatement, Peter decided to be diplomatic in his response for his DI had gone off alarming saying he was being left out of the interesting cases just because he was new and not in the 'Club' of DCI Webb as he called it. A few choice words were added to his outburst which Peter knew were uncharacteristic of the normally quiet and diligent DI Davis; he put it down to frustration. He understood.

"I will talk to him and explain what I want to do, you will still be working on the Soper case but under DI Davis and with PC Krane; how near are you to finishing the fraud case?"

"A day, maybe two it depends on the demands of the CPS".

"Good we will have a meeting later today with you and everyone".

Toni went back to her office a plan of action in mind. She was sure the abduction and murder were linked. She suspected there may be other missing children as yet unknown, small teams would not have the resources if what she feared was true.

She sent texts and left messages for all concerned to come to the station at three this afternoon. She then went along the corridor to Superintendent Munroe's office.

Toni spent some time laying out what had happened so far and her intentions of creating a stronger task force to investigate.

"I believe this may be the sign of something much bigger Sir, I have a feeling if we dig a little deeper; we will find more children missing under similar circumstances, much more than the normal runaways. Constable Busion and her team are working on it now. I may be wrong I think the boy dying was a mistake, I don't believe there is a deliberate killer let alone a serial one, if what I suspect could be happening is true, then it may be better if it was. These boys have been taken for a purpose and not a savoury one I fear. I am waiting for the autopsy result, but I suspect it will be inconclusive".

Walter Munroe had known Toni long enough to trust her gut when it comes to difficult cases. He was fearful however that he would be taken to task if he allowed her to go too far before informing his bosses. He would give her a little more time but would at least send a memo informing them a possible politically sensitive case may be pending depending upon ongoing enquiries, a small insurance but one that may become necessary later to safeguard his position.

"You know I have relied on your instincts in the past and given you your head, so I am not going to stop you now. Just remember with so many people involved it will be difficult to prevent a leak and if the press get hold of this it will warn whoever is responsible and give them time to cover their tracks, not to mention the public response".

"If that means parents are able to better protect their youngsters I won't mind too much, perhaps a small carefully worded press release from you will give some warning without alerting the abductors, think about it Sir. In the mean-time I will keep a tight rein on those involved so hope we can keep it in house".

"You know Toni it seems to me this investigation may become too politically charged if young children are being abducted and we don't warn the public, we may need to call in outside help, don't let it get out of hand, keep me in the loop at all times, I'll think about that press release and let you know".

Toni agreed, but knew Munroe was preparing to cover his arse somehow and eventually handing the cases over to the Serious Crime Unit in London even though he was reluctant to give it away too easily. When she arrived back at her office Jonny Musgrove was sitting in the chair with the cushion reading what seemed to be the murder file.

"Well where have you been hiding boss, tucked away somewhere quiet and me bearing news you have been dying to hear too?"

The jibe did not go amiss, Toni and Jonny had a friendly relationship allowing for light-hearted banter when they were in private, which reverted to the expected more formal only when working together.

"What news is that?"

"You know very well what news; I have the full autopsy report and it makes very interesting reading. I am surprised you didn't wait for it when you were with Doctor Taylor".

"You are SIO so I didn't want to cramp your style on your first big case as a DI. Of course, I want to know so stop larking about what is so important for you to be sitting here".

"Not conclusively murder could have been accidental, what do you make of that".

"I thought certainly not deliberate, manslaughter maybe, what are the pathologist's conclusions".

"Well there you go again. Death was by suffocation, caused by being in a confined space for a long time, either a very small space or a very long time. The blood shows saturation of carbon dioxide to an extreme level and acidosis in samples taken. There were quite large traces of Zopiclone, a hypnotic usually prescribed in the form of a sleeping pill for adults. In children and at this level it could cause unconsciousness and delirium on waking. No sign of sexual interference, no physical abuse or restraint. He seems to have been cared for, considering he had been missing a month; His clothes were clean as was his body with signs of shower gel where he hadn't rinsed properly, so had access to a bathroom recently. There was some indelible ink on the back of his hand, like a re-entry stamp used in clubs and at events like car shows unfortunately it had almost worn away so no indication of where it had come from. They are carrying out tests on the skin to see if an image can be recovered, but don't hold your breath. His clothes revealed some traces of straw like material which when analysed turned out to be animal feed, so maybe he was he kept on a farm. He had signs of excrement on his inside thigh, his bowels were empty so the Doc thinks he defecated at the time of death, apparently not uncommon, so whoever moved him must have cleaned him up which explains the lack of underpants. His stomach had the contents of a meal taken probably ten hours before, almost fully digested so don't know the constituents. If they had wanted him dead would they have bothered to feed and keep him clean? One interesting finding, there were almost invisible sites on both arms where needles had been inserted into small veins, the report favours they were more likely for taking blood samples than giving injections; they had healed sufficiently to have been made over a week before death".

"You know what, Jonny, this confirms my thoughts, I'm of a mind the missing boys are linked with some others we have yet to identify. Let's have everyone together this afternoon, you organise that okay. I am going to bring in DI Harrold Davis and run the investigation as a joint exercise with you as team leader".

"If we spread our search to other Counties and even the Met maybe we are going to have a job containing this, it may be taken out of our hands by those upstairs".

"I'm aware, so we will confine our investigation to local boys for now; Compton will build up a picture of what has happened in the Home Counties and the south east, we will not involve the Met at this stage until we have confirmation of our ideas. I hope to God it is just local and we can deal with it quickly, anything more and the Super will probably call in the big guns anyway".

Chapter 7

The room was full to bursting, the officers requested attending as well as those normally resident.

"Thank you for coming everyone however today it is a closed meeting so those not invited please go and have a cuppa or a walk if you fancy it, don't come back until we have done".

A few grumbles from some as they left the room which took a couple of minutes to clear, ready for the CID teams and their back up officers.

"PC Krane will you check there are no hangers on or ear-wiggers before we start".

Krane checked the squad room door to find no one in hearing range or even in sight.

"All clear Ma'am".

"Good, now let me make it clear we need to keep what I am about to tell you close to your chest. We expect to keep this away from the press, so no leaks. I'll have the balls off someone if it leaves this station from any one of you, hear and note well".

She cast her gaze around the room catching the eyes of most as she made her point.

"What we tell the press will come from me and me alone. We have no confirmation as yet but the death of young Kenneth Swift was not necessarily intended, we are inclined to think maybe not murder, so keep an open mind. Kenneth along with the missing boys Michael Soper and John Digby we believe are just some of several children who have gone missing over the past few weeks and maybe even longer. We think just boys, or at least by the method that has come to light, were abducted at shows or events concerning cars. The coincidence provides a strong suggestion for a link, with one or more perpetrators. The children come from low to middle income homes, no high rollers inviting ransom demands so they are being taken for another purpose, we don't know what yet.

Constable Busion and her team are now searching Counties outside our vicinity to find any similar events. She is concentrating on boys around twelve years old. Our immediate concern is for Michael Soper as he is from our area and has been recently taken so the trail is fresher, this does not exclude John Digby or any others we find, even if not on our patch. We are pretty sure these are connected so find one lad and we may find the others. This is going to be a big task so am bringing in DI Harrold Davis and his team".

Harrold was not paying much attention, he looked up a little surprised as he thought he had been side-lined as far as this case was concerned. Toni turned and spoke to him directly.

"How are you with your fraud case Harrold?"

"Almost there, Ma'am we just need approval from the CPS for what we have submitted. I don't think it will take up much more of our time. We can get started with this new case straight away if you like, Constable Krane can deal with the CPS if they have any remaining problems".

"Good, good, if we find a definite link then DI Jonny Musgrove will be SIO with DI Davis as number two. I will be involved to deal with any inter County difficulties, the press and to fill in if any new leads come to light. We will keep the murder file alive for the time being, Compton will be coordinator for this. At the moment we have three children two of which are still missing but it could become more. We will treat them individually for now but keep the murder file for Kenneth Swift as the central information source, the other boys will have separate files. Information where there is any crossover from the other cases should be copied to it. Thoughts or questions anyone?"

A murmur rumbled round the room with a shuffling of position from those standing, no one moved all keen to hear more. DC Peter Andrews had been taking notes, his mind now awash with thoughts and questions.

"Why boys, all around twelve years old and why car shows?"

That's three questions Peter let's take them in order. First boys are more likely to be given freedom to travel than girls of the same age; also on the whole boys would be more trusting of strangers. Any child younger than twelve would generally not be allowed to travel alone. At twelve or so they would be more susceptible to abduction being physically weaker in comparison with say a fifteen or sixteen year old. To parents a car show or similar would not seem to be a threat whereas maybe a disco or pop concert might be. The car is a big attraction for a young boy and parents would easily be induced into letting their sons go to a seemingly safe daytime event.

One thing to bear in mind we have no proof yet these events are indeed linked abductions; it is just a theory; even so we cannot rule out girls from the theory either. I want to keep it simple for now. DI Musgrove will work on the case of Kenneth Swift and DI Davis will take on Michael Soper's investigation. I will look into the case of John Digby. Regular updates to me will pick up any genuine links if we have proof these events are linked then we will approach the whole investigation in a different way. That's it everyone we'll come together here tomorrow morning, good hunting".

The two lead detectives spoke together for a few moments, separating to the two ends of the room with their assisting officers. Toni left and went up to her office hoping her delegation of the case to Harrold was the right move.

Chapter 8

Marty was nervous, he was ready to transfer the next two kids onto the customer; he was now one boy short for next month's delivery, but how was he to know young Ken would peg it; he seemed healthy enough, it was not his fault he had followed instructions to the letter. He would try to find another lad in time and hoped Jake would not be too angry if he couldn't, after all he had done well with the boys he had found so far, the text he had sent to explain about the dead boy had been ignored the reply only told him the pick-up date and times.

He had no idea what had caused the boy to die; when he unlocked the room he thought the lad was asleep. The damn light was not working, 'must replace that bulb' he thought. He moved into the shadows to shake the lad but was shocked when he tried to raise him. He was stiff and cold. No one had touched him in fact all the boys had been well looked after, so he must have died of natural causes or maybe there had been a reaction to the drug he'd been supplied with which to subdue the boys. He was not fazed by the dead body; in the past he had been involved in eliminating others for his bosses on more than one occasion. He quickly opened the other three lockups to find the coloured kid Anton asleep, the boy Michael using the toilet and John lying on the mattress crying. He took them all a pack of biscuits and some doctored cans of lemonade, watched them whilst they drank to make sure they would be quiet and compliant as the move was due soon. He returned to the end compartment looked down at what was once a living child seeing him as only a damn nuisance needing to be disposed of. He decided to move the body to a public place near the boy's home and well away from the farm.

He would make it look like the lad had just arrived there under his own steam. When found they would think he was a runaway who had been living rough and had died in his sleep. The park in Basingstoke seemed as good a place as any. When he came to lift the body there was a terrible smell, finding the boy had shit himself. He swore out loud knowing he couldn't move him to his van like that, the only solution was to undress him and remove his mess filled under-pants. He threw them away after wiping him down with some wet-ones and redressing him, not perfect but at least the smell had gone. The stiffness which was present when he had first found him was subsiding so was able to fold him head to toe squeezing him into a large hold-all. He carried it easily to place him under the toolbox in the back of his van. The van carried a false copy of a legitimate number plate from an identical vehicle that would disguise his presence if anyone should take an interest; the underside of the large tool carrier would hide the body of the boy from prying eyes. He dressed in navy blue overalls, black beret and gloved hands. The park at Basingstoke was dark and silent at one am as he parked close by the row of trees along the road adjacent to the gate. He dropped the bag over the wall then easily climbed after it. He placed the boy under the tree adjusting his position to look like he was sitting, asleep. Two minutes later he was driving away sure he had not been seen, but not worried if he had been, there was nothing to trace the boy to him; he had not done anything to him anyway, the kid had just up and died and that was that.

The boys were sedated and compliant, drugged just enough to move on their own but unable to resist. The ambulance arrived, Marty unlocked the compartment and led Anton out, he walked him up the steps into the back of the vehicle laid the boy on the stretcher bed and strapped him in minutes later John was taken from his compartment and secured the same way. He never saw the driver, as soon as the rear door slammed shut he drove off the two boys were gone, leaving Michael ready for next month's collection. He sent the agreed text, knowing he would not have anything more to do until the show at Peterborough in two weeks. The camper van shows were good hunting grounds and Peterborough one of the biggest, he was sure he would be able to replace the dead boy in good time.

He returned to the container behind the barn where his latest acquisition was lying asleep on the makeshift mattress.

The inside had been divided into four compartment cells, each with its own small door from a narrow corridor. A mattress and blankets with a porta-loo in the corner were the only comforts. A small light operated by a motion sensor in the corner allowed them to use the toilet and eat but would extinguish a few minutes after they had stopped moving. He recovered the empty biscuit packet and cup, a cheese sandwich with a new cup of lemonade set in its place. The boy would wake soon, eat the sandwich and drink the drugged lemonade. Marty would let him have some exercise tomorrow and a shower, it was small effort for him now with only one to look after and the drugs seemed to make them totally controllable following his instructions without question.

This one had been really easy, the boy named Michael, was a simple catch on the first day of the show; he had watched him closely knowing he was a possible candidate with his head under the bonnet of the XJS chatting to its owner, obviously a Jaguar fan. His mate moved away and a short while later the XJS drove off to be part of the parade. Marty's XJ6 was not in the same class as the fully restored XJS or the sporty E types, but still attractive bait for the young boy, he made his move.

"Are you going to watch the parade young man"?

"I may do in a minute I'm waiting for my friend to come back he's probably gone to the MG stand. Is this your car mister"?

"Yes, a sixty seven LWB four point two XJ6, do you want to see inside"?

"Can I"?

"Of course"

Marty opened the driver's door, Mike slipped his trainers off and climbed in to sit behind the wheel. Marty opened the rear door and sat immediately behind him pointing out the controls and explaining the history of the car. Mike was familiar with the model but enjoyed hearing the man talking enthusiastically about his car.

"The rear of this one is non-standard you know the seats recline with armrests and it has a cocktail cabinet and tables built into the back of the seats in front. There is an electric glass partition too come and see if you like".

Marty opened the offside rear door and moved over to make room for Michael. He stepped out from behind the wheel moved to the open back door and sat next to Marty in the larger than standard rear. Marty opened the hidden cabinet showing glasses and some cans of drink. He let down the walnut table in front of the boy and raised the glass partition with the press of a button in the armrest with its built in radio tape player.

"I've never seen that before".

"It was ordered in long wheelbase format by the original owner to be chauffeur driven, are you thirsty, would you like a drink I have lemonade"?

Mike's mum would not allow him sugary drinks, except on special occasions but he thought this was one time she wouldn't mind.

"Yes please sir that would be great".

Marty opened the can and poured the fizzing liquid into the prepared glass passing it to Michael.

"Here you go, what your name lad"?

"Michael sir, thank you".

"Drink up. Cheers Michael".

Marty raise the can and took a swig of the remaining lemonade whilst Michael thirstily downed his glass in three easy swallows. Michael asked if he could see under the bonnet, he liked viewing the engines as their owners usually polished every part so they looked better than new. He went to get out but felt a little woozy not able to rise.

"Oh dear mister, I don't feel very well".

"Just sit back a moment Michael and close your eyes it will pass".

Ten minutes later Marty was at the gate leaving the show ground his package unconscious covered in a blanket on the back seat.

Marty had no idea what happened to the boys when they left him, he did not care much, they were a commodity just like any other; acquired for sale, the two boys now gone meant a package would arrive soon containing two thousand pounds for each, in used notes; his sole interest was in these payments. He thought perhaps they were being used by wealthy paedophiles or as slave workers, so what! If parents didn't want to lose their kids they should look after them better.

He never had anyone to look after him when he was a kid and he'd managed okay. He never knew his parents, having been in care since a baby, being passed from one foster family to another until he was adopted at thirteen by Mr. and Mrs. Reynolds, a farmer and his wife; adoption was permanent he would never have to move again he thought his luck had changed at last someone actually wanted him. He tried to love them but by then he had been desensitized to the point where he had little empathy and no emotional response to the pain of others. As time went on he came to realize they only adopted him as it was cheaper than hiring someone to help with the farm. He play-acted the part of a caring son for his new 'Mum and Dad', in this way it seemed like a real life, a life he'd never had before. He was made to work hard for them on the farm, in exchange they looked after him well enough but all in this family were emotionally quite cold although his Mum showed him some affection and protected him sometimes from the worst bullying by his strict Dad. It continued for many years until when Marty was thirty-two his Dad became ill and died. To Marty's delight and surprise he discovered he was to inherit the farm and not his Mother. If he hadn't he would have left for sure but as it was he continued to work the land for a while. He thought about selling but had not got around to it, his life here was easy now having allowed his Mum to stay as it was more convenient than the alternatives; she helped to run the farm, did the cooking, washing and she never poked her nose into his new business it was a pleasant relationship.

His downfall started when his newfound freedom led to him going into town to the clubs. He developed a gambling habit and soon ran up some serious debt with even more serious people. They sucked him into becoming party to their criminal activities and in order to save himself from their retribution he complied without question. He was wiry and strong, from years of toil on the farm, with no qualms about physical violence he became an enforcer for Jake Snell, one of the gangland bosses, the one who held his gambling marker was Henry Giles, Jakes boss. He was forced to quit betting until he cleared his financial obligation to Giles but by then he had become completely entrenched in the easy life, forever under Jake's and Giles control. The remoteness of the farm and the suitability of its buildings led them to persuade him to take up his current occupation. They did not really have to force him either, it was better than being a bouncer at their nightclubs; he more than enjoyed the work and it was easy money.

Chapter 9

DC Compton Busion was struggling, she had been going through the Jaguar models matching the type thought to have abducted Michael Soper, she was surprised at how many there were and had no way of deciding which one might be the car they sought. This car show business worried her, thinking. 'If it is just one guy then the cars used to abduct these boys must be sufficiently attractive to lure them away. Michael Soper was taken in a Jaguar, yet to be identified. John Digby in a kit car perhaps and our dead lad Kenneth Swift from Brands Hatch in a vintage car of some kind'. Instead of looking for a particular vehicle she decided to look at all the registered Jaguar owners instead, to see if any one person owned more than one vehicle that might fit the bill for all the abduction scenarios. Unfortunately, there was no existing automatic search program and manually it would take forever; she picked up her phone and called IT.

Toni occupied her next several hours trawling through all the reports that had been mounting up as the uniform officers submitted their house to house enquiries as well as the interview transcripts with the parents and friends of the boys. Nothing unexpected had come to light just confirmation the boys had gone missing, probably abducted. She was still waiting for the updates from Compton concerning her wider search. She did not want to go down and pressure her personally so sent a gentle e-mail to see if there was anything new. The e-mail response was almost instant.

'I was just going to call you, come and see!'

Toni did not hesitate she locked away her files, switched off her computer and was on her way down in a few minutes. Compton was waiting the significant report displayed on her screen.

"I have come up with another missing boy, Anton Biggs, he went missing on thirteenth September from a Camping exhibition held at Olympia. We did not pick up on it till I widened the search as the missing person report originated in London".

"Looks similar but not exactly the same as the others".

"Oh but it is Ma'am in all major respects; Anton is thirteen, comes from Newbury, close to our area, the day of the event is a Saturday as was the others, the 13th of September to be exact and although it is a camping exhibition there is a large section devoted to vintage camper vans which is what Anton specifically went to see. He also travelled with his friend Gregory Simpson, twelve, who was 'with him one minute and gone the next', his words when asked what happened. I have the full report from the police unit based at Olympia. Apparently, the local force always provides a presence at the shows held there, it is one of the larger venues for these events. Anyway, Gregory went to them near the end of the day having spent most of it searching for his friend. He went missing when they were looking at campervans. By the time the police started searching the show was closing down, it was the last day so the whole place was chaotic with stands being dismantled vehicles coming and going; most of the camper vans having already left. Both sets of parents turned up at Earls Court Road police station. The investigation is being conducted from there, nothing so far".

"You're right, it does have all the hall marks, does this help or cloud the issue, are we really seeing some true connection here or leading ourselves astray?"

"Ma'am I'm in the middle of a search for cross matching multiple vehicle ownership. We don't have a program as yet but IT have come up with an idea using the DLVA data base. We have started with our Jaguar list seeing if any of these owners have more than one vehicle. The search is ongoing at the moment, it is slow as each owner has to be looked at individually; we have found six matches so far but have only just started. We know our guy owns or has access to a Jag, if we find some who also own a kit car, a camper van or another vintage car it gives him the means to go to all these shows as a legitimate exhibitor".

"I like your thinking, but you will have to be lucky, the chances are, even if he has all the vehicle types you are looking at, they may not be registered in his name. We know he used a false number, name and address at the Reading show, so some of his cars may not be registered at all".

"I know all that guv but these vintage car owners are very possessive of their precious vehicles. I don't know what else to do there are so many to sieve through and have nothing else to identify him by".

"Good luck, I'll go through this new case here and see if anything comes to light".

Toni returned to her office to download the report from Earls Court. She wondered how her two DI's were getting on. They would be going through the case material and getting on with the legwork, interviewing the witnesses not yet questioned and reworking those the uniform guys had flagged as interesting. She wouldn't interfere, tomorrow morning's meeting would be soon enough. She settled down to read the file, noted Anton and his friend Gregory were black, no thoughts their colour was significant just whoever was doing this was not just choosing white boys. She wondered if it was only boys, girls could be going the same way maybe, being lured by different means.

Her original idea young boys were given more freedom did not quite ring true in today's culture, girls were more advanced than boys at twelve or thirteen and were certainly not accepting the stay at home image of the previous generation. She did not know the statistics regarding missing young people she would have to investigate, guessing and surmising would not cut it; more work for DC Busion's lot, or maybe not, Toni decided to follow this line of enquiry herself.

Missing boys and girls were on a par as far as numbers went, but the girls were on average three years older which lent support to her earlier idea boys were given more freedom at the younger age. She was just looking at statistics not individual cases, she felt perhaps she was over complicating things by following this line of enquiry so put it to one side for now, especially as there were no current cases of interest in Hampshire.

Chapter 10

Alfred Bailey hated waiting at the Channel tunnel terminal, he just wanted to be on the road. He arrived at Folkestone terminal and went through the auto check-in more than pleased to find there was no delay, the security check was minimal as usual; the only thing they were interested in was to ensure your gas bottle was disconnected and turned off. He passed through the dual passport control and would be sliding into his allocated train carriage slot very soon and on the other side in less than an hour. This was his second trip with a vehicle that was new to him, the van he had been using before was a bit slow and quite old, this one was almost new. He loved driving this van he would like to buy one like this and with a few more trips he would have enough be able to get his hands on a good second-hand model. Travelling for his own fun and without the restriction of the job and the fear of being stopped was something he looked forward to. The two kids who were transferred from the ambulance earlier this morning were sleeping at the moment and would be quiet for at least a couple of hours so he wouldn't have to stop for ages yet. The compartments in the base of the converted campervan were well hidden so he had no qualms about their being discovered. No one checked much on the way over to France as almost all searches were concentrated on vehicles travelling to the UK; the French didn't seem to care much anyway, no one there had stopped him before. Once he reached the transfer point near Abbeville he would collect his cash and be on his way back. A good dinner, a comfortable night in the Calais hotel, buy some wine in the morning then through the tunnel, return the mini-bus and home by teatime. Job done.

The drive from Calais towards Boulogne was easy, he left the N road onto the A16 motorway towards Abbeville, picked up his toll ticket at the pay-point, aiming to stop at the 'Aire de Beaufant' a quiet wooded rest area some twenty miles on. He had plenty of fuel for the journey so did not need to stop except at this rest station where the facilities provided were only a toilet and picnic area. At this time of year there were few people around a lorry or two and the odd car maybe. He could easily park out of sight, take the boys to the loo one at a time and give them their drug laced drink without arousing suspicion. This would be the only stop on route, the transfer would take place at a house, different from last time, in a remote area a couple of miles off the A16 motorway junction 24 near a place called Cressy. Earlier he'd entered the coordinates he'd been given into the sat nav and studied the map to make sure he knew where to go.

The stop went without incident as did the rest of the journey up to the motorway toll station at his intended exit. He drove into the narrow barriered gateway where normally he expected to find someone in a box collecting the toll; the left hand passenger window wound down ready to pay, he had his ticket and a ten euro note in hand, to find it was an unmanned station. He couldn't reach to insert the toll ticket into the required slot from his right hand driver's seat so had to climb out of the van walk round the front to gain access to the pay point machine. His French was poor but managed to follow the instructions except that it rejected his ten euro note, he tried again without success. Finally, he was forced to insert his credit card which was accepted. The automatic barrier raised as he climbed back in, swearing at the infernal machine under his breath not liking there was now a record of his presence by having used his personal bank card.

The sat-nav. took him along its computer calculated route to arrive at a derelict and empty looking house which stood alone at the end of a narrow lane. There were no people or vehicles visible, he checked his watch to see if he was early, but only by twenty minutes. He made a struggled five point turn in the narrow area at the front of the house, the van now pointing down the lane ready for his departure.

He waited in the van watching for a car or someone to arrive from down the lane. The knock on the window made him start to see a short dark haired young man signalling for him to get out; he complied.

"Monsieur, sil vous plait ouvrez les portes pour les garcons".

Alf didn't speak French but understood what was wanted. He opened the rear door and raised the false floor revealing the two compartments where the boys were lying asleep. Another man came out from the house front door, moved over to the bus, leant in and lifted out one of the boys and carried the unconscious bundle inside, he came back and was able to walk the other lad, who was by then more or less awake, through the same door. The first man watched as Alfred closed the van door, when secured he handed Alfred a packet but said nothing. Alfred took the packet without question, feeling uncomfortable in this man's presence he climbed into the bus and drove off with the watching Frenchman visible in his mirror till he turned back onto the main road. A few kilometres down the road he pulled off into a layby to check the package he didn't trust these French. Inside was two thousand euros in notes as was agreed. He split the cash into two bundles and put them into the inside pockets of his coat. He opened the underfloor compartments removed the bedding and stored it in the vans wardrobe; placed the toolbox and some vehicle spares in the spaces vacated by the children, if discovered it would look normal and less like what it had been used for. He played servant to his paranoia by waiting long enough to ensure he was not being followed, fired up the willing motor and put his foot down on the gas pedal to quickly reach the autoroute's generous speed limit glad to be away and on the road back. This time the toll machine took his cash and was soon skimming along free of fear; he thought perhaps he would skip the hotel and catch a late ferry instead of using the tunnel tomorrow. The tickets were cheap enough less than the cost of a night in the hotel in fact. He could have his supper and buy some wine on board ship.

He knew he had made a wise choice as he was able to board a ferry leaving very soon after his arrival at the port. He was now sitting in the food hall with a plate of curry and a glass of beer as the P & O's Pride of Kent left the harbour bound for Dover.

An hour and a half later he was sitting in the queue leading out of the docks when a police officer directed him to the customs shed. He pulled into the covered building, lowered the window to be greeted by a young constable.

"Good evening sir just a quick check, would you switch off your engine and open the rear door please".

Alfred thought 'Thank goodness I didn't try and pick up anyone in Calais'.

He climbed down and opened the double door revealing his two cases of wine sitting on top of the false floor. The officer peered inside with his torch sweeping all around the interior of the bus.

"Where have you come from sir"?

"Just been over to Calais for a day trip, pick up some wine and have a look round you know".

"You did not go out on the ferry today did you"?

"Err no, I used the tunnel this morning and was going to come back tomorrow but didn't fancy stopping after all".

"Did you go anywhere else other than Calais"?

"I did go out of town for a bit just for the ride like".

"Where was that then"?

"I don't know really I just drove for a while and then came back, no place special".

"Can I see your passport please Sir".

Alfred went to the cab and removed his passport from the glove box and gave it to the officer wondering what the hell was going on.

"Wait a moment please Sir".

The officer moved over to an office at the side of the customs shed and disappeared inside. He came out some minutes later with another officer.

"We are going to search this vehicle as what you have told us conflicts with our record of your movements".

Alf knew there was nothing to be worried about, they couldn't know about his movements they were just trying it on, wanting to look big, even if they found the false floor he would express ignorance, the van was not registered in his name and he had hire documents to prove his legitimate use.

The search of the van indeed led to them finding the false floor.

"Please sir can you explain what this hidden compartment is used for?"

"I have no idea, I only hired it for a couple of days. I suppose it must be for securing tools or something I didn't even know it was there. The hire documents are in the glove compartment, I'll get them".

The search had revealed the tools in the hidden compartments however they were not taken in by those few items in a space obviously designed for something else. However, nothing was found that would allow the officers to detain this man or his vehicle; except their experience told them he was not telling the whole truth. They decided to let him go for now, so as not to alarm and deter him from future activities where they may catch him out. There was now a flag against his name and the vehicle whereby every port would keep an eye open for him and his travel movements in the future.

"No problem Sir that's alright, here is your passport all is in order, it is just vehicles like this are used for smuggling asylum seekers from Calais and we have to check, sorry for the inconvenience".

Alfred was a little apprehensive they seemed to have let him go too easily, he kept an eye on the rear mirror in case he was being followed. Perhaps he was just being paranoid again as he could not see any following vehicle. He avoided the motorway and stopped at a garage on the A20 for fuel and a coffee. If anyone was following, he would have spotted them by now. He felt foolish, hundreds of people get stopped and searched every day, in any case he had nothing for them to find, except maybe the money and he had kept that in his pockets out of sight.

The two customs officers watched him leave.

"That Alfred Baily is a wrong'un for sure".

The officer was logging the search of Alfred's van and his passport details into the computer.

"We had nothing to hold him on but, the bus was definitely built for smuggling".

"His story of driving to nowhere did not ring true. He was up to no good. I'll log him on to the watchlist and the van too. We need to check on this vehicle's movements with the French and our own CCTV coverage. I'll verify the owners are a genuine car hire company".

"Passport control will give us a history of his travel in the past, he is not just doing this for a few bottles of cheap wine".

Chapter 11

Jonny and Harrold were sitting opposite each other at Harrold's desk.

"After you Harry, have you any thoughts how we divvy up this lot"?

"I'm not sure Inspector, I wasn't expecting the Chief to include me, I haven't had time to even look at the file, she seemed to want to do it all by herself, at one point she was even taking Andrews from my team you know, what changed her mind"?

"You will get to understand her ways soon enough, she is a hands-on type, as you guessed, very intuitive, like a bulldog once she has the scent, she is not a glory seeker, will give credit where it's due, just wants results. If she trusts you she will give you all the rope you need and will support you to the hilt, she may step in a bit heavy sometimes but there is usually a good reason. Best interviewer I have met, has witnesses and villains alike giving up information with them thinking she was doing them a favour. I think she is testing you, if you are as thorough with this as you are with the fraud case you won't go far wrong".

"So, I'd better be careful then Inspector, I must admit I haven't paid much attention to these cases because I thought I was being pushed to one side, will you fill me in where we are now".

"Of course, we are going to need as many heads on this as we can and yours is better than many. By the way call me Jonny when we are together like this, save the formal Inspector stuff for when we are outside, I hope my calling you Harry is okay, or do you prefer Harrold"?

"Harry is fine".

"Right down to business. When you read the files, you will see all the details, our first indication of a problem was when the boy Michael Soper went missing from the car show at Reading. Our next was when Kenneth Swift turned up on our patch dead, he also went missing from a car show this time car racing at Brands Hatch, he died of asphyxiation and was dumped in the park at Basingstoke. John Digby has also gone, this time from a kit car show at Esher. Compton has also found a lad Anton Biggs who disappeared from a camping show at Olympia, this one is not our case as he comes from Newbury but the similarities are too close to ignore. The Chief suspects they are linked; so do I and there may be more; Constable Busion and her team are looking for other missing persons similar or at least closely matching the same scenario. I am going to concentrate on Ken you should start in with Michael. Read the file, chat to Compton and get your team up to speed. Well meet tomorrow first thing and you can then give me your plan of action, okay".

"Thanks Jonny, you know what, this is the first time anyone here has paid me any real attention".

"Don't worry about your position here Harry you will fit in well soon enough, most people are wary of newcomers at first; the officers here are young, clever and keen, just don't push them too hard and you'll be fine".

Harry had been thinking he would never become accepted at this station, that was before today, but now possibly things were changing for the better, anyway this case was going to be more interesting than his usual trawling through masses of paper evidence and dealing with manipulative bent accountants.

He sat at his desk for the next two hours reading the files and all the peripheral reports of the other cases. He checked the interviews with neighbours and the people at the car show. He studied the CCTV footage and came to the same conclusion as his colleagues these missing boys were all be connected. He decided to go and pick Constable Compton Busion's brains for she had the reputation as the go to person for wheedling out information on the internet and databases. He had never had any real contact with her before except an introduction when he first came to Basingstoke although he had seen her about the station quite a lot, one thing he noticed she never seemed to go home. He'd nodded hello on occasions but had never used her skills.

His fraud cases had taught him a great deal about the use of computers to cover up illegal money manipulation and as such had developed a nose for hidden information. He had his own way of uncovering information from the seized computer systems of suspects digging out evidence of their wrongdoing. He wasn't a forensic accountant but well understood the minds and ways of those that were and had great respect for the officers who were able to ferret inside the maize of the W.W.W.

Until two years ago Compton worked alone alongside the detectives. Her efforts had so impressed the Super she was given an office and new computers one floor down from the main squad-room, she now had two young officers helping and since the system upgrade last year her little team had gone a long way in helping CID and also other police departments in their investigations. DCI Webb had a special relationship with her for she kept records of all the cases in a unique filing system with access for all officers who had an interest. Harrold knew she had been looking into the connection possibilities and specifically trying to trace the owner of the Jaguar who had abducted Michael Soper.

As a matter of courtesy Harrold knocked on her door before entering, she hadn't heard the knock as she was wearing headphones but looked up and gave him a beaming smile when he walked in. He was quite disarmed by the radiance she emitted.

"Hello detective, and what can I do for you Sir".

"Good morning, Constable Busion, um… I've taken on the Michael Soper case and hoped you have something for me. The Chief said she had spoken to you and you were doing some kind of cross matching search, any luck with that"?

"We are getting there, I have twenty six candidates so far but we are only halfway through the first pass, so expect it to double".

"Seems a lot of possible suspects, would you please explain your methods, perhaps I can help".

"We started with over seven hundred matches to the particular car so cutting it down to fifty or so is not bad for the first run, unfortunately we are doing most of the work manually. IT are working up a program that will cut out lot of the work; by IT I mean one constable whose main job is maintenance; keeping all our old computers running keeps him busy so it's taking a while for him to write and test the new programme; we won't have much to work on for a while".

"Will a second stab reduce it even further"?

"I hope so but only a small percentage, let me explain. We know Michael's abductor used a not too rare Jaguar XJ6, but we don't know the exact year or model. At least two other children were abducted at car shows or venues. We are searching for owners of multiple vehicles that match the probable types used. Sports cars, camper vans and any vintage type of transport displayed at an exhibition. Our assumption is if one man is doing this he will have access to all these cars, so we are eliminating the owners of just one car first and then two cars and so on we hope to find someone who owns four or more vehicles that would do the job. So far we are at the three car level, we think any more will be so unusual for them to be flagged up as a possible suspect".

"I like your reasoning but it's full of holes, what if the suspect does not own the cars or if he does he may have them registered in another name"?

"We know, so are cross referencing the possibility of hired vehicles and using common addresses as well".

"Well you certainly have your work cut out there young lady, I'll let you get on with it then".

"Yes, Sir thank you, I'll call as soon as I have anything".

Detective Inspector Harry Davis walked slowly back to his desk thinking about how he was to proceed, pleased to know, despite his earlier doubts, he had the backing of a good team. He had been very apprehensive about the move to Basingstoke and as such put up a bit of a barrier when he first arrived. His family were still living at their home in South London, a police house which came as part of the job. He had been in the force from back when the accommodation privilege was normal although the practice had ceased for new officers, it still continued for those of a certain age. He did not want to move the family to Basingstoke until he was sure of his position here so had been living in digs for most of the time with the odd days at home. This recent change left him in a more positive frame of mind he hated the uncertainty; Annie his wife desperately wanted to move away from London also his son Joe was coming up to sixteen about to leave school and go to sixth form college, a fortuitous time to consider a move. Chief inspector Toni Webb had assigned Detective Constable Peter Andrews and Constable June Owen to him on his first day. They were respectful but not particularly friendly at first. He had been brought in to help with several cases of fraud as this was his area of expertise. He was hoping to get away from these typical City based crime he had been working on for the last four years with a move to the country, the decision to change was beginning to look good. The fraud case was successful largely due to his persistence, knowledge of accounting and computer crime.

Peter and June were willing to learn and had mellowed towards him, which went a long way toward the rapid and successful result. Now at last he had a case where he could maybe help someone, Jonny Musgrove had put him at ease and even the Chief had taken on a less dominant role. He called Peter and June Owen together to lay out his plan.

"Peter have you studied the CCT footage from the show"?

"Only briefly, Compton picked up the car details as it left the rear gate but not much to see there".

"That's not enough Peter, please get hold of footage for the whole day, if we can see the car entering as well as leaving we may be able to get a picture of the driver and any shots available from other cameras. Try the local press they would have covered the show and maybe one of their photographers got a shot of our lad with the car. June I would like you to re-interview Michael's friend Jerry Franks, we can't rely on the Reading police interview report, at the time of the first interview he was under severe stress and may have inadvertently missed telling us something important, the lad may remember something new with a gentler approach. I'm going to work with Constable Busion, I have an idea which may speed up her search. Any questions"?

They both shook their heads and offered a "No Sir" as they moved back to their desks to take up their allotted tasks.

Harrold had an idea and wanted to run it by Compton so returned to her office to find her still at her desk headphones round her neck.

"Hello again have you a minute I would like to run something by you"?

"Yes, Sir no problem".

"Do we have a detailed list of all the entries of Jaguars to the Reading show"?

"Yes, but it is not possible to identify our man specifically as the information is very sketchy. Some entered online, some by post and a couple turned up on the day".

"We can eliminate the genuine exhibitors, as their vehicles will be registered at an address that agrees with their entry. I suspect our guy turned up on the day paid in cash and gave a false address. If we look at the other venues where the boys were abducted he may have used the same method and if anything cross matches such as an unknown vehicle number or false address we will have confirmed a connection to the abductions if nothing else".

Compton smiled; she liked this guy's thinking.

Chapter 12

Sleep eluded Toni, she perched on the end of her bed, clothed only in the baggy T shirt she preferred to use as pyjamas, overlooking the woodland grove from her bedroom window; the view that would normally please her troubled mind was still in darkness, the moon's gentle glow was not enough, she couldn't see much; now too awake to even think of going back to bed. The trees swayed in a gentle breeze of Autumn the shiny hardening leaves reflecting an eerie lunar driven light casting shadow and flashes of light across the bedroom walls like fireflies dancing. Her fear for the missing children had played havoc with sleep and the need to be at peace, her thoughts flitting from one scenario to another like the moon driven flickering images in her room. Why take these particular children from their families, she mused, it was no simple thing to do? There were many more vulnerable kids on the street who would be much easier to subdue and seduce away without them being reported missing, what is so special about an 11-year-old boy from a good home that made it worth the risk? The question almost answered itself, it had been there all the time in the back of her mind festering away keeping her awake, a good home meant a well looked after boy. Street kids were malnourished, often on drugs usually sickly and carrying God knows what infections. Healthy bodies are what they are after; the blood samples taken from Kenneth were used for something, a chill ran up her spine again when she thought what they might be for; 'please be wrong she pleaded with herself, please be wrong'.

No chance she would sleep anytime tonight; the shower called, letting the hot stream and soft gel attempt to wash away the unthinkable, the jets of water caressing her skin providing some temporary relief. An hour later a coffee and a change of clothes saw Toni set off for the station before the dawn chorus enriched with sound the trees and their dying leaves that had earlier triggered her ghastly enlightenment.

Out of habit, on the way up to her office, she glanced into the soon-to-be deserted squad room where the night duty uniforms, nearing then end of their shift, were waiting to go home, none looked up ignoring her fleeting presence. No matter, in a few short hours it would be buzzing with her teams preparing for the day ahead, by then she would have a good idea how they should proceed; if she was right the Superintendent would want to offhand this to the Serious Crime Unit based in London, before then she would want to make sure her ideas were not just her overactive imagination.

Compton Busion's office was two floors down from Toni's she took the stairs slowly as it was only just six am and whilst she knew Compton would be in early she did not expect to find her there yet, so stopped off again at the squad room. Two officers remained; the others having left on the dot of six. This time they did not ignore her and gave up a welcoming, "Good morning Ma'am".

"Coffee still on the go lads"?

The younger of the two responded at once.

"Yes Ma'am have a seat, I'll get you a cup; milk, sugar"?

"Just black thanks".

She took the seat, vacated by the young constable, opposite his older colleague.

"How's has your night been err…"

"Constable Peters Ma'am".

"Yes, um.. Peters I remember now, you must be on permanent nights we don't cross paths too often do we"?

"No Ma'am we don't, quiet night for us mid-week, near the end of the month you don't find many people about; Traffic had an easy one too. It will be different next week, payday for most, so the town centre will be busy on the weekend and so will we no doubt".

The young constable brought her coffee.

"Thanks, no need to stand attendance on me carry on with what you're doing".

"Oh, we have finished for the night Ma'am just waiting for the dayshift to come in for a handover then we'll be gone".

"Not much to report then"?

"No, only a missing girl, her parents were here half the night..."

Toni sat bolt upright and stared her heart racing.

"....No real problem though patrol found her at three am. She went missing after she left her friend's house a bit late and missed her bus. Apparently, she fell asleep in the bus shelter not realising the last bus had gone".

Tony's heartbeat had jumped a notch at the mention of the words 'missing girl' and stayed beating rapidly for several minutes even after the safe return was revealed. Amazed at her sudden emotional response she rose quickly finishing her coffee in one quick gulp grimacing at its lack of sweetness needing to get on with her task. She thanked the two officers and left.

Surprisingly Compton was already at her desk, Toni was still not expecting her to be there even though she had taken longer than she meant with her squad room diversion. Compy, as she was known to most, was always early the first to arrive and the last to leave, especially when she was on a charge.

"Morning Ma'am what can I do for you today. The missing boys I suspect"?

"Of course. Don't you ever go home young lady"?

The rise in her voice asking the question but not expecting an answer.

"We have come a long way since yesterday boss, DI Davis came up with an idea; it shortened our search quite a bit, his knowledge of searching for computer fraud has many similarities to our own cross-referencing programs. Anyway, I think we have something he can work on at last".

She pressed the print button and waited the minute for the machine to respond then turned to Toni, handed her several printed sheets.

"Let me explain Ma'am. Page one is the list of possible suspects there are twenty-two in all. They are in order of priority; as you can see I have marked the top three as being the most likely. There are full details of these three, one page for each. The details of the other nineteen are limited, contained on just these two pages. I can get more on these if we need to, they must not be excluded entirely even though they are lower priority we do not have their full history and of course I could be completely wrong and have nothing else panning out. I'll keep on working as IT will soon have ready a new search and match program, I'll let you know of any changes but for now it's up to your guys; old fashioned footwork needed eh"?

Toni scanned the list of names, Duke Kingswood, Frederick Marshall, Richard Foxhall, Martin Reynolds, Peter Smithson She stopped at five, thinking these would be more than enough to be going on with. All five owned jaguar cars of the type used to abduct Michael, some also owned campervans and the first three had several older model sports cars whereas Reynolds had only the Jag an old Alvis plus a large white van with several vintage motor bikes. She discounted Smithson as he had a red soft top Jag, which did not match what they were looking for, and two old Austins; she'd come back to him later if none of the others showed promise. All five lived in the southern counties. Busion had given full details of their addresses, marital status, job description and criminal record where there was one. Only Kingswood and Reynolds were known, Kingswood for breach of the peace some ten years before, bound over, nothing since. Reynolds had two youth offences for assault, suspended sentences and one later charge of credit card fraud five years ago for which he was found not guilty. No details there.

"Thanks Compton this is good stuff it gives us something to work with, has DI Davis got all this?"

"Most of it, Ma'am he was here really late last night so is already on his way to interview Kingswood. I believe DC Andrews is also on his way to seek out Marshall".

Toni returned to her office and powered up her computer finding a longish message from Davis to Jonny Musgrove laying out his plans for the day with a copy to her. He was following up on Kingswood and Foxhall, with June Owens whilst Peter Andrews was to deal with Marshall and Reynolds. Nice to see he was keen and was ahead of her in tracking down the Jaguar or more to the point, it's owner.

She returned to the list of possible suspects noticing near the bottom the name of a Company rather than an individual, A.C.H. of Newbury. She noted that is where Anton Biggs hails from. It seems this firm have a stock of old cars of all types which they hire out for special events. Weddings mostly but sometimes for use on TV and Film sets. She wondered why Compton had included it on the list. There was a list of cars they had available for hire. It included a Jaguar and an old type 2 VW Campervan a Rolls Royce and various other makes.   A star against three of them with number 1, 3, and 4. Cross references to others on the list. Duke Kingswood rented a Jaguar from this company on the weekend of Michaels abduction, Richard Foxhall has several vintage cars and often lends them out through A.C.H. Martin Reynolds hired the VW Camper van on several occasions. It seems Compton had thought the hiring of vehicles added to the probability of their being suitable candidates for interrogation.

Toni's restless nature would not let her sit at her desk she would not interfere with her teams' investigations but would go to A.C.H. just to see how they operated. She headed down to Compton's office on her way out.

"Constable Busion please tell me how do you get all this information"?

"Most of the vehicle stuff is from our special link to the DVLA but most car hire companies leave their computers online nearly all day, I just call up their website with a list of the cars they have for rental and log in as if I was going to hire, hey presto the door is open and in I go. They often have no security to speak of to protect their records not even a password".

Toni was not sure if it was legal so would try and get an official copy of the data during her visit.

"Please come with me".

Compton looked up in surprise.

"What right now Ma'am"?

"Yes, constable, I am going to visit this A.C.H. I think they are a key suspect from your list and I may need your expertise".

"I will need a moment or two to shut this down".

"No problem, I'll wait in the car park".

Toni left, leaving Compton obviously somewhat bemused, she did not really need her on this visit but thought it would be good if she spent a little time out of the office away from her beloved computers; it might give her an insight into what her information gathering led to. Although Toni had looked through the list, more detail and a better feel for what had caused these particular suspects to be selected could be learned on the journey to Newbury. Toni walked slowly to her car and arrived only a moment before Compton came jogging along with a laptop under her arm. Toni laughed to herself seeing her officer still attached to the very machine she was trying to get her away from. She pointed forcefully at the offending MacBook.

"You don't need to bring that with you".

"Oh. I'm sorry Ma'am, I thought you wanted to be given more information about the list, it's all in here. Shall I take it back"?

"No, no it's fine, and by the way don't mention we already have the information you downloaded from their computer".

"What information is that Ma'am, I can't recall"?

"Just so, get in".

The journey time was not wasted Compton went through the list quickly explaining how they'd prioritised the suspects and also added much more detail concerning the ones at the top of the list. She also learned A.C.H. was run by a Terry Scofield, his only previous record having been caught by a speed camera three years before, thirty-six in a thirty limit, not exactly a villain.

The company operated from an industrial complex on the outskirts of Newbury where he had three adjoining units, he lived some ten minutes away on a small private development. Married to Juanita with two girls aged eleven and sixteen.

They found the industrial units were erected in a simple square development amongst some forty others. There were no gates and only a light wire fence surrounding the whole site. She noticed that A.C.H. was alarmed and had several security cameras and movement sensor lighting. The large roller doors to the left and right were reinforced so obviously the cars were valuable enough to be well protected.

They parked on the front outside the middle unit where there was a small door and a window with a sign above; A.C.H. Ltd. and a telephone number. Toni exited her car and indicated for Compton to follow her.

The door was unlocked so they entered a small reception area with several chairs and a sliding window behind which sat an elderly woman.

"Good afternoon, can I help you?"

Toni showed her warrant card.

"Good day, I'm Chief Inspector Webb and this is Constable Busion, I would like to speak to Mr. Scofield please".

"Oh, okay I'll call him, he's in the back, can I tell him what's it about"?

"Just call him please".

She left her seat and disappeared through rear of her office, coming back a few seconds later. She unlocked and opened a side door and poked her head out.

"Please come through".

They followed her through her small office out the back where they found themselves in a workshop are. A tall man with dishevelled hair in navy overalls stood up from under the bonnet of an old Austin and walked forward wiping his hands with a not too clean rag.

"Hello, I'm Terry Scofield, I won't shake" waggling his still greasy hands and fingers, "but welcome to A.C.H. what can I do for you, I don't have any old style police cars in stock but I can probably get one if you need it".

"We are not here to hire a car sir but would like to ask you a few questions about one of your customers".

"Better come into the office a bit more comfortable".

They followed to a half glass room set in the corner of the garage workshop.

"Please have a seat I won't be a moment".

Indicating the need to deal with his dirty hands. He returned after a short while having washed and removed his overalls.

"That's better; now who is it you want to know about, what have they done"?

"Well actually there are two persons of interest Duke Kingswood and Martin Reynolds, we don't know if they have done anything but I understand they have both hired vehicles from you".

Terry didn't ask where Toni had come across that bit of information but leaned forward to his already switched on his computer.

"Give me a moment, I can print off their records. I know both men, they are regulars with me. Sometimes they hire, other times I use their cars and bikes for other customers. Most of my business is weddings a little film work and for TV sometimes. Films are the best they often hire for weeks at a time, TVs not bad but they only hire for a couple of days or so".

As he talked he was tapping the keys followed by a buzzing of the printer in the corner, responding with the promised sheets of data.

"Duke's wife is a photographer she does weddings mostly and he doubles up as a chauffeur so he uses more luxurious cars like our Roller or the Bentley. It is no too often as he tries to persuade their customers to use his Jaguar whenever possible, to save on costs. Martin however likes to go to the shows and sometimes he doesn't have a suitable vehicle so borrows one of ours. We have a reciprocal arrangement as we use his motorcycles or Alvis for our film and TV work. The vehicles and dates of hire are all here".

Toni took the sheets of data even though she already had the information thanks to Compton's possibly illegal hack. She noted the record only went back to the beginning of the year.

"Do you keep information for last year as well"?

"Oh yes we archive everything to a memory a bank each year, but it is not available on this computer. I could make you a copy onto a memory stick of any year if you like, but it will take me quite a while as it is all mixed up with the accounts, correspondence and the service records and everything we do, I'd have to search manually you see, could be a couple of hours".

"That is not necessary just now, Constable Busion will give you a link to our system so you can send it to us later when you have more time. I would like just the records for the last couple of years concerning our two already discussed men, plus any customer who might be on the list of names she will give you".

"Good I am not too busy at the moment so I will do that for you later today you should have it by tomorrow, here is my card it has our website and e-mail".

Compton used her laptop to pass the list of names to Terry Scofield's computer and checked to see he had her e-mail address for the return. She indicated to Toni all was okay.

"You have been most helpful Mr. Scofield, thank you, we'll be in touch later if we have any questions about what you send".

"Would you like to look at our collection"?

Toni did not have much interest in old cars but was hoping for this invitation, she wanted an excuse to have access to the possible offending vehicles without seeming to be pushy, she agreed with a smile besides conceding to Compton enthusiastically nodding her head.

"We have a few minutes to spare so that would be nice thank you".

He grabbed a bunch of keys from his desk drawer a big smile on his face, obviously proud of what he was about to reveal.

"Follow me. We have two garages this one contains the older cars the other the later models and vans".

Compton followed closely with Toni lagging behind. He opened a door between the workshop using a key and a security keypad. Inside the fine collection was parked nose to tail with a small gap between each row. There were nine different cars in here he wandered to the front with Compton in tow explaining each cars pedigree as he passed. Toni stood in the centre half listening and half studying the data she had been given earlier. She did not spot the vehicles she was interested in so after some time she indicated she needed to move on.

"You have a wonderful stock of cars here, could we have a quick look in the other garage before we leave"?

"Of course".

He turned and left by the door we came in, he locked it before crossing to another the other side of the workshop. Another keypad negotiated led them to a similar sized area. This time however there were some more modern vehicles including a Vanwall racing car, two old type delivery vans. There were two campers and three Jaguars here which is where Toni's interest lay, the weekends when Anton Biggs went missing from the Camping exhibition held at Olympia and of course the missing Michael Soper.

"I see from your information sheet Duke Kingswood hired a Jaguar on the third and fourth of October".

"Yes that would have been the white XJ6, he had a wedding Saturday if I remember rightly and his car was in the workshop".

"What colour is his Jaguar"?

"British racing green with cream leather, very nice car, it has a full length sunroof which he decks it out with white ribbon for the weddings it looks great.

"Ah, yes fine, I also note Martin Reynolds hired a camper van on the twelfth to the fourteenth September, which one was it"?

"Err. It would have been the type two VW, over here, the grey and maroon model, he always has that one".

"Can I look inside"?

"Sure I'll open the door".

He fumbled with the big bunch of keys, eventually opening the sliding side door. Toni looked in and noticed it was clean but a little dusty here and there.

"Do you valet the cars when they are returned"?

"Not always if they are not too bad we wait till they are let out again then give them a good going over, ready for the new customer. Sometimes they stand for a few weeks between hiring so we would be doing the job twice over if we cleaned straight away".

"Has this one been cleaned since Reynolds had it".

"I doubt it, he was the last one to hire this one and he always returns it clean enough".

"Mr. Scofield I want you please to lock and leave this vehicle as it is, kindly give the keys to Officer Busion here. I want to get a forensic team over to examine it in detail. Constable Compton please call and arrange for a team to come here at once".

"What is going on here, what if someone wants to hire it out"?

"I'm sorry sir I believe this van may have been used during the commitment of a crime and needs to be examined. We will be careful and respect your property but it is a possible crime scene so must remain untouched. It may reveal nothing; in which case you will have your van back today. If it shows signs of illegal use we may need to remove it to our laboratories for a while".

"Bloody hell! I wondered what was going on why did you want to know about Duke and Marty what have they done. Will I get it back in one piece, it's worth thousands you know"?

"Of course sir, we may not need to remove it yet so don't get too worried, as for the two men we don't know yet if they have done anything but we do need to illiminate them from our enquiries".

"Can't help but worry. I worry all the time you know we have a huge amount of money tied up in these cars and they don't all belong to us we let them out on their owner's behalf for a commission. The security and insurance are so damned expensive we only just make enough to live on. Most of our own cars are financed, we own just a couple outright. Another few years and it will be okay but we can't afford to lose even one really".

"Okay relax young man, I'll do my best to see if the forensics can do all they need on site here, so we won't have to take it away. Does anyone else work here with you"?

"Just my wife Juanita she does the accounts and office work a couple of days a week".

"Ah the lady at the front office".

"Oh no that's Joan she only comes in part time when I am working on the cars, maintenance and cleaning; I usually man the front desk".

Toni had dismissed Kingswood and the white Jaguar hiring as suspicious although the date was right the colour was not, she'd have to check the wedding though just to be sure. She'd reserve her judgement of Terry Scofield for now; he was over co-operative she thought but maybe it was just her suspicious mind. His use of the first names Duke and Marty showed a familiarity she would follow up on if necessary later. If his vehicles were involved she'd look at him differently but for now would treat him as the innocent fellow he appeared to be. Compton returned from the car a few minutes later.

"SOCO are on their way Ma'am, won't be too long they are on the A39 already".

"Thanks Compton, we'll wait till they get here you can give them the keys and observe if you wish, I'll get our Mr. Scofield started on his list from last year".

Toni and Compton left one hour later, leaving SOCO well into their work, and Terry Scofield hard at it producing the details they had requested. Toni was eager to see the results of the interviews that Jonny's and Harrold's teams had carried out during the day but would wait till they were back at base and for them to come to her. She was finding it difficult to hold back and let them have a free reign; her little trip to Newbury being an example of her not letting go entirely. They wouldn't say anything to her of course, she was the boss and Newbury was well outside their plans for investigation at the moment, or it was until the discovery of the Camper van, its link to Reynolds and the day of Anton Biggs disappearance. She'd call a meeting to pool data and dump this lot into Harrold's lap; he wanted to be involved more so this would be his chance.

She feared most of the boys had long gone but maybe there was a chance Michael was still somewhere where she hoped he could be found alive and well. Her instinct told her they were close, one of the names on the list would be their quarry and when they tracked him down they would find Michael or at least have an idea where he might be. On her return she found Munroe had left a message requesting an update, Toni sent an e-mail with the details, not wishing a long confrontation in his office.

Chapter 13

All the case personnel were together except for DS Melanie Frazer, it was getting late, the sun had long set and the darker nights of Autumn were looming large no one was going home for a good while yet. The group of detectives were gathered around DI Jonny Musgrove's desk, the rough horseshoe of chairs on which they sat were touching arm to arm with no way out for any, unless Harrold or Jonny, who were at each end, moved to make space. Toni was seated at the apex, the white board facing her had been brought close up between the two lead detectives. The uniformed officers who had been brought in to help, stood behind surrounding the detectives eager to learn of their progress, even Compton and her two helpers had left their den to be present. Toni sat silent intending just to listen and observe hoping she could keep her resolve to do so at least until the end. Jonny Musgrove opened the proceedings.

"A lot of progress has been made today and I hope by the end we may have a plan in place that will lead to a result. Earlier today DI Davis and his team conducted interviews with the suspects from those at the top of the list produce by DC Busion, we will take the reports of those interviews along with some forensics gathered by SOCO at the vehicle hire company A.C.H. Limited. I have discussed a theory of what may be going on with Chief Inspector Webb and have the detailed autopsy report for Kenneth Swift. We have discovered certain things today leading us to send DS Frazer with a uniformed officer to watch the home of one Martin Reynolds. I will explain what has led to this action but first we will go through today's events".

Harrold stood and turned to the white board which had an enlarged version of Busion's list and the names of the missing boys.

"Right, to start, I went with Constable June Owens to visit Duke Kingswood and Frederick Marshall whilst DC Peter Andrews went to deal with Richard Foxhall and Martin Reynolds. Our approach was to present ourselves as crime prevention officers who, following a bout of stolen valuable older vehicles, were checking with owners of vintage cars to make sure they were aware of the problem and their cars were secure. Our questioning asked if they had been out in their cars recently and had they noticed anyone following them, in this way we hoped we could get a feel for the suspects without rousing their suspicion. Duke Kingswood was at the top of the list, however on arrival at his home I found him an unlikely candidate. Although he had the type of vehicle under scrutiny namely a green Jaguar, this vehicle had been in the local garage under repair during the week Michael was abducted, this was confirmed by a later visit to the repair shop. On Saturday he was acting as chauffeur for a wedding using a hire car from ACH Ltd. More of the hire company later. His wife who acted as photographer at the wedding confirmed they were both at the church, the wedding reception venue or the couple's home all day. We have confirmed this with phone calls to the catering company and the bride's father. They say they were also working at weddings on the other Saturdays we are interested in. I have not confirmed these yet but have no reason to doubt their statement. Our next call was to Frederick Marshall, he lives alone and is eighty two years old, he no longer drives but keeps his old cars in a garage adjacent to his home, I inspected the Jaguar XJ6, an Aston Martin

DB3 and an Austin Big 6 in this garage, it was obvious these vehicles had not been used for a very long time. I had a chat with Mr. Marshall and although he never uses the cars any more he can't bear to part with them, he never lends them out in fact he'd had them put up on blocks to protect the tyres and has the batteries removed and regularly put on charge. A local lad comes in every now and then to keep them clean reconnects the batteries and starts the engines, he says they haven't been on the road for more than three years, not since he gave up driving. I have dismissed him as a suspect or a source of the abduction car".

Jonny now turned to Peter Andrews indicating for him to continue.

"I went to the home of Richard Foxhall along with two uniformed officers. He lives in Basingstoke on the Popley estate, he was not at home at the time. I spoke with his neighbours who confirmed he was currently on holiday with his wife and twin seven year old sons. They were touring France in their camper van and had been gone over week, they did not know when they would be back. I asked about his Jaguar and where it was kept as there was no garage at the property. He apparently keeps it in a block of garages in the next street. On return here I checked with the Brittany ferries at Portsmouth they are due back in six days when they will have been gone for three weeks, which means he was away when Michael was abducted. We may need to check further to see if the Jaguar is where it is supposed to be and has not been let out but doubt it will prove to be a suspect vehicle".

Peter paused a moment to let the reports made so far sink in and to answer any questions. All remained quiet waiting for what he was about to reveal next.

"The outcome of where our next suspect leads us, namely Martin Reynolds, will determine if we have to expand our search, I think probably not. He and his mother live on a farm off Laverstoke Lane south of Laverstoke village which is on the B2406 between Basingstoke and Winchester, the lane further south joins the A303. There is one road leading to the farm but several tracks across the land that could lead back to the B2406. At this moment DS Mel Frazer is on watch at the farm as we strongly suspect he may be involved. I and the uniformed officer Constable Jacobs drove to the farm along the lane in a marked police car, as we neared the main farmhouse we were met by Martin Reynolds with a not too friendly manner. His exact words were 'What the bloody hell do you lot want?' I introduced us both explaining the reason for our visit and asked if we could see his Jaguar and any other vehicle that may be at risk. He told us to 'bugger off, my cars are my business I don't need you and yours nosing around', he then went to the house and slammed the door. We turned the car around and left however I parked up the lane some six or seven hundred yards so I could have a view of the property. Beside the main house there were two large barns and some smaller sheds. There was little sign of farming activity apart from a few chickens in the yard I couldn't see any livestock. I had a bad feeling about this guy so called DI Musgrove with my concern who dispatched an unmarked car with DS Frazer to continue the watch whilst I returned to the station to follow up on Reynolds and make my report here. He has some minor form and has been known to associate with other criminals, a bit of a heavy too acted as a bouncer in some of the lower class night clubs and one time bodyguard to one or two London villains".

Jonny looked across the desk to Toni who waved her hand for him to continue.

"Thanks Peter, now to the cruncher, DI Davis will you please continue".

Harrold Davis stood knowing the Chief had given him the opportunity to cement his position here by providing him with the evidence she and Compton had obtained at the A.C.H. hire company, all he needed to do was present it and set in motion the follow up action.

"A camper van hired by Martin Reynolds from A.C.H. at Newbury was found today to have fingerprints of Anton Biggs on three different places inside the vehicle, we are waiting on DNA results from samples taken to act as confirmation. Fingerprints of Martin Reynolds were also found in the same vehicle; DNA from the steering wheel is also under analysis. Various fibres and hair were also removed and are under comparison with samples taken from the home of Anton Biggs. This van was hired over the weekend when Anton went missing and CCT footage from the security cameras at Olympia shows this van, or one just like it, entering and leaving. The plate used at the show was not the one on the van when it left ACH but had been change for a made-up number not DVLA issued. The vehicle was entered as a late exhibit on the day, under the name of D. Thompson with a false address and payment in cash. This ties in with the method of entry for the Jaguar when Michael Soper went missing. The van was returned to ACH with its original number the following day. There was enough evidence here for a warrant to be issued to search the farm and arrest Reynolds, which we will do shortly. We should wait for DNA confirmation but DI Musgrove and I agree we should act tonight. Before then DCI Webb has something to add".

Toni stood and with a grim face looked at her officers wishing what she was about to say would not turn out to be true. As she looked round she saw the Super had entered the room and remained standing quietly by the door, he half smiled at her, likely an encouragement he was supporting her actions but also hoping she was wrong.

"Thanks everyone for your efforts, if this man is our abductor, which seems most likely, then we will probably have to hand this over to the Serious Crime Unit as I believe he is just a small part of something much bigger than we can deal with alone. We will still be involved in some role of course but we cannot keep this to ourselves we just don't have the resources. Your recent fine work may save at least one of the lads from a terrible fate and prevent many more from following that path. I have thought long and hard about why these particular children were being taken, at first I believed it was for sexual exploitation or even for slave working but that did not ring true. I and the Superintendent have come to the conclusion these children are most likely being taken abroad, their kidneys and possibly other organs extracted for use in an illegal transplant business".

She paused a moment, there was complete silence for just a second then a universal murmur of disbelief echoed round the room, followed by chatter growing louder and louder as the officers began to vent their feelings and ask questions of each other.

"Quieten down please, I know this outrages everyone and we may be wrong, let us hope so, but I have studied the alarming statistics and everything points in that direction. If I am right we must stop this foul trade now".

Further emotional reactions from the officers produced a hubbub that grew in intensity as what had been revealed began to sink in. Jonny then stood and called for silence.

"I know this is a lot to take in but now I need you all to prepare for what comes next. Records show Reynolds has a registered shotgun I also think he may have other weapons undeclared; he is also known to have been violent in the past so we will take an armed unit with us as a precaution. Constable Krane will you organise that please. We cannot approach the farm by car without being seen or heard, so the armed response unit will proceed on foot and be in position before we drive down the lane; they will be ready to respond but only if needed. I have a radio link to them and sole command over this unit, no one fires a shot without my say so. All open communication will be on channel four, other channels will be allocated as per protocol. Please check your radios and allocated channels before you leave. Once in place one car with DI Davis will go in as before, I will be with a second vehicle ready halfway down the lane. A SOCO team will wait in the lane but will only proceed to site when I have given the all clear. DI Davis will take over from me if I have a problem. The lead car officers will attempt to make an arrest, and although there is only one road in and out there are various tracks that could be used if he attempts to escape, these all meet at the river and lead to one exit point by a bridge on the B2406. Two cars will cover that exit. Any questions"?

No one responded all eager to get on with it.

"Remember there may be one or more children on site somewhere and he may use them as a shield so no untoward reaction please, if a life is in danger step down and let him go. I have a helicopter on standby available to follow him should it be needed. Reynolds mother is also on the premises and may be totally innocent so be aware. I have been in contact with DI Frazer; there has been no sign of movement at the farm up to now so let's go to it and remember everyone wears jackets and I mean everyone. Let's go"?

The room emptied quickly; within half an hour they were mobile and on their way.

Toni waited for the room to empty then moved over to the door where the Super had been waiting.

"Looks like we might be lucky Sir".

"Let us hope so Toni if we find even one child it will be a blessing and may open the door to where the others might be".

"I suggest you contact your pals in the Met to see who this Reynolds hangs out with".

"Already on that Sir, if Reynolds is our man then he is being controlled by someone and I want to know who".

Chapter 14

Marty was most put out by those nosey coppers calling just when he was going to feed and let the boy have a shower, he thanked goodness he was not in the barn when they came, they may have seen something and been suspicious. His Jag and the Alvis were in the large shed which he used as a garage, his bikes were in the smaller one next door, he'd thought they were safe enough way out here but if those coppers were right and some thieving buggers were on the prowl nicking vintage cars he'd better put some proper locks on his sheds; tomorrow he'd park the old tractor and van in front of the doors, they'd have a job to get in then. If they came when he was here he'd hear them in the lane and would send them packing with his twelve-bore. It was a bit late now for the boy to have a shower that could wait till tomorrow but he would go and give him his sandwich and special drink before Marty had his own supper. He wondered what Mum had cooked for him tonight he hoped it was his favourite steak and kidney pie, if not he'd ask for some tomorrow.

Not the hoped for pie but a very good second best, he'd had his fill of an excellent liver and bacon dinner with tinned peaches and ice cream for afters; she was a good cook his Mum and although she wasn't his real mother he had come to look on her like she was. She had looked after him and had even shown him affection in small doses unlike his bully of a Dad. He wasn't sure if she knew what was going on with the boys but suspected she had a good idea, although she never questioned him about it and always did as he demanded without hesitation. A rare spark of fondness for her had emerged over the years. He went to the fridge and took out a couple of cans of Stella deciding to settle down in front of the tele with her for the evening. Half an hour later, both cans consumed, he was dozing in front of his Mum's favourite game show feeling full and happy. Mum was in the kitchen during the ads making her second cup of tea when, without thinking, she automatically answered the unexpected knock on the kitchen door.

Chapter 15

Harrold spoke on the radio to Sergeant Frazer who reported all was quiet at the farmhouse. He and the three uniformed officers drove slowly down the lane dipped headlights lights needed as it was becoming quite dark. They pulled up twenty yards from the front of the farmhouse door, so far so good; there was no response from the house to their vehicle lights. The officers left the car and moved cautiously towards the building, two uniforms went around the back as planned, Harrold and his colleague went slowly towards the front door. They could see the flickering of a TV through the drawn front curtains and hear the sound of canned laughter from the same source. Harrold was pleased it seemed their approach had been undetected. He was about to knock on the door when his radio unexpectedly burst into life.

"Boss, boss! Quick come back here you should see this. Oh my God".

It was a call from one of the officers who had gone to the rear of the farmhouse. Harrold ran around behind indicating to his constable to stay put at the front. The back door was wide open, the two uniforms either side staring down at a woman lying face up just inside with blood all over her chest. Harrold bent and checked for a pulse even though it was obvious she was dead. He told the officers to remain where they were. He called through the door.

"Police officer coming in please show yourself".

There was no reply he didn't really expect one; he removed two plastic gaiters from his pocket and was putting them over his shoes as he called Jonny on the radio.

"You had better get down here Inspector, we have the body of an elderly woman just inside the rear entrance to the house, I believe her to have been shot, I don't know if anyone else is inside I am going in, the area is not secure please approach with caution".

Harrold then called again through the door.

"Police officer here, I am coming in now, if anyone is there please show yourself".

Harrold took a little comfort from his flack-jacket as he carefully stepped over the body and entered the kitchen, the door to the hallway was open and he could see light from the flickering television shining through from the open door of the living room. He moved slowly sweat breaking on his brow anticipating something dreadful was about to happen, nothing did. He cautiously peered through the door to see the hair of a man's head over the top of an armchair, his arms hanging loosely either side. Harrold entered the room, saw that apart from the seated man it was empty. He moved round to face the chair; the man's eyes were open unseeing with a reddish brown hole in his right temple. He checked for a pulse the man was dead. He went upstairs and looked in the three bedrooms and the bathroom to find them empty and undisturbed, he left the way he came in not wishing to further contaminate the scene. Another call to the SIO Jonny Musgrove as he moved round to the front.

"Sir, in addition to the woman there is the body of a male in the living room we need to get the doc and SOCO down here now".

The radio message received as Jonny arrived at the front of the farmhouse he didn't bother to reply as they came face to face.

"What the hell has happened here Harry"?

"Looks like an execution, the killer went in through the back door shot the mother then into the living room and took out Reynolds as he sat in his chair, I'm presuming it is Reynolds and his mother. Couldn't have been long ago both bodies are still warm. I have done a quick check of the house no sign of the boy, shouldn't we be looking for him?

"You're right get a search started will you please Harry SOCO are only a few minutes away, they will take over here, I'll call the pathologist. Why didn't Mel spot anything she has been here since Andrews left this afternoon"?

Jonny used the open channel 4 on his radio.

"Sergeant Frazer come down here at once. The armed response team should stand down and wait in their vehicle, thank you; all others meet Detective Inspector Davis outside the large barn no one except SOCO are to come within twenty yards of the house".

Melanie Frazer pulled up along the lane behind the cars already parked there the SOCO lads in front were suiting up preparing to go into the house; she jogged the last few yards wondering what had happened and why she hadn't seen or heard anything.

"What has gone on boss how did they get by me"?

"That should be my question were you asleep or something"?

The look Mel gave him was enough.

"Sorry Mel I didn't mean to....., I know you would be on the ball, tell me what you did see"?

She ignored his obviously frustrated accusation and accepted his immediate retraction without comment.

"Well nothing Sir, either I or Constable Jacob had the binoculars on the house at all times. You lose the overall picture when using them, so we took it in turns to scan close up whilst the other kept a wider eye on the house and grounds. The woman came out the front on one occasion to empty some rubbish and later she went across the yard and threw some feed down for the chickens. Reynolds came out of the house just before it got dark and went into the big barn carrying a package of some kind, I couldn't see what it was though, he was there for about five minutes and came back empty handed. I could see some movement in through the front window but when it became dark the curtains were drawn so only dim light was visible and some flickering probably a television, I was too far away to hear anything much. Nothing else after".

"Did you see any movement from the areas behind the house or hear anything unusual a gunshot maybe"?

"Not when it was light but after dark it was impossible to see anything beyond the buildings, nothing heard that comes to mind and as far as hearing a gunshot goes we wouldn't have still been sitting here now would we"? A question unanswered. "It's pretty quiet out here just a little birdsong. Is it true Sir are they both dead"?

"Yes Mel I'm afraid so, someone got here before us and shot them both. They must have used a silencer or you would have heard I'm sure; it seems like they knew we were coming and didn't want this guy to talk to us, but how did they know, is there a leak in our camp or was it just bad timing? What a bloody mess. Anyway, we can't do anything here until forensics have done their job and the pathologist removes the bodies so let's go and help with the search".

A uniform constable came over until he was within shouting distance of the two detectives.

"Detective Musgrove Sir you must come and see this I think we have found where the boy might be".

They both swivelled at the same time almost knocking each other over in their haste to move. Mel was the first to get to the officer. "Where"?

"Follow me it is in the big barn, there is a converted container inside with rooms. The doors are open except for one which is sealed tight with a mortice lock we don't know where the key is, they are trying to break in at the moment".

Jonny pushed by the constables who were crowded in the barn all trying to help but just creating confusion.

"Right everyone stop what you are doing, all of you except DI Davis and Constable Andrews please leave. I know you are keen to find the boy but you have just buggered up a valuable crime scene with your size twelves, we will find and open the door with a key, trying to break in will take much longer. It is too dark to continue a useful search of the area now so please return to your vehicles and await further orders. Peter go to the house call on the SOCOs to look for the keys they are probably bunched together somewhere. Harrold go and organise an ambulance if the boy is in there he will need help for sure".

Peter returned after what seemed forever, but was less than five minutes, with three bunches of keys.

"They were all together on hooks behind the kitchen door, I don't know which one so I brought the lot".

Jonny looked and saw there were mortice type keys on each bunch so the only way to find what they wanted was to try them one at a time. He set Peter to the task; it took a few tense minutes when the third key of the second bunch hit the spot, it easily turned the offending lock and allowed the small square door to swing back. They peered inside it was dark but as soon as Jonny stuck his head inside a small ceiling light came on. A combination of fear and joy welled up in his rapidly beating heart; tears came to his eyes when he saw the small child curled up in a foetal ball on a skinny mattress. The smell was appalling as he stepped in to feel the frail body was warm and responsive. He lifted him into his arms and carried him out of that evil hole into the fresh air, the tears now streaming uncontrolled, unnoticed down his face. The paramedics were waiting outside the now taped off area, he walked over and placed the boy gently into their waiting skilled hands.

"Please take care of him he is very precious; I think his name may be Michael".

Melanie placed her hand gently on his shoulder a soft smile for him to lift his spirits. She could see he was moved by the discovery.

"One saved boss as much as we could have hoped for. When forensics have extracted everything from here we will have a good idea who else he has had locked up and probably lots more. What do want us to do now"?

Jonny had recovered enough to take on board her question but had no idea how to answer.

"God help me Mel I don't know our only witnesses are dead, all the other children are gone. I suppose we must leave it to SOCO now; they will have their work cut out what with the house, the container and the sheds, they will be here for ages. I want to wait for the pathologist before we leave. Where is DI Davis now"?

"He's following some tracks that appear to have come along the pathway at the back of the house shall I get him"?

"No he'll be back when he's ready, I'll leave you to close the site send everyone back who is not needed. Arrange watch teams on eight hour shifts to remain here during the site investigation, two officers should do it. I'm going to meet Doctor Taylor she should be here soon".

Jonny switched to channel 11 his direct line to the DCI.

" I don't know how much you picked up what has gone on here Ma'am but we found both Reynolds and his Mother dead on our arrival".

"Yes Jonny I got that much what about the children"?

"There was just one alive I can't be sure but I think it is Michael I only have his photo to go on; we need to confirm it's him before we speak to the parents, remember our mistaken assumption before. He has been taken to the hospital at Basingstoke an officer is with him".

"Leave it with me I'll check his identity before we inform anyone. No sign of any other children I suppose".

"Sorry just one boy here. Reynolds had a set-up with four separate rooms in a container, they all appear to have all been recently occupied, hopefully there will be plenty of traces, fingerprints DNA and other stuff. With luck we'll soon know who was being kept here, the labs are going to be busy for sure. What is worrying me Ma'am is how did they know we were on to Reynolds; someone's been talking out of turn at least or maybe worse. I'll finish up here and come back as soon as the pathologist has released the bodies".

"No Jonny go home when you have finished it'll be late enough nothing more you can do in the dark; get some sleep you will be no use coming back here in the early hours knackered. Come in later tomorrow when you have rested, same goes for Mel and Harry let them know, that's an order".

"Okay okay, you're right of course it's just what is happening is making me want to grab hold of these animals and do… whatever, you know don't you…. I won't sleep till we stop it".

"Yes you will, just go home Jonny as soon as you can. We'll get them tomorrow".

"Fine, I promise I'll do my best, see you tomorrow then. You hear that Mel; we have to go home now".

"I wish; shall I tell DI Davis he has to go home too".

"No joking apart, the boss is right really but I doubt if I will sleep much after seeing that in there".

Jonny wasn't referring to the dead bodies, he'd learnt to accept them as part of the job but the nightmare container with its cells for children and the thought of why they were being taken hit him in a way he had never felt before.

"You and Harrold finish up as soon as you can and follow her orders, she seems to think sleep and fresh minds will do the job much better tomorrow. Where is Doctor Taylor, Davis and Krane too I want to know where they are"?

Mel called the two officers on channel 4 to report in. She couldn't contact the pathologist unless she used her mobile so decided to wait for her a little longer.

"Davis here, we've found some tyre tracks at the back of the house, they look like an off road bicycle tyre to me they go quite a long way but it's too dark to follow, we need daylight to find where they go, it may be how our killer got here unseen".

"Okay Harry make sure SOCO take a cast then come back to the house front".

"P C Krane Sir, I am on my way back with the firearms unit to Basingstoke to disarm, will you need me to come back after; did you find the boys we only heard a part of what happened on the open channel"?

"You have no need to come back here Keith we will all be leaving soon anyway and yes we found one lad I'm almost certain it is Michael Soper, I would like you to contact the constable who accompanied him in the ambulance. I don't know his condition but he was alive at least. He will be at Basingstoke Hospital soon. Check if the officer with him has been able to confirm his identity, then arrange for a family liaison officer to collect the parents and take them to the hospital but not before you have confirmed it is definitely their son, get the FLO to give me a call later. We won't interview him till we get the all clear from his Doctors. Any problems call me if not, we'll see you tomorrow".

"Okay Sir, no problem, I'll be in first thing".

"Doctor Taylor has just called my mobile, Sir, she is sorry but it will be another fifteen minutes before she gets here".

Jonny scowled mumbling under his breath. Mel was not happy; Jonny's reaction to finding the lad in such conditions was obviously stressing him out. A harshness in his voice and the way he demanded to know where everyone was well out of character. Perhaps she should offer to finish up with Harrold Davis and let him go home. The thought only crossed her mind for a second she knew he would never accept. She'd take on as much as she could tonight here and give him time to recover his composure.

"Jonny I will go and make sure SOCO prepare for Debbie's arrival, anything else you want me to do"?

"Whatever you want, we can't do much till Doctor Taylor has finished with the bodies and SOCO have cleared working in the house, the containers and on the vehicles. It is too bloody dark for us to start searching we'd probably go trampling all over important evidence. It's a bloody mess, we are going to be here for days when I want to be looking for the other boys. I tell you what Mel, I know its late but try and get hold of transport tonight so we can remove the vehicles back to base first thing, it will save us some time".

"Sure Sir good idea, but what we get from here will open up a whole load of stuff we can follow up on, we will just have to wait for the forensics to give us some answers and a good starting point".

"You're right of course I'm just impatient, I wish Doc Taylor was here".

As he spoke the red Sirocco of Debbie Taylor arrived fifty yards short of the taped off area. She retrieved her bag from the boot and changed into her working white suit where she stood.

"Sorry I'm a bit late detective Musgrove, it seems today has been a busy time for us pathologists, four suspicious deaths in just the last six hours not including yours; well where are they"?

"Hello Doctor, that's okay, we have had enough to do here but need you to do your stuff before we can get inside. SOCO have finished at the back door area where the dead woman is located and are currently in the front room where the second victim will be found; by the time you have finished with the woman they should be clear there too".

120

Jonny walked round to the back of the house with Debbie following; he'd left Mel a little way up the lane waiting for the vehicle transporter. She would show him where to turn as he would need to back down the last hundred yards or so as there was no room to manoeuvre a large vehicle at the bottom of the lane.

"I hear you found one of the boys alive, how is he and do you know who yet"?

"I think it is Michael, but it's only from the photo, we made a mistake before so need more positive confirmation but I'm pretty sure it's him. He was unconscious or in a deep sleep, probably drugged. I am waiting for the officer who accompanied him to the Hospital to call me".

Debbie took photos of the prone corpse, knelt by the woman's body looking intently at the wound in the centre of her chest. She leant forward and smelt the area, then felt her face and arms; she was quite cold and rigor had set in. She spoke into the mike at her shoulder.

"A white woman approximately sixty years of age, appears to have been shot in the chest where there is a smell of gunshot residue so shot from fairly close range less than a metre, apparently fell back and I would think was dead almost at once".

She inserted her special thermometer piercing the side of the woman and into the liver.

"Dead about six hours, near to eight pm last night".

She then turned the body over noting the settlement darkening of the skin on the back, buttocks and legs taking photos as she carried out her examination.

"She died where she fell. Damage to the back of her head is consistent with the fall; there is no exit wound so I should be able to recover the bullet; no other visible signs of injury. Body to be bagged and removed to Richmond for autopsy".

Debbie stepped over the woman and proceeded into the living room with Jonny close behind. The SOCO lads by then had finished and moved out through the front door. She approached the body from behind the chair moving slowly round to the front taking in the position and general appearance of the dead man. She carried out her examination in a similar fashion to the woman taking pictures throughout.

"A man of about forty, slim and in good condition generally. His hands and nails are clean inconsistent with farm work. The same temperature as the woman so died at about the same time, eight pm last night. A single gunshot wound to the right temple, again from close range, some burning would indicate from just a few inches, the autopsy will confirm. I would think dead instantly. The position of his body and lack of defecation would suggest he was completely unaware of the shot, possibly even asleep at the time. Death was instant. He died where he sat. No exit wound and no sign of other injuries".

Debbie switched off her recorder and turned to the CSO responsible for transporting the bodies.

"You can do the woman as soon as the van arrives but for him I suggest you wait for rigor to relax before bagging".

Debbie left the house and walked over to where Jonny was waiting.

"Well there you have it detective, don't quote me but it looks like an execution of this man, the woman was just in the way. The killer probably used a silencer or the victim would have been alerted when the woman was shot, he was almost certainly asleep when killed. A professional kill so I presume no cartridges were found so maybe a revolver, or more likely he picked them up before he left. Close range shots with no exit so unlikely a revolver but we can't rule it out. We will know more on the type of weapon when I recover the slugs; our pickup van is on the way to bag up and transport them back to the lab so we will do the autopsies first thing. Is there anyone to do the ID".

"No known relatives however we have prints for the man so can confirm his ID from those so you can start as soon as you like. I go along with a silencer being used as Mel was on watch when it happened, she saw and heard nothing; we arrived just after eight so think they were killed only a short while before, when DI Davis found them he said the bodies were still warm so we were just too late".

Three hours later the SOCO lads were finishing up with the house and the container. The CSIs had collected a great number of items that would allow them to put a picture together of what had been happening here. The bodies had been removed with Debbie long gone. The cars had been checked and were loaded aboard the transporter. Time to go and get some sleep, the night shift uniforms would remain on site till tomorrow. Jonny Mel and Harry said their goodnights and were on their way home. Jonny would come back and do his search tomorrow.

Chapter 16

John Digby's eyes were opening to a room he had never seen before. He felt weak as if he had had not slept at all. Most of the day had passed with nothing to eat or drink for several hours, his mouth was dry and his stomach was rumbling. The bed on which he was laying had no covers, he was still shoeless in the clothes he had been wearing since he left home; how long that was he had no idea. This room was much larger than the metal box of earlier, with light creeping in through the covered curtains. He tried to sit up but as soon as he did his head began to spin forcing him to lay back eyes closed. The couldn't care less feelings of earlier were fading fast fear creeping in to take its place.

Anton Biggs had been aware of his surroundings for some time but was afraid to open his eyes. He remembered the journey in the van but had pretended to be asleep. He'd had an idea the drink they kept giving him was making him sleepy so swallowed only a little every time even spitting it out the last time when no one was looking. He tried to stay awake but still fell asleep after they put him in the room. He was wide awake now so sneaked a look around the room; on seeing he was alone, he sat up. The bed was soft with a dirty mattress and no covering; he was warm enough but his bare feet felt uncomfortable, light from the partly covered window showed it was either very early in the morning or the sun was beginning to set. On hearing someone at the door he quickly lay down, again feigning sleep. He heard two men talking in a language he did not understand. One of them grabbed his arm and jabbed him with a needle, the sharp stab made him cry out. A few seconds later he disappeared into darkness.

Doctor Francois Aureol pulled the mask up over his mouth, his mind closed to the thoughts that had brought him to this. His youthful oaths and ambitions destroyed long ago. His skill as a surgeon had not diminished but the use to which they were now being used ate away at his soul; his weakness of character had allowed him to fall under the control of these evil men where their threats made him selfishly fear for himself regardless of what abominations he was being asked to do. He tried to justify his action by concentrating on the recipients, on those who would benefit from the procedures he was about to perform. The sometimes death of the donors he blanked from his thoughts at the time but had no way to resolve the dilemma that saving one or more lives at the expense of another had any real justification.

He moved in; the two living beings were sedated ready for him to begin. His medical support staff seldom spoke, they carried out their tasks responding to his directions without question, he wondered what hold the men had over them that made them complicit. The young woman with the diseased kidneys had been kept alive by dialysis for some time but had reached a point where death would come soon but for what he was about to do. The woman was opened and her right kidney exposed, he could see the innate organ, treatment having failed to deliver any hope of its recovery. He ignored the offending lump of useless flesh preparing the vessels and tubes that were to feed the new kidney with blood and the urinary tract connection from this now redundant and useless flesh. He turned to the donor, cutting in with the same deftness as he did to the woman, this time exposing a fully functioning kidney; a fresh young organ only in the early years of its role in supporting the body in which it was created. He hesitated for a few seconds but proceeded to remove the pristine renal gland tying off the vessels as he went. The boy's incision was closed and he was taken out of the theatre to recovery. The newly removed kidney was then placed in the woman's right pelvic area, the arterial and venal blood vessels were placed adjacent to their new recipient organ and the careful task of connecting the vessels began. Drugs to prevent rejection were administered, all that was needed now was for the new organ to prove functional by her passing some urine and his involvement was over. Three hours from start to finish and it was done. None of his patients remained at the facility where he performed the operations, as soon as they were stable, they were removed he knew not where. The donor was either removed at once or remained if a second transplant was scheduled. Today, thankfully, there was just one procedure. Two new patients were due tomorrow, one would be for him, there was no let up, his task masters were not to be ignored. He knew the donors were unlikely to survive, he had a good idea what happened to them when they left his operating theatre, it wasn't something he wanted to think about. He stepped away removing mask and gown in one motion, he just wanted to leave and go to his hotel; his sweat soaked body demanded a shower, his guilt blasted mind several large Pastis.

Chapter 17

Toni lay awake waiting for the light of the morning to peep through her bedroom window before she rose. She had deliberately kept away from the scene at the farm wanting to let her teams have the freedom to conduct their own investigations, however, enough was enough, today she would take a more active role; the terrible events she suspected were happening elsewhere had to be stopped and pussy-footing around was not going to cut it. Eggs on toast and two strong coffees with just a little sugar were a needed breakfast for it was going to be a long day and her strengths were going to be tested. Dressed in her usual light blouse, dark grey slacks and matching jacket her hair brushed back, no make-up today, she was ready for business.

Early as usual she found the station was in the process of night to morning shift change over, Toni went straight to her office she did not feel like exchanging banter with any of the officers coming in or leaving. Unbeknown to her the CSIs and her detectives had been at the farm from before daybreak even before she arrived at the station they had made good progress.

Information was piling in as they uncovered evidence at the farm. It was being relayed to Compton Busion as fast as it was discovered, she in turn was keeping Toni updated. Some fingerprints had been matched already, others and DNA samples were on their way to the labs as well as fabric fibre and hair samples from the cells in the container. One significant discovery concerned the death of young Kenneth; fingerprints had been found confirming he had been imprisoned in the last cell of the container. The ventilation duct to that cell was blocked with debris from an old bird's nest to such an extent there was no possible air flow. It is almost certain he had been left too long with the door shut causing him to slowly suffocate. DI Davis had tramped through the pathways at the back of the house following the bicycle tracks he had discovered the day before. They terminated some mile and a half away at a point where the path joined the B2046. There were some car or van tyre tracks on the verge at the same location. He had the CSIs take casts of the bike, car tyres and some footprints found at the junction of the road and path.

The boy they found was indeed Michael Soper he had woken from his drugged sleep during the night and was reunited with his overjoyed parents. No one had formally questioned him yet just enough to establish his identity and to confirm he was abducted from the car show in a green Jaguar. The doctors found the drug Zopiclone, among others, in his system; same cocktail as found in young Kenneth Swift.

Too much information was arriving for one person to take in and evaluate, it needed coordinating and whittling down to what was significant and that which corroborated what they already knew. This was a task Compton and her team would revel in. Toni gave her a call asking her to process everything relating to the boys in separate groups and flag up areas common to all four. Finding Reynolds and recovering Michael was not the end of this case not by a long chalk; she called Jonny asking him to order all officers return to base; once together Toni could consolidate the information and instigate a plan of action. There must be a way of finding those who had controlled Reynolds and the route along which the boys were being sent. Speed was what was needed here if there was any chance of saving those lads recently abducted and maybe others from sources they did not know about.

She called Jonny and Harrold to her office; although she wanted Jonny to run the meeting she intended to include DI Harrold Davis in the loop at the start, she was finding it hard not to take over, this move was a real effort but she knew a necessary one if she was to get the best out of her team.

"Good work you two last night saving the lad was a real success and what you have dug out of the scene today gives us several tracks to follow up on. What you decide to do next will determine whether we will be able to track down the other boys; I know the chances of saving them are slim but we must try. I will be briefing the Super after this meeting, I will do my best to keep this with us for now but I suspect he will want to involve Serious Crime sooner rather than later, if he does we will have to hand everything over and lose all control. At best they may second one of you to assist during the hand over whilst they get up to speed. They may of course have been looking into similar incidents from a different point of view, I have no idea about that though, they are a secretive lot, if they have been working on illegal organ trading, then what we know will no doubt help them so we shouldn't be too reluctant to give up what we have. Anyway, in the meantime let's see what you think. Harry you go first".

Harrold hadn't been prepared to speak at this time as he thought DI Musgrove would be the first choice as SIO and would be leading off. Pleased to be included like this and in an investigation of some real significance, made him glad he had moved to Basingstoke; he resolved to make every effort to expunge the negative attitude he had displayed during his first few weeks here. He would show everyone and especially the

Chief that he would be a real asset to the team. His hesitation was momentary, he was sure no one had noticed. They had.

"Yes….Ma'am….Whoever killed Reynolds must have known we were coming or even was warned we were watching; they obviously knew him and his farm well enough; coming in along the track rather than the road meant he could get to the house without warning and avoid us too. Although we have bike and vehicle tracks they are not going to be much good as we have no idea where they came from. What worries me is someone has information about us and our movements, Reynolds was key in finding where the boys are being sent, as soon as we were on to him they took him out, it looks like we have a leak".

Toni thought the same but was not one to go off without proof and bandying it about they had a spy in their midst would only warn whoever it was and she did not want that. She had in mind a way to ferret out any bad egg without them being aware so decided to scotch the idea of a traitor in their camp immediately.

"I don't think it likely Harrold, they knew something was going to break when the boy died I'm sure the decision to remove Reynolds was taken well before we knew of him. These people are very careful, getting rid of him as soon as they could even before the intended to pick up of Michael, it was just luck they got there before we did. Reynolds will not be the only one procuring for them so removing him was their way of shutting us out. Losing one donor source was a small price to pay for protecting their anonymity. Carry on".

"Err yes I see; you are probably right, always looking for the bad guy me. What next ah yes, we have the CCTV data of vehicles on the A303 around the time of the killing, currently under scrutiny we may get lucky and see something, a car with a bike rack or a van maybe. The cars we found in the barn come garage the Jaguar in particular have given us Michael's fingerprints and some others, from what appears to be small hands, maybe from earlier abductions. The other car, a vintage Alvis, also has one set of prints of a similar type. Some phial of liquid was found in a drinks cabinet in the rear of the Jaguar, under analysis as we speak, I'll let you know as soon as we have any results of this and the unknown prints. One more thing there were several made up number plates in the garage, clones of similar models".

"Thanks Harrold good work. What do you have Jonny"?

Jonny was aware Toni was trying to encourage and induct DI Davis into the team as quickly as possible so accepted the change of protocol where even though he was lead officer he was given a temporary second spot here during this briefing.

"Right boss, what we have here is a bit of a waiting game with lots of forensic results pending, the labs are prioritising our stuff and feeding the results though piecemeal, but in the mean time we have identified the four boys we know about were definitely in that container with DNA and finger prints of others as yet unidentified; Constable Busion is spreading her search to try and find out who they are. Now it seem likely Reynolds kept the boys until they could match the blood sample with prospective recipients, I can't see Reynolds taking blood samples himself so someone must have been here to do that, there are prints and samples of an unknown adult who has been in all four cells on more than one occasion. He will have come to the farm by car so we are looking at the CCTV of vehicles that came along the A303 and turned off onto thee A2406 also those coming up the 2406 from Winchester. There are cameras close to both junctions either side so we can see those coming along the A303 but not going further than the turn off, the same goes for the Winchester Road junction. It will take a quite a while I know, but if we find a regular coming and going we may hit upon the guy's car who took the blood samples. Another vehicle will have used the route regularly too, the one picking up the boys; I can't see Reynolds being allowed to see where they were going so he is unlikely to have delivered them. He must have made contact somehow to let them know when he had a new captive, there was no landline so probably by mobile phone, we didn't find one in the house so whoever killed him must have taken it. Well see if one is registered to him but I doubt it, they will have used untraceable phones and off the shelf sim cards".

"It looks like you have a lot to go on with; if we are lucky with the forensic and CCTV results they will give us some leads to follow up. Carry on and keep me informed of any significant development".

Toni left the squad room and made her way up stairs, she needed to brief the Super and see which direction he would take. Her mind was wondering how to set a trap for whoever was leaking information or at least find out if there was indeed an internal leak or if some outsider had found a way into their systems. I could all still be just coincidence, her inner feeling told her otherwise.

Chapter 18

Henry Giles was a man of extremes. He was extremely ugly, ugly in his manner, character and appearance. He cared for no one except Henry Giles. He was always extra careful to protect his position and defended it with extreme violence. He hardly ever made threats, he didn't need to, his reputation was enough for anyone who came under his influence to know the consequences of even the slightest mistake. The only man he trusted, Jake Snell, was never far from his side, willing and happy to do his bidding. Not privileged with a formal education in the formal sense Jake had a more than a cunning mind understanding the ways of the street and the underworld in which he lived. He had been with Henry since they were kids, both still living in Camberwell where they were born. Neither had ever worked but lived off the efforts of others through extortion and pimping among the several nefarious enterprises Henry had acquired through fear and violence.

They had both been arrested a couple of times when they were younger, but witnesses had mysteriously disappeared leaving them with no convictions. The local police had been told not to waste resources being so undermanned, as were most forces, they had limited time and almost no chance of securing a conviction anyway so followed orders and left them in relative peace to carry on.

If it became necessary Henry didn't bother to make threats, he just carried them out, or rather Jake did. Reynolds was the latest to receive his treatment. The business of selling kids for body parts had been kept very quiet; a very lucrative enterprise had annoyingly become vulnerable to the recent events involving the police. That idiot Reynolds had put the whole enterprise at risk by letting the boy die and stupidly leaving the body for all and sundry to find, at least Henry had found out in time and had dispatched Jake to eliminate him before they too became vulnerable.

The police were well aware of their business in most respects but the abduction aspect of his little empire had been instigated by his hidden boss and as yet had not become known by the police or anyone come to that; he wanted to keep it that way; the accepted status quo and quiet life would vanish if they lost control of this particular activity. His boss whom he had never actually met in person certainly had some pull with the local police, for they left him in relative peace. He often wondered if it wasn't someone in the police themselves that ran his business. He thought back to when he was arrested by a cop called Vale for a drug possession bust; a DI who let him off with a caution provided he did some snooping for him. He gave up a couple from the opposition; it led to a biggish drug haul which seemed to satisfy Vale. He heard from him a few times after but not for a while. He was picked up three years ago by some guys he never saw as he was blindfolded. They explained in detail he was no longer running his own show and would receive orders from elsewhere. The detail was excruciatingly painful, he was in no doubt what was required; his missing little finger a reminder of his expected continuing loyalty. If Vale was this controller no way was he going to look there, much too dangerous.

Henry decided to order a complete shutdown, with all traces of the operation to be removed or destroyed. The collectors must go about their normal and legal business with any planned abductions cancelled at once. If by some chance the police outside the locals discovered what they were doing at Reynolds farm and it led to other collectors being identified and they made searches, he wanted nothing found that would lead back to him.

"Jake contact the collectors, tell them to shut up shop now and clean up their sites and I mean clear everything showing they had been involved. If they have a visit from the police remind them to say nothing; oh, then order them to destroy and dump their mobile phones, we'll send them new ones later".

"Okay Hen, what about the kids who are left"?

"There wasn't time to move the boy left at Reynold's farm so he is gone; thank goodness the girl was transferred to Joe's place in Sidcup earlier or we would have lost her too. Call Alf Bailey and get him to pick up the kid in the van direct from Joe's and get across the channel with her today. There won't be time for you to do an ambulance pick up so phone Joe to get the girl drugged up and ready to go then clear his place of any evidence; you will have to give Alfred Joe's address. I'll call the 'Froggies' to be at the house in Abbeville to collect her".

"Wouldn't it be better to just get rid of her"?

"She's too valuable, we've already lost the money for the boy left at Reynolds place. I really don't like any of the drivers knowing where the collectors live but speed is essential here. Dumping her would mean too much risk especially if the cops have a handle on any of the collectors. No, neither of us can go near anyone in the chain, we don't know who is watching. Sending her to France is the best option, it can be done without us showing ourselves. I know it means we are exposing Alfred but he doesn't know much about what is going on and for sure he won't say anything about us even if caught. We can start up again later when all quietens down".

The phone call to France did not go well, an unscheduled delivery was not accepted at first but Henry applied some pressure and threatened to cut off all future supplies, they conceded reluctantly and agreed to have someone at the Abbeville house that evening but insisted they weren't ready and had nowhere suitable to keep her. They decided if they were to take on an extra donor outside of schedule they were not going to pay for her and told him as much. Henry Giles made a mental note of that fact for future reference; no one gets away with not paying their dues. He wondered if this was worth all the trouble, maybe it would be better to just kill off the girl and dump her somewhere; he was in two minds; if he was to get rid of the girl he would have to cancel everything and as the move was arranged already she would soon be out of their hands; he decided to let the planned transfer go ahead. The Frenchman's lack of cooperation would give him leverage in the future if indeed there was a future with them. He vowed to try and find an alternative customer so he could tell the Frogs to get stuffed; he was unsure if the boss would go for a change of customer, he had no idea what their arrangement was or what was happening to the kids. Best leave it for now they'll be pissed off enough without him poking his nose in their business.

Chapter 19

Alfred was surprised to get the call from Jake. These trips were usually organised with plenty of notice and the subjects were delivered to him; he'd never had to go and collect anyone before. Jake gave him specific instructions over the phone which he never normally did, in the past he would be asked to meet at a café, a library, a supermarket; always somewhere different he would be given a piece of paper with his instructions which he had to destroy soon after, they seldom spoke during these brief exchanges, all the information he needed was written down. The mobile phone was supplied by Jake, he was told in no uncertain terms, for the sole use of arranging these meetings and not for any other calls, this was the first time that had changed. He used his own phone as usual to book the channel tunnel for six this evening enough time for him to collect the van from the hire company, get to Sidcup and back to Folkestone. His flat in Maidstone was central to all the places he wanted to get to so had plenty of time. The delivery was to be at the same house in France as before, this was new too, he normally never went to the same place twice. He was not getting paid in France this time either, Jake promised he would be paid in pound notes when he came back, he didn't mind or doubt Jake's word and wasn't worrying about not being paid, it was just 'all very unusual'. His paranoiac mind was twitching all over the place, he wondered what was going on with those in charge, he would have to be careful on this trip he needed to take care of himself first and foremost, he still had in mind the nosey customs men at Dover who stopped him on his way back last time, it was a good job he was going through the tunnel he did not want to meet up with those two again. He collected the van from the garage in Sydenham as always except a small problem, the man there was not expecting him. He said he normally had a text from the owner to say Alfred was coming so he had to wait whilst a phone call was made to confirm it was okay to release the vehicle. He also had to park his little Fiat in the street this time, the garage guy said he had no room as several vehicles were due in the following day. Another out of norm event played on his mind as he drove towards Sidcup.

The small holding in Sidcup was tucked down a long lane well off the main road. Alfred pulled up outside the low building as instructed and waited. A few minutes later a man and woman emerged from the greenhouse type building with a young girl being supported between them. She wasn't able to walk without assistance or even stand. Alfred opened the back of the van to reveal the hidden compartment where he had already placed the quilt and pillow. The couple lifted the girl and placed her inside, she curled up immediately and fell asleep at once. Alfred covered her and closed the compartment. The woman moved away towards the house a bit further down the lane. Joe passed Alfred a bottle of 'doctored squash'.

"Here take this. I've never prepared anyone for this before they normally take them in an ambulance, I gave her a shot of stuff they sent me by courier an hour ago and she has been asleep since then. She should stay asleep for a few hours at least, give her some if she wakes just half the bottle should keep her out for another three or four hours".

"Thanks, hope the stuff you gave her works okay; I don't want her waking up too soon. I'm Alfred by the way. Do you know what is going on, why the change of routine"?

Alfred took the bottle and tossed it onto the cab seat. They shook hands, oddly like old mates even though they had never met before.

"Hello Alfred, I'm Joe, the injection knocked her out straight away; she should be out for quite a while, so they told me and no I don't know why the change in routine I never like to ask, too risky being nosey with these guys. All I know is they have shut me down and told me to clean up all traces, I'm a bit worried the cops have wind of what is going on, but I'm sure it is just they are being extra cautious; they did say it was only temporary and they would be in touch soon. Quite frankly I'll be glad of the break".

"Well Joe, I'll be on my way. Good luck, hope we never meet again eh"?

They both laughed a nervous kind of chuckle as Alfred swung up into his seat and started the engine. A short wave of farewell and he was gone.

Alfred was very intense, his mind in a whirl; the change of routine had thrown him already and the brief conversation with this guy Joe had made him even more concerned. Everything seemed to be shutting down in a hurry and here he was lumbered with the task of taking this girl out of the Country with no back up if anything went wrong. He knew the French would run a mile if there was anything amiss, he wasn't confident they would even be there. He had no way of speaking to Jake that was always an incoming call, he could only text; besides he had been told to ditch the phone so probably Jake would have done the same, he would keep it for a while just in case. He was on his own he would have to make decisions to protect himself. He must make the delivery, or he doubted if he would live to explain why he hadn't, Henry Giles was not a forgiving man.

The drive to Folkstone was slow but uneventful, he was an hour early and did not want to hang around inside the terminal. He left the A20 on the hill above the tunnel turn off where there was a services, a large lorry park and a filling station with an outside toilet. He filled the van with diesel and moved it next to the loo. He climbed through to the rear where he opened the cover to reveal the girl still asleep. He gave her a gentle shake; she stirred and opened her eyes. He helped her to sit up.

"Young lady you need to go to the toilet now".

He had not transported a girl before, it had been fine with the boys for he could control them easily, he was unsure how to deal with a girl especially using a toilet. He helped her stand and moved her to the driver's door. He walked her staggering figure to the toilet and let her go in on her own standing by the door. She went in without any questions. He waited a while, but she didn't come out. He knocked and called with no response. Embarrassed he opened the door to find her sitting on the seat, knickers round her ankles fast asleep. He tried to wake her, but she was unresponsive. He lifted her with his left arm round her waist and pulled up her underwear with his right hand. He carried her to the van pushing her up into the driver's seat her clothes all awry. He didn't see the man coming up behind him.

"You all right mate what's up with the girl"?

Alfred was stunned for a second the shock caused him to almost lose his voice; regaining his composure quickly with the need to reply to this interfering stranger right away.

"Were okay thanks, been travelling all night, my girl's a little car sick and very tired, we'll be on the train soon going to France on holiday you know".

"Oh right, it just she seemed to be in distress; is she okay"?

"She'll be fine just needing some sleep; we'll be camping tonight on the other side".

"That's nice, she your daughter like, what's her name"? The man persisted with his annoying interference.

Alfred ignored the questions he just wanted to be somewhere out of the way of this inquisitive bugger; he put on a false smile with a finger to his lips indicating he did not wish to wake the girl and replied in a loud whisper.

"Thanks for your interest but we're okay, must be moving on you know, don't want to miss our slot".

Alfred climbed into the cab moved the girl over to the passenger seat and belted her in. The man's question made him think; he didn't even know her name and here he was about to hand her over to God knows who. He didn't have a daughter although he had been married a few years back, there were no kids to consider when he and his wife separated. He wondered how he would feel if she were his daughter. He then drove out of the garage sweat running down his back, his fear dismissed the paternal thought; emotion was getting the better of him, what had he let himself in for, he had to think, it was too dangerous to take this girl abroad but what choice did he have. He stopped a hundred yards away in the lorry park and moved the girl into the compartment swearing under his breath. She had not been in a condition where he could make her drink the doctored juice so she could wake up any minute, what if it was during the check in or as he was going through passport control, that would be a disaster; he must find somewhere quiet and make sure she was going to stay asleep. He had no idea if Joe had prepared her properly for the long journey like the guy in the ambulance had always done; had he given her too much of the injection or not enough? His instincts were telling him he was heading into a situation out of his control he must step back and be rational get his head together and not let his emotions run away with him. Think, think! What could he do to avoid going to France and yet not incur the wrath of Jake and his even worse boss Henry? He could just let her go and say the girl had escaped. No that wouldn't do. He could kill her and say she died of too much of the drug but what would he do with the body and Jake would still blame him and probably kill him too; he didn't think he had the bottle to kill her anyway; stupid thinking like this. Perhaps if he changed his plans and went on the ferry instead; he could throw her overboard. The ideas were getting more and more ridiculous by the minute but then he had an inkling of a plan that might solve his dilemma. Maybe just maybe he could get away with this if he just held his nerve. Yes, it could work, he would have to think it through make sure his story was watertight, he could lose the girl and not be blamed as the whole thing would appear to have been out of his control. Jake would be cross of course but would have no reason to hurt him, he probably wouldn't get paid but that was a small consideration. He wasn't so sure about how Henry Giles would react, but it was a chance he might have to take. He sat for a while finally calming down wondering if maybe he should just make the trip, give her to the French and be home in the morning. He would have to make up his mind soon as the departure time was fast approaching.

What Alfred didn't know was the man at the filling station had watched him leave, he'd thought the situation was odd so had noted the van registration number. 'It wasn't right the girl having her underwear all exposed like that and her Dad not giving her enough care. Maybe I'm being nosey, but you hear a lot about these girls being abducted and the like. Maybe he wasn't even her Dad at all, he certainly seemed nervous; I'll report it later when I get home, the police would know what to do'.

Chapter 20

Constable Busion called DCI Webb as she had come across something she thought might be connected to their cases.

"Ma'am I think you should come and see this, I'm not sure if it is significant".

Compton and DI Davis had set up an automatic computer search scanning the reports of incidents involving any combinations of children, camper vans and vintage vehicles originating from all stations in the south including London. It loaded these into a file which she studied every evening before she went home; tonight, one report stood out. While she waited for Toni to arrive, she printed off a copy.

"What is it Compton you sounded excited"?

"It's this report Ma'am. The police at Folkestone have apprehended a man in a camper who had a young girl on board. He apparently reported to the police at the channel tunnel terminal that he had found her wandering along the slip road to the terminal. At first it seemed he was genuine, but on checking his number plate it had been flagged as suspicious by the customs police at Dover a week before; they suspected he may be bringing in asylum seekers. He was alone at the time so Dover customs didn't hold him, just sent out a warning, as records showed he had only hired the vehicle the day before, and an underfloor compartment where they though one or even two people would fit was full of tools. Now here is the interesting bit. A Jack Meaker who worked at the service station on the A20 reported a man in a camper van was acting suspiciously with a female child in the toilets, he spoke to the man who was very cagey and who left in a hurry; he noted the van number and time.

He reported it to Folkestone Police. They contacted Dover and the Tunnel security to stop and question him should he attempt to leave. That request came just half an hour after he tried to pass this girl off as a lost child. There is not much more, do you think this is connected, what do you want me to do"?

"An abducted girl instead of a boy perhaps, this is new but not out of the question. Well done young lady, this is ringing a big bell it would be nice to go down to Folkestone, but it is a long haul; find out who is running the case get me their number. I'll be in my office see what else you can get. By the way does it say how old this youngster is"?

"No, you have everything there that I have, wait a second; the investigating officer is a detective sergeant Mike MacManus, here is his number".

"Thanks Compton I'll let you know if it is related after I talk to this sergeant MacManus".

Toni hurried to her office and called the number straight away, to her surprise a girl answered the phone.

"Oh, I was hoping to speak to a sergeant Mike MacManus is he available please, I'm detective Chief inspector Webb from Basingstoke CID"?

"Speaking Ma'am, my name is Michelle, but everyone here calls me Mike, sorry for the confusion, how can I help"?

"That's alright sergeant, I understand you have a fellow in custody who had a girl on board his camper van without a good explanation as to how she got there, I've seen the interforce report but it's very sketchy would you please update me with the current situation. My interest stems from our having had several youngsters abducted in camper vans and the like and we suspect being transported abroad, I won't go into details over the phone but there may be a link to your guy".

"Right, I'll give you what we have but I will need to confirm with my DI before I go too far, he's not in at the moment and may not be back tonight".

"Of course, give him a call if he doesn't come back soon; let him have my number he can ring me anytime day or night. Now, just a few simple questions to start, they will let me know if we need to collaborate or if yours is just a one off and nothing to do with our case. How old is the girl, do you know her name and what is her physical condition"?

"She is about twelve years old maybe a tad younger, but we have been unable to talk to her yet as she appears to have been drugged. She has been sent to the local hospital with an officer on watch; no ID of any kind as yet. Physically healthy and well cared for apart from the sedation".

"What about the man"?

"He's been lying through his teeth keeps changing his story as we catch him out in one lie, he comes up with another. Also, what he says conflicts with a witness. His name is Alfred Bailey, not much of a record though small-time stuff, you can look him up. He's clammed up now and demanding a brief, we are waiting for our witness to come in and do an ID. What we can't understand is he wasn't stopped and searched, but handed over the girl to the security police at the Tunnel in person, why on earth would he expose himself like that"?

"I don't know, but it seems there are definite similarities to our missing kids. Was she wearing any shoes"?

"Come to think of it no she wasn't and there weren't any signs of them in the van, how did you know that"?

"It's a feature we've seen before also ask the medics to check her for the drug Zopiclone, a positive would clinch it. I think he could be part of the same team who have been abducting kids in the Southern Counties. I'm convinced he's worth interviewing, don't forget get your DI to give me a ring and seal off the van, SOCO will need to go over it with a fine-tooth comb. I think I should mention one of the children was killed by this lot and we suspect several others have suffered a similar fate, maybe your guy had a conscience attack and couldn't go through with what he'd been asked to do, but don't you dare let him go before I say so, no matter what your DI says or his brief comes up with".

"Will try Ma'am but I have to do as I'm instructed by my DI. I have your number; I'll tell DI Finch soonest. Abduction and murder eh, we don't get many of them in Folkestone".

"Neither do we in Basingstoke thank goodness. Depending on what your DI says I will probably be down in the morning, look forward to meeting you then, goodbye and thanks sergeant".

"Ma'am".

Toni went down to Compton's office and gathered together copies of tyre mark casting photos, evidence collected from the Reynold's farm, including the prints and DNA profiles of the boys kept there. She wanted to see if they had ever been in this Alfred Bailey's van. She spoke to both DI Jonny Musgrove and Harrold Davies to set their teams searching CTV coverage looking for this vans number on routes around Reynolds farm and anywhere else they could think may be relevant. The hire company that owns the van needed to be investigated. Harrold could handle that also a search of Alfred Bailey's home would be a job for Jonny. None of this would be possible until she spoke to this DI Finch, collaboration was essential if this was to go ahead. Toni requested DC Andrews accompany her on this visit; Harrold was more than happy to release him; he knew Peter being there was almost as good as going himself. The female sergeant Mike had been very forth coming but she wasn't sure if Finch would be the same; she knew how close minded and secretive some detectives could be especially if they had a sniff of a big case.

She couldn't wait too long for this DI to ring her she would have to ask the Super if he would smooth the way before everyone in authority went home for the night, she wanted to be on her way at the crack of dawn.

Superintendent Munroe listened to Toni's request.

"If what you tell me pans out this could be a big break Toni. Wait here I'll give the Folkestone Super a call".

Superintendent Munroe picked up the phone consulted his desk roller-card. He knew it was a bit old fashioned of him to have such a device but found his card holder a quicker way of looking up phone numbers and addresses than scrolling through a computerised address book. Most Superintendents knew each other to some degree, from early days in the force, through conferences, interforce policy meetings and sometimes when cases overlapped, as appeared to be the reason here. He spoke for several minutes, Toni hardly able to hear what Munroe was saying and certainly not what was being said by his opposite number.

"Well Toni, it seems you are free to go down to interview this Bailey and our SOCO team can go over the van. One provision he and the van stays with them and when it comes to any prosecution, they will be the lead".

Toni was not happy with the limitations but had learnt enough of police politics that expressing her opinion at the wrong time was counter-productive, she crossed her fingers and lied.

"Of course, Sir, no problem; I'll be there first thing. Thanks for smoothing the way".

"I'm not sure how smooth it will be Toni, apparently DI Finch will not let this go easily and will want to be in control. Throwing your rank at him won't cut it so tread carefully".

"Don't worry Sir, I'll be discreet and soft as butter".

Chapter 21

It was six am Toni was waiting outside her front door when the car pulled up on time. She had asked Peter to drive, having dispatched the SOCO team well ahead, she wanted time to study the files on the journey. She knew they would be able to identify prints and tyre impressions fairly quickly on site and hoped this would have been carried out prior to her arrival at Folkstone nick. A print match to one of the boys would give her the power to question Bailey on her own terms and override any objections that may be raised by Finch. DNA would of course have to wait. Perhaps he would be fully cooperative, but reputations of stubbornness are not born out of nothing; she would defer judgement.

The journey was uneventful but slow even at this early hour; there's no coastal motorway and hated the idea of using the M25 so resorted to the A roads meandering through Hampshire West and East Sussex to Kent finally arriving later that morning at the police station in the centre of town. It seemed the desk sergeant was told to look out for her arrival; as soon as they started up the few steps to the front entrance a tall, thin and grey haired officer moved to greet them, he almost clicked his heels as he stood to attention speaking with the deepest voice Toni had ever heard outside of an opera house bassist.

"Morning Ma'am, DI Adrian Finch welcome to Folkstone".

Toni stopped and nodded acknowledgement.

"Thank you, Detective, DCI Toni Webb and this is DC Peter Andrews. I presume our SOCO team have arrived"?

"Yes, Ma'am they are with the van in our yard at the rear; before we start Superintendent Walker would like a word Ma'am if you would follow me please; the Constable can wait here if you don't mind".

Toni gave a look to Peter indicating for him to stay put.

"Lead on detective".

She followed him along a corridor and up a short flight of steps to a mezzanine floor at the rear of the building. Finch knocked and waited for the 'come' whereupon he opened the door and offered Toni to enter. She walked in to find the Superintendent already standing his hand held out in greeting.

"Superintendent Walker; DCI Webb welcome, please take a seat".

She took his hand briefly, smiled and sat down noting DI Finch had remained outside. The Super's office was large and airy, the window behind his desk overlooking the courtyard below, littered with various vehicles and the odd officer moving across the compound.

"I just want to say we hope what happens here will help with your enquiries but if it turns out to be not connected all data collected by you and your team will be handed over to us. DI Finch will be present at all times".

"Of course, Sir your cooperation here is much appreciated, I'll be getting on with it then".

She stood about to leave when the Super made a parting remark making her wonder how much Munroe had said to him.

"I hope to God you are wrong Webb, children for spare parts surgery isn't something I can contemplate easily. Do what you have to".

Surprisingly Finch was not outside so she retraced her steps to the front desk where she found Peter chatting to the desk sergeant. She addressed him formally not wanting the other officers to see the familiarity which existed between them.

"DC Andrews have you seen DI finch"?

"Yes, Ma'am he said to meet him round the back where SOCO are working on the van".

"Fine let's go, which way"?

"Straight through the long corridor and out the back door he said".

Toni led the way eager to get to grips with Bailey, she'd rather leave the CSIs to do their work undisturbed. The van was under cover in a large shed on the far side of the compound. DI Finch was standing alongside a female officer which Toni assumed was DS MacManus. Sure enough as they approached Finch introduce his sergeant.

"Thought you would like to see the van Ma'am and the hidden compartments before you interview our man. You'll see why his story that it is for keeping tools is a load of bunkum. Do you want to speak to your chaps"?

"Not necessary they will find me as soon as they have anything worthwhile. You're right about the hidden space though, worth seeing. Where is Bailey now"?

He's in a cell at the moment, shall I bring him to an interview room"?

"That would be good, I'd like to study him for a while before we start. Put him in the room with a uniform officer at first then leave him alone whilst I watch, ten minutes or so should be enough".

Finch marched off smartly leaving DS Mike to show them the way.

"Follow me Ma'am; the DI is a bit put out you know; the Super intervening did not please him. By the way he didn't mention it, but they tested the girl and found considerable traces of the drug Zopiclone like you said. He will seem to cooperate as instructed but considers this to be his case so be wary, he can be quite devious".

"Why the warning sergeant"?

"Let's just say some of the 'old school' are in it for less than noble reasons; it is certainly not my way; where kids are concerned, I would join forces with the Devil if it would help".

"I'm not the Devil, Michelle I can assure you, but I can be a bit of one when necessary. I take note of what you have said".

She wasn't sure if the warning was genuine or given to deliberately muddy the waters. A DI and their DS were normally very close and would back each other to the hilt; she had doubts about this unsolicited confidence so let the sergeant walk ahead and spoke quietly to Peter.

"You hang back when we get to the viewing room stay outside, wander around a bit, chat to the uniforms tell them you are here as just my driver and I won't let you near the case. What I really want is for you to find out more about our DI Finch and Sergeant Mike if you can. Station gossip can be very revealing".

"No problem boss I love a good chinwag, the desk sergeant seemed friendly enough I might even wheedle myself a cuppa".

"That's my boy, a cup of tea and canteen chit-chat; lovely. Showing them your bullet wound will get them eating out of your hand".

They both laughed at the quip intended by Toni to lighten the mood, but it brought back memories he'd rather forget. Being shot in the leg on a case during a confrontation with a psychopath was no laughing matter, however the exit wound was bang in the middle of his right buttock leaving everyone in the station asking him, how come he got shot in the arse, which was now a standing joke among his colleagues.

Chapter 22

Alfred was sitting at the table with a uniformed copper standing in the corner watching him. That Detective bloke had been at him for ages twisting his words, so he didn't know whether he was coming or going. He said he didn't believe his story of finding the girl on the side of the road but couldn't understand why not. No one had cautioned him, and he knew that's what they were supposed to do, or he thought so. They had not charged him with anything either. When he asked for a solicitor or lawyer, they just stopped questioning him and put him in a cell. He had changed his story about where he had found her to fall in line with what he thought they wanted to hear so much so he couldn't remember what was said. If they asked him again, he would go back to his original plan and stick to it, after all he had given her up as a lost kid, they should be thanking him not giving him a hard time. The watching policeman suddenly turned, opened the door and left, he was on his own; he sat for a while expecting someone to come in and start again but no one did. His mouth became dry not from thirst but a nervous reaction of anticipation unfulfilled. Alfred couldn't sit any longer he stood and began to walk round the table, he could see the camera in the corner but didn't know if it was working or not. Were they watching him?   He moved in front of the mirror saw his unshaven features and noted the skin around his eyes had become dark through stress, he would have a good sleep when this was all over. He wondered if anyone was behind the mirror, he tried to peer through the glass but could see nothing, perhaps it was just an ordinary mirror. He sat again, waiting for something to happen. The paranoia stuck again what if it was all a set up and Jake had informed the police somehow, perhaps it was their way to get rid of him; no Jake wouldn't do that, but the bastard Giles would for sure. He was in a spot of bother and he knew it, '*I must keep calm and say nothing*' he rested his head in his hands and felt the fear creep into his heart.

Toni knew he was ready, Bailey had, in the twenty minutes he was left alone, become ready to concede, a condition an hour of questioning may have never achieved. She, DI Finch and a uniformed constable entered the room. At her request Finch remained standing out of the direct line of Bailey's vision but wanted him to be aware of the detective's presence. She sat immediately opposite Alfred and waited whilst the constable set up the recorder but did not switch it on. The constable left the room and closed the door behind him with a loud click the sudden noise made Alfred sit up and remove the hands supporting his head. He looked at Toni and turned to look at Finch then back to her, expectancy and fear in his eyes; she waited a full minute before starting.

"Mr. Bailey or perhaps I can call you Alfred, I am Detective Chief Inspector Webb, I've been called in to help you resolve this situation. I know it must seem we are a little heavy handed but where children are concerned we cannot be too careful I'm sure you understand".

Alfred nodded, confused at the gentleness this black women was showing towards him.

"This interview is informal no recording or anything I just want to find out what happened then we can all go home. You said in your original statement you picked this girl up from... where was it now"?

Toni pretended to shuffle through her file looking for the answer.

"It was on the road just before the tunnel".

Alfred couldn't resist, his vow to say nothing vanished at that moment. He wondered if they had sent for a solicitor like he had asked.

"Ah yes that's it, are you sure it wasn't a bit earlier you could easily have been mistaken with the location in the rush to get to the tunnel"?

"I suppose it's possible I don't really remember".

"Could it have been at the service station when you stopped for fuel, it's understandable to become confused with you wanting to help someone in trouble and yet not miss your crossing"?

He never trusted those blacks he had met in London they were always after your money or worse. She seems different somehow but he was not too sure, should he change his story.

"I don't remember that; I did stop for fuel but don't know if she was there before then or not".

"That's alright I don't want you to say something just because I suggest it, all I want is the truth as you remember it. Now let us look at your van and what we found inside".

"It's not my van I just hired it yesterday, I gave the hire documents to the other officer".

He turned and threw a glance at DI Finch as he spoke.

"That's true but you have used it before haven't you"?

"Yes but only once, I like to do trips to buy wine, a hired camper is ideal to have a day or weekend away I only have a small car see, nothing wrong with that is there"?

"Not at all it must be fun, I wish I had the time. Now here's my problem the compartment under the floor seems to have been used to transport people".

"No, no, it is for tools I told the other one, but he kept shouting at me that I had been bringing in asylum seekers".

Toni realized then Finch had not been interested in the girl at all but was trying to score a people smuggling charge against Bailey. urging him to confess. She wondered why there were no tapes of the interview or why Bailey hadn't been cautioned; now she knew. Finch was waiting to brow beat him into submission before recording anything. Mike's warning was also more understandable now. She would not pursue the line Bailey had just opened up. She couldn't see his face from where she was sitting but hoped Finch would think she was unaware of his motives and hadn't picked up on what Bailey had just said.

"I don't think it was used just for tools. We found some bedding material in the compartment and there seems to be child sized fingerprints inside too, how do you explain that"?

"I can't, I'm not the only one to use that van, it's on hire to all sorts of people".

"But the prints we found belong to the girl you found on the roadside. Did she open the hidden compartment and climb inside"?

"I don't know she could have done when I wasn't looking. You've got the girl she is safe now why won't you let me go, I've done nothing to her"?

"I'm not saying you have, but someone has; I intend to find out who. Very young girls don't go wandering the street in her condition by chance now do they. If it wasn't you who drugged her and put her in the compartment, then you know who did. The fact you handed her over as soon as you could shows you never wanted to be part of what has happened; it will go a very long way to mitigate whatever charges you may face. I suggest you consult with a solicitor before we interview you formally do you have one"?

"No, I don't, I asked for one yesterday you know; I don't have any money to pay for one though is that why no one came"?

"I don't know but will arrange for the duty solicitor to come and see you, at this stage there will be no fee".

"Thank you. I didn't mean no harm to anyone you know but I didn't have any choice you see".

"I understand Alfred, but we must get to the truth and I know you want to help; you do that for me and it will be alright in the end".

Toni and DI Finch left the room, the constable outside then re-entered. Finch turned to Toni with a smirk on his face. She now had a good idea why Finch didn't send for a brief when Bailey had asked; he was a bully; what he said next confirmed it.

"If you think he will fess up after that display you've no chance. Once he has seen a solicitor you'll end up with a 'no comment' to every question. You should have left him to me".

Toni didn't respond verbally to his rude comment but moved her face close to his, pointed two fingers at her eyes and pulled the lobe of her ear, all with a broad smile.

"Whilst we wait for the solicitor to do his best to confound us, a cup of tea would be good Inspector if you wouldn't mind".

Finch nodded with an affirmative grunt pointing the way, wishing he had kept his mouth shut. Her petty 'look and listen' reaction had left him unsure of himself wondering what this woman was up to, he'd keep quiet for now.

"Canteen's this way" he paused before completing the, not so courteous, "Ma'am".

Alfred was in despair; here he was now in the very position he was trying to avoid. This woman copper must have some notion of what he had done or why was she handing him the opportunity to get away with a lesser charge by telling of Grimes and Snell. She can't understand his situation, giving up either of them was not an option, if he did and went to jail, he would be dead in a week, he didn't go much on his chances if he got off scott free either. There must be a way perhaps the lawyer they give him would be able to help.

They returned to the room, Toni asked the constable to turn on the recorder and leave. Toni opened the proceedings.

"Interview commencing with Alfred Bailey, those present Chief Inspector Toni Webb....".

The interview formalities were completed by Finch, Bailey and the solicitor Markham stating their names for the recording.

"Alfred Bailey I am about to question you formally, there are no charges at this time however I must caution you. You do not have to say anything, but it may harm your defence if you do not mention when questioned something which you later rely on in court. Anything you do say may be given in evidence. Do you understand"?

"Err. Yes miss".

"Alfred earlier today we had a conversation establishing you voluntarily gave up a young girl to the security police at the Channel Tunnel check in. You also stated you found her wandering somewhere on your journey to the tunnel. Is that correct".

He looked at his solicitor who nodded.

"Yes, that's right".

"Is it true you cannot remember exactly where you found her".

"Yes, I was a bit confused not wanting to miss my train but didn't want to just leave her somewhere".

"How come she spent some time in the hidden compartment in the base of your camper"?

"She must have climbed in when I wasn't looking".

"Oh, I see whilst you were driving looking at the road".

"Yes, that must have been it".

"A bit difficult, when I tried I couldn't lift the cover unless I pulled really hard, I don't think a small child would be strong enough; perhaps you let her get in there when you picked her up".

At this point the solicitor interrupted.

"You are trying to put words in my client's mouth, he has already stated he doesn't remember exactly what happened".

"I'm just trying to jog his memory with suggestions. All I want is the truth about when and how she got in there. Okay maybe he will remember later just a simple question or two requiring a simple answer".

"Was she with you when you were at the service station"?

"Yes".

"Did you take her into the toilet"?

"No, she went on her own".

"What happened next"?

"She fell asleep on the loo, I had to lift her out".

"Was it the drugs she had been given made her fall sleep"?

"Yes, I suppose it could have been".

"Then you admit to giving her drugs"?

"No, no I didn't give her anything like that, it must have been before she was with me".

"Did you give her a drink"?

"Yes, some lemonade, she was thirsty".

"Did you give her the lemonade from the bottle we found in the van"?

"It was all I had, it's what was in the van already".

"Who left it there, the hire company"?

"Maybe; I don't know".

Again, the solicitor interrupted.

"Stop there. I advised my client to be cooperative as he has done nothing wrong, but you are introducing trivial questions just to confuse him. He delivered a girl he found in distress to the appropriate authorities in good faith and all you can do is badger him about where he found her. It seems to me you have no evidence of any wrongdoing so if you are going to proffer charges, I suggest you do so now or we are leaving".

"Wait here. Officer DCI Webb leaving the room. Leave the tape running I will only be a few minutes".

Toni indicated for DI Finch to remain where he was. Her departure took her to the rear yard where SOCO were still working on the van. She had a brief conversation with the lead SC officer and returned to the interview room. She looked directly at the solicitor ignoring Alfred

"Now here's the thing I will be charging him, but what charge will depend upon his answers to some straight questions. I now have overwhelming evidence that children other than the girl have been transported in that particular van, and your client appears to have been the sole user of the vehicle in question. I believe your client has been coerced by others to transport these youngsters, maybe against his will, I don't know. If he decides to help us this will go a long way towards how he is dealt with by the CPS. If not, the charges will be very serious indeed. I suggest you have a word and advise him accordingly".

Toni shut off the tape; she and DI Finch left the room. Finch was more than angry, as soon as they were outside he held onto her arm turning her to face him.

"What the bloody hell is going on here, where did you go"?

She removed his hand from her arm and held on to it much tighter than he expected, pulling his face very close.

"Don't you dare grab at me! You forget yourself DI Finch you are not dealing with one of your submissive minions here".

She let go and stepped back her hands held up in a submissive position, waiting. Finch realised he had overstepped the mark as touching a senior officer like that was more than offensive.

"I'm sorry Ma'am I don't know what came over me but it was my case and you have cut me out completely. My Super told me to keep you under control; he would give me a real hard time if I just let you walk all over us".

Toni understood his frustration; she would feel the same in his place; so decided to adopt the friendly approach and keep the DI in the loop and see where that would lead. His helpful behaviour would be more acceptable to her than what would almost certain become obstructive if she shut him out completely.

"I'll let it go this time but do anything like that again and you will end up walking the beat; understand"?

"Yes Ma'am I'm so sorry".

"Let that be an end to it". So you think I am trying to cut you out do you? Well you don't know the half of it Adrian not by a long way. Alfred is part of an evil group of men who will not stop their dreadful trade unless we do something about it. Look Adrian I am not intending to keep things to myself, but I now know much more than I did when we started. I am going to trust you to do the right thing here by putting you fully in the picture. Will you calm down and listen for a change"?

"Yes Ma'am" Finch replied feeling bewildered, no one had stood up to him in a long time.

"First, in Hampshire and nearby Counties we have had several youngsters abducted using camper-vans and old or vintage cars. These have taken place at special events and shows over several weeks and probably months. This is an organised team; the targets being healthy well cared for 12 year old children; we suspect they are being shipped abroad initially to France where they are being stripped of their organs, murdered for their body parts to supply the illegal transplant trade".

She paused to let the awful truth of what is taking place sink in. In those few moments Adrian's face and body language had changed from red and aggressive to pale and submissive.

"We have already found one child dead and have luckily recovered one other before he was moved. We know of two more boys who were recently shipped across the Channel. Now here comes the crunch my SOCOs have just confirmed the van you have here has the prints of those two boys and probably their DNA too. We tracked down one of the abductors to an out of the way farm, but he was found dead when we got there. Murdered by whoever is operating this disgusting business; they are serious and dangerous people they even killed his elderly mother. I think your man in there took those boys abroad and was about to do the same with our young girl but got cold feet. He knows who these people are or can lead us to them. I'm not trying to take your case away from you I just want to help save these children".

Adrian Finch stood unable to speak, what was he doing thinking he knew better than this black woman Chief Inspector, she didn't get that rank for nothing. Her forgiving him a serious transgression, her openness in confiding in him he'd seldom met before, most officers played their cards close to their chests, this woman was a new breed; up front for sure and honest, she almost certainly was. His own idea that Albert Bailey was ferrying asylum seekers, and this troublesome girl just one of the invading 'nobodies' he had brought in was a no go from the start. He was so far off the mark. He had made no attempt to identify her, in fact he had dismissed this child as being a worthless foreigner. Now this woman's *'Look and Listen'* mime made sense, she wanted him to learn her way. He was fully aware of his shortcomings and prejudices, always seeking the easy bust, twisting the evidence to fit his perception of the crime, not concerned for the victims and even less for the suspects; he was not nice and he did not like it. The Superintendent always wanted convictions regardless, personal advancement uppermost in his mind. He was not always like this; not how Adrian wanted to be but just the way he had been indoctrinated over time.

What had he been thinking, this girl needed his help and he had ignored her situation completely, ambition always seemed to get the better of him? He now needed to deal with a wave of guilt he had never felt before, finding out who this young girl really is and returning her to her family would be his new priority.

The thought of kids being cut up for their organs made him shudder, remembering the agony he had suffered as a boy when he watched as his father died from the result of a road accident. He didn't know it at the time, but his Dad had donated his organs to be used after his death. His Mum told him several years later at an age when she thought he would understand, the pride he felt at his Father's consideration for complete strangers had stayed with him always. The thought some bastards were belittling his Father's selfless gift of life knotted his stomach, the result of the revulsion he felt filled his mouth full of bile. Anger followed, mostly at himself his Superintendent and at Alfred Bailey. He swallowed, hard. A pivotal moment had arrived for DI Finch.

"Wow, this is terrible, I've been a fool, if you don't mind Ma'am I'd like to go to the hospital to chase up the identity of the girl".

The change in his face and demeanour, as Toni spoke of the terrible fate of these kids, was clear, she was surprised for it seemed to have made a much bigger impact than expected.

"I can see you are angry; you know what Adrian I felt like that too when I discovered the plight of these youngsters, but we must tread carefully if we are to get the best result. Your Super said you were to stay with me at all times, but I don't have time to wait till you come back from the hospital".

"Don't worry about that, do whatever you need, I've been a stupid 'shithead' with this case trying to get what I want regardless. I'm not going to do this anymore the Super can go and whistle, so you get back in there and nail this bastard".

"I want to find the other kids and stop this traffic so need to act now; I'm not overly concerned with charging Alfred too soon, he must be petrified at the moment; imagine how would you feel with only two choices, he can either give up his bosses and face their almost certain fatal retribution, or he can take the rap and serve his time. Self-preservation will win out every time, so we must give him an alternative which is more acceptable. Good luck with the girl, let me know whenever, okay"?

"As soon as I know you will".

Good. I'll go look for my constable I need someone else in the room during the interview unless your sergeant Mike would be available".

"I don't know. Try the canteen on the first floor they could both be there if not someone there will have seen them".

They parted, Finch out the front door and Toni up the stairs. The canteen was easy to find the noisy chatter heard emanating from the open doors well before she arrived. DC Peter Andrews and DS Michelle MacManus were at a table in the corner heads together unaware of her approach.

"Well well, is this what you do Peter when I'm not looking, drink tea and chat up the locals"?

Michelle looked up alarmed, Peter turned and laughed.

"How we doing boss"?

"Fine; looks like we have something solid here, follow me and I'll bring you up to speed but first let me have your news".

Michelle was slightly taken aback, half stood and made to leave. Toni put a hand gently on her shoulder forcing her to sit back down.

"No, you stay right there young lady you need to be part of this too. Go on, Peter let us have it, what have you found out"?

Peter wasn't sure how far to go, he felt embarrassed speaking about Finch with his number two listening.

"I don't know if you want me to, you know, in front of sergeant Mike".

"No secrets here Peter, Mike has broad shoulders I'm sure".

"Well I spent a while with the desk sergeant, he liked to gossip as they do. I learnt there was some competition between the DIs here; pressure from above. He didn't exactly say they bent the rules but there was a definite hint some suspects' rights were maybe being abused. Mike here..."

Peter paused and received a go ahead nod from the Detective Sergeant at his side.

"... has been open about her relationship with DI Finch. She has not been happy for some time as he tends to select the evidence to fit the crime. Sometimes the villains deserve what they get but on occasions she feels he goes too far where quite minor offenders get brow beaten into giving confessions for more serious crimes. If she says anything he loses his rag and she has to back down. The Super is worse, he pushes his DIs for quick results, only interested in a high clear up rate and thinks the sun shines out of Finch's you know where".

"A problem in many stations I think; it's hard to beat the establishment".

Toni looked at Michelle with a sympathetic smile, the sideways look hinting it was even harder for a woman.

"I do believe however you will be pleasantly surprised Mike; our Detective Finch has had a miraculous change of heart; at least on this case and maybe for good, we will see. I wasn't sure if he was faking it but something he imagined, or what I said shook him to the core. A surprising and complete turn-around in attitude; by the way he has gone to the hospital to ID and help the girl get home, well out of character I would think".

Michelle took a deep breath, this was rubbish, no one changes that fast, she wondered what was going on she couldn't believe it, Finch was a bastard and would always be a bastard in her eyes. She'd have to see the change first-hand before she would be convinced; it was just a show for the visitors benefit.

"Bloody hell he would never do that, showing feelings for a victim is not his style. He must have another agenda I wouldn't trust him Ma'am, I really wouldn't".

"Let us wait and see; in the meantime obstacles to our investigation are apparently no more, so let's go to it".

All three entered the interrogation room. As agreed, Toni sat opposite Brian Marchant the duty solicitor, Sergeant MacManus in front of Albert with Peter standing in the corner under the closed-circuit video camera.

Peter carried out the preliminaries with the tape introducing the room occupants for the record.

"I don't think we have met before today Mr. Marchant, but I hope you understood the gravity of what I said before".

"No, we haven't met and yes I have discussed the situation with my client and advised him of his rights, but until we have some idea of the evidence against him; I have told him to say nothing".

"Well there have been some developments since we last spoke. Analysis of the contents of the bottle, which your client admitted he gave to the girl, was shown to contain a specific drug found in one other child victim and also in the body of another who died whilst in the hands of your client and his collaborators.

Before I commence this interview Mr. Bailey you are not under arrest at this time, but I reiterate you are still under caution. Do you understand"?

"Yes".

"Alfred you heard what I said before concerning the evidence we have; it clearly puts you in the frame for abduction of a minor at least and possibly conspiracy to murder. The evidence is now overwhelming and if we proceed it is certain you will go to prison for a very long time. Now here is a question for you, what do you do if we proceed? You have two choices, very difficult ones too"

"I don't have any choice. If I speak I'm done for".

"First you can let those evil men go 'Scott Free' whilst you serve your time. You know they won't thank you, instead they will find a way to get at you in prison. Second, you can tell me who they are, so we can put them away. What do you pick Alfred, prison and possible retribution, or prison and the same"?

A long pause to let her words sink in, he would see he had no way out; he would die in prison and not from old age; she waited a full minute before coming to his rescue.

"I'm certain you would like me to find another way"?

Alfred Bailey was in shock all he had done was a simple delivery and now his life would be in ruins and death will come soon or would when Jake or Giles found out where he was. He wasn't safe even in this place. He looked at his lawyer who held up his open hands as if to say it is up to you. He certainly didn't relish either. He really should keep quiet and say nothing; but it seems this woman was offering a way out.

"What do you mean another way"?

170

"You must first tell me everything you know, no holding back no embellishments either, just the plain old truth".

"That's no good they will kill me for sure, what do I get if I speak out"?

"If I know exactly who they are and how the system works I can find a way for these guys to be put away without them knowing you were even involved".

This was a bit of a stretch Toni had no idea how she could achieve such an outcome but needed Albert to snatch at the carrot she was offering even if it was a tenuous one.

"That's impossible if you even approach them or make enquiries they will find out and will know it was me. I bet they are trying to get at me even now. I'm cursed either way".

"That you are Albert; keep silent and your position is no better than if you talk to me. So why not give them up and I will find a way to protect you".

"You mean a witness protection thing"?

"Not exactly, maybe better; they go to prison and you get your life back".

"I don't see how you can, even in prison they will have control; they never forgive or forget you know. If I do what you want what guarantee do I get"?

"Absolutely none but it is a better option than any other. I'll go now; leave you to talk with Mr. Marchant and take a little time to think about it. You either speak up or when I return you will be charged and released on police bail to await trial".

"No, no you can't, I don't want bail; they will think I have shopped them for sure; I won't survive even one day you've got to keep me here, keep me locked up".

Toni did not respond but rose from her chair slowly and left pointing for Peter to do the honours with the tape.

Sergeant MacManus followed not knowing if this woman intended, or was even really able, to keep Bailey safe. Was this vague promise of a lifeline real or just a ruse to get him to speak; that throw away at the end, hinting at bail, was a peach.

"Cup of tea Mike, Peter, we'll let him stew a bit, he should come through don't you think"?

Mike nodded smiling, enjoying the methods of this deceptive lady, leading the way to the canteen, she couldn't resist the question almost knowing the answer in advance, thinking this DCI Toni Webb is clever, a bit devious but okay.

"Would you really let him out on bail"?

"You're kidding, no chance, Abduction and a Murder charge will be what he gets if he starts in with the 'no comment'. The best I can do for him then is to keep him isolated at least until trial. I'm sure it won't come to that. He'll talk, you'll see. Ah thanks Peter".

Toni and Mike accepted the tea and biscuits offered, the three sitting in silence each with their own thoughts about what would happen next.

"Ma'am, do you have any idea who he is working for"?

"No Mike. The man Reynolds, we know abducted and kept children at his farm; he was out best lead; he was one step below whoever is organising this, but he was murdered before we could get to him. Alfred here is further away as he probably took the kid from Reynolds or someone like him, there could be another level, or even two, higher in the chain we don't know as yet. For now I am grateful we have broken this chain, maybe it's the only one I doubt it. Early days; if Bailey coughs we may be one step nearer, patience is the game here. Tread gently Sergeant, 'slowly, slowly catchy monkey' an expression often used by my old boss which has proven true more than once".

"When are we going back in"?

"What did I just say Peter, patience, we will wait till Marchant calls us then we wait another half hour; in the meantime go and see if SOCO has finished with the van, if they have send them home no need to wait for us".

Chapter 23

The buzz of Toni's mobile interrupted the dunking of her biscuit, she popped the soggy mass into her mouth as she pressed the accept call.

"Hello, Ma'am Constable Busion, hope I'm not interrupting anything I could call back if you like"?

Toni knew Compton Busion had information for her that couldn't wait, or she wouldn't have called. Toni swallowed the remains of the custard cream before responding.

"No, it's fine what do you have"?

"Thought you would like to know, The SOCO lads have finished at the farm all evidence has been collected. Confirmation of matches to the boy's DNA we already know about, but additional traces have revealed two others were kept in those cells, a Sean Brightwell eleven years old from Reading and a twelve year old girl Freda Spring from Newbury. Their prints and DNA profiles were on record from the missing person reports. The girl was reported just over two weeks ago but I'm afraid the boy was from six months back. The reports are a bit skimpy on how they disappeared. No real link to car shows and the like as yet, DI Musgrove is interviewing the parents today he may find something. I'll send a picture of the girl just in case she is the one you have there, it's not very clear but it might help. I'm sending her prints to the SOCOs at your site so an ID should be possible if it is her. There is plenty more stuff, but it needs sorting and prioritising before I dump it in your lap".

"Much appreciated Compton. What about the shooter did DI Davis come up with anything yet"?

"Oh yes the pathologist recovered the bullets from both bodies. They were from a 2.2 and have been matched to a killing four years ago. The victim then was Lance Miller a witness for the prosecution of a low life called Henry Giles charged with extortion. The case never came to court. Other witnesses failed to come through, said they had made a mistake. The gun was never found. Henry Giles has a side kick Jake Snell, just as evil as his mate apparently.

The off-road bicycle tyre is very common to all makes so no joy there the vehicle tracks at the exit from the track to the road are from an early Land Rover, the tyre type and wheelbase are a dead giveaway. We have CCTV of one like it going east on the A303 with a bike on the back but no number plate visible and no further sightings. Difficult to trace; there are hundreds still around especially in rural areas".

"Thanks Compton that's all good stuff, text me anything else you think might be useful, oh and a picture of the girl please. One other thing get hold of DI Musgrove to get a warrant and search Baileys place, I'll text you his address in Maidstone, he will need to contact the local police first don't want to step on their toes, he can call me should there be a problem and for sure if he finds anything significant. I know it's an imposition just one more thing you could look into when you have time, someone is leaking information to the outside, recently the villains seem to be one step ahead all the time, would you look into anything unusual going on with the computers or the files, no rush it may be nothing just me being paranoid".

She wondered if Alfred Bailey, Henry Giles and Jake Snell were associated? She could ask Compton to check but thought she would give the task to Michelle MacManus, keep her sweet, let her be part of this without Finch breathing down her neck.

"Mike, I have just had some information that you could check out for me. See if Alfred knows a Henry Giles or Jake Snell both from London, known villains I would think".

"Yes, Ma'am no problem".

"One other thing did you see the girl before she went to hospital"?

"No. Finch said she was an asylum seeker and would be dealt with by immigration after she was released from hospital, so no need to get involved".

"How do I get hold of Finch"?

"His mobile would be quickest I think".

She gave Toni his number.

"I'll get on with Giles and Snell then shall I, where will you be Ma'am, in the interview room"?

"No, I'll wait here I have some calls to make, Albert can wait till you return I don't want you to miss anything, let him suffer a bit longer eh".

DS MacManus left. Toni turned to Peter.

"Compton has come up with those two names, from a firearm forensics match. I'm hoping Bailey has some connection to them in which case we have some extra leverage which will surely get him to speak a little more freely".

Toni held out her empty cup to Peter with a smile of anticipation dialling the number Mike had given her.

"How about another whilst we wait for Mike to do her stuff and see if they have some more biscuits. Hello Finch, where are you"?

"At the hospital Ma'am, what do you want?"

"How is the girl"?

"Better, out of danger sleeping now. I haven't spoken to her the doctors won't let me in yet".

"Look I'm going to send you a picture, it's a bit out of focus but see if it could be her and let me know straight away".

"You know who she is; what's her name"?

"Look it may not be her; the picture is crap, I want to be sure before we get the parents involved, just look and call me okay".

Toni sent the picture knowing each time the image was transferred it down-graded just a little. Would Finch be honest and tell he the truth about the likeness. She waited it seemed an age. Her phone buzzed.

"Yes"?

"I don't know, it could be her. The hair is different, longer now, the face does seem like it could be her but it is too blurry for me to be sure; what is her name"?

"You get those doctors to wake her now; you find out her name then call me back when you know okay".

She still was not sure of the DIs motives, but he had at least been straight about the photo. She'd wait a while and see if he came back with an answer. Another age passed before the call, only ten minutes in real time but forever when you are waiting.

"The doctor said her name is 'Fred' that can't be right can it she's a girl and that's a boy's name".

"So is Mike, detective. Hang on I'll call you in two minutes. Peter run over to the van see if Soco has matched the prints sent by Compton; come straight back".

Peter was gone and returned almost running a little more than two minutes but quick enough.

177

"They match Ma'am, who is she"?

Toni called Finch with Peter listening in.

"Good news Adrian, I think her name is 'Fred', Freda Spring that is, I'll have family liaison contact her parents; she was taken two weeks ago from Newbury. Thank God she has been saved; by chance and not through much effort from us".

A fond memory from the past had often steadied her in times of doubt; a childhood lesson from her Father to her and her brother *'listen my young ones, expect less but strive for more and you will not be disappointed'* Less wasn't acceptable; she was very disappointed. *'I'll try harder Dad'* she promised to a loving image in her mind.

"Stay with her Adrian see what you can find out. Interview the parents when they arrive. Call me with anything, okay. I'm going in with Bailey anytime now, just waiting on confirmation of a couple of things. When you've finished get back here and we can go through everything. It will probably be very late but if it works out you can be here to make the arrest, something to please your Super however I will probably have him put in protective custody well away from here".

She smiled at Peter.

"That little carrot should get him moving don't you think".

Not needing to answer Peter, smiled back. Toni sat a while making notes in readiness for the next phase. Mike returned and handed Toni a printout.

"Looks like you are right Ma'am, these two have been noted as persons of interest by the Serious Crime Squad in London. It doesn't say what the SCS are looking for my grade doesn't give me access to much, but I did manage to get a list of names of those identified as either meeting with them or phoning them during the last six months. Some thirty-two regular contacts, if you look down near the bottom, Alfred Bailey is there, four calls and one meeting".

Toni thought of her old colleague now a DCI in the Met. 'smacks of Colin Dale this, I'll give him a call later but first things first'. They made their plan of attack and left.

Chapter 24

"Mike in answer to your earlier question Giles and Snell are our next target. I will open and you can take over, when it comes to the names okay".

The three detectives took their places in the interview room however this time Toni sat immediately opposite Alfred Bailey. No smiling faces this time; serious business.

"Alfred Bailey, a reminder, you are still under caution, but in the light of further evidence I must warn you a serious charge is pending".

"Can't get any worse than murder and that's what you said last time. By the way I didn't kill anyone, you can't prove I did neither".

"I said conspiracy to murder; that will only get you ten years, but if we charge you with child trafficking it will be double for each offence, you will never come out. Don't carry the can for those who threatened you and forced you into doing something you didn't want. Let us put them away for life and we will protect you. Sergeant Michelle will ask a few questions a simple yes or no answer will do, but you can tell us more if you think it will help; if you are not sure please consult your solicitor".

Mike opened the file in front of her without Alfred being able to see.

"Did you really find the girl at the roadside as per your earlier statement"?

Marchant intervened here.

"I have advised my client he should cooperate but not say anything that may incriminate him; however, he has decided to tell you everything as long as your promise to protect him is kept. I did tell him your promise is easily broken and holds no legal weight. It's up to him I can do no more".

"We don't make promises lightly especially where the life of anyone is threatened all I can say is we will do our very best. Now please answer the question did you really find the girl at the roadside"?

"No".

"Were you asked to collect her from someone"?

"Not asked I was told".

"Who told you"?

"No comment".

"Okay, let's see now, ah right, were you told to take her across the channel"?

"Err, Yes".

"Was it Jake who told you?"

"Yes….No… I don't know. Who is Jake"?

"Jake Snell, he is a mate of yours isn't he, you must remember you have made enough phone calls with him".

"No comment".

"No comment to what; that was a statement of fact; I never asked a question"?

"No comment to Jake".

"When I asked you if it was Jake who told you to take the girl your first answer was 'Yes', why was that"?

"I don't know".

"Fine, let's move on. Where did you pick her up"?

"I thought your questions were going to be answered with a yes or no".

"Okay here's a simple one. Are you frightened of Jake"?

"You're kidding, too bloody right I am he'd cut my throat if he knew I was talking to you".

"The same goes for Henry Giles I suppose"?

"That maniac he's bloody crazy, kill you with a look he will".

"You seem all upset, so you do admit to knowing these the men. Did they threatened you and forced you into taking children abroad"?

"I didn't have any choice it was take the kids or they'd do for me".

"They still will unless you help us".

"How the hell did you get their names I never said anything"?

"They won't know that, but do you think us police are fools, we have had those two in our sights for a long time. Now I want you to tell us everything you know and with luck we will arrest them without your having to be a witness of any kind. I can't promise you won't face charges it will depend on what you tell us and the CPS being sympathetic. How did they pay you"?

"What. I didn't do it for money, they gave me enough for travelling and stuff but that's all".

"So, the four thousand euros we found in your flat is not yours"?

"It's what I saved from expenses; I wouldn't use hotels I'd sleep in the van".

"A very generous expense account or a lot of trips to have saved so much".

"I'm careful".

"Really, we'd better check with your bank to see just how careful you are".

Alfred was beaten, they had him all ways and he didn't want them to find the rest of his money. He needed to change the line of their questions away from his personal finances so decided to capitulate and give them a little of what they were after.

"Okay, okay, you win ask your damned questions".

"Where do you pick up the children"?

"I don't, I usually get a text message to meet somewhere, always different. They give me a piece of paper with instructions where to hire a van and wait for the kids to be delivered. They come by ambulance. This time it was different I had to go and collect her".

Mike realized too much information was being given at once, she would have to break it down by being careful with her questions. She decided to let Alfred go on, she would come back to specifics later".

"Where was that"?

"Sidcup".

"Come on Alfred, Sidcup is not enough tell me everything about this pick up why was it different"?

"It's a bit complicated but Jake gave me instructions over the phone which he never normally did, in the past he would ask to meet me in a public place; he would give me a piece of paper with his instructions which I had to destroy. I used my phone as usual to book the channel tunnel. The delivery was to be at the same house in France as before, normally I never went to the same place twice. I collected the rental van from the garage in Sydenham as always".

Alfred was sweating profusely; he stopped to wipe his brow with the back of his sleeve.

"I drove to this small holding in Sidcup where a man and woman came out with the girl. She climbed in to lay down in the hidden compartment she fell asleep at once. I covered her and closed the compartment. The man passed me the bottle of drink. I asked him if he knew what was going on, why the change of routine he said he didn't know but said they have shut him down and told him to clean up all traces. He thought maybe you lot had wind of what is going on. I left and went to the tunnel. I stopped at the services to fill up and check the girl; she needed the loo. It was then I had second thoughts; they told me the boys were being taken for adoption or something you know for people who couldn't have kids. It didn't seem the same, this girl was out of her skull she even fell asleep on the bog, I had to lift her off like, that wasn't right. I thought the whole business was wrong, so I did what I did, gave her to the security at the tunnel. That's it, I had no idea how I was going to explain it to Jake he wouldn't believe me if I said she had escaped, I was so scared, then you came along with all your questions and now I'm buggered".

"Quite a story now I will need you to go into detail, the name of the guy and the location of the Sidcup pick up for a start, the garage in Sydenham, next the address of the drop off in France. You said you had been there before, who did you take then. Write everything down here, names, addresses everything here, that will do to be going on with".

Toni stood and interrupted as Albert took up the pen and paper held out by Mike.

"I'm leaving now but if I am going to help you avoid the wrath of these men, I want to know what hold this Jake Snell and his mate Giles has over you, don't try and water it down, the full facts, think about it Albert don't you dare try and cover your arse, I'll know okay. Now get on and give the sergeant everything she wants. Your cooperation has been exceptional and will be noted in the file".

She did not mention she would return with DI Finch to charge him and make the arrest. Let him tell it all before he gets what he deserves. One thing she wouldn't let those lowlifes get to him, he didn't deserve that, he may have had a change of heart, a bit too late, he would do his time in prison. She felt at a loss with no office to go to so made her way to the canteen knowing there at least she could sit down. The room was almost empty so took the table and seat she had occupied before. She removed her notebook updating the record of events so far. She read through her notes to see if anything needed her attention; she reached for her phone wondering if Finch was on his way back.

"Hello, detective Toni Webb here Adrian, how are you getting on"?

"Good, good. I'm just about to leave I'll be with you soon. The girl has recovered enough to go home later today, I had a chat with her parents and briefly with Freda herself. Your Detective Musgrove had already spoken to them before we knew she was safe; he may have more detail than I could get today. She went missing whilst with her friend at a motorcycle race meeting at Snetterton. Her mother had taken them there for a day out, she dropped Freda and her friend Mary at the gate and was to pick them up after the meeting a few hours later; apparently, the girls are both avid fans of the sport. No details how she went missing. I'll look into it later unless DI Musgrove will follow up. Freda doesn't remember much, but from her description of the cell where she was kept I think it may have been a similar place you told me about where you found your boy Michael. She did say she was recently moved to another location where she was kept in a normal room with a proper bed. No memory after the move".

"It all fits in with what we have learnt before. Her prints and DNA were found at the farm. I'll leave it to Jonny Musgrove to liaise with you later on the follow up. I'm in the canteen at the moment; I'll wait for you here so we can update each other before we go in for you to charge Bailey. Sergeant Mike is in there at the moment getting his statement down on paper. Alfred has folded and will give us everything he has in the way of addresses and names; he believes in exchange for protection. I'm not sure how we can cover that, maybe you have an idea or two there. See you soon".

Toni hung up and selected another number.

Chapter 25

"Colin".

"Is that you Toni, how you doing"?

"I'm fine, very well in fact; glad I got you, all okay with you and the family"?

"Yes of course, not spoken for a while have we. What can I do for you this fine day, I'm sure you're not phoning for a social chat"?

"I could be, I should be; but sadly no I'm not. I'm calling because I need your help. We have a serious problem here which seems to extend into nearby Counties and London too. Someone is abducting kids from our region and selling them abroad".

"You mean girls for the sex trade"?

"No, they are mostly boys about twelve years old, but some girls too. We think, or I do anyway, they are being sold for their organs. Transplants to order".

"What on Earth makes you come to that conclusion"?

"A gut feeling; the targets are very specific well cared for and healthy, all of an age where the organs, like kidneys are almost fully developed and are prime to give the best results. We have recovered one boy and one girl from six kids we know about, they were being held in conditions designed to keep them in good condition but drugged by someone to the point where control was easy but not damaging. One boy was found dead we think an unintended accident, a big mistake on their part as it made us aware of their activities".

"It's still a stretch; organs for sale from children I find that hard to believe. They are more likely to be for the sex trade; I don't know what's worse".

"That's true, but then you'd think they would pick simpler targets; the waifs and strays on the street those no one would be looking for, taking these family raised kids is not easy and it attracts unwanted police attention, yet they take the risk. 'For what'? I asked. I was bemused so did some research and found the trading of organs worldwide is massive; hence my conclusion. I may be wrong and hope I am, if not the children already taken abroad are probably long gone or even dead. Anyway, whatever the motive kids are still going missing and I need to stop it".

"Okay so suppose I go along with it what do you want from me"?

"I'll text you a list of names of our suspects see if anyone in the Met is looking hard too. They have been flagged up as persons of interest when we did a general search; what I don't want is for us to dive in on these guys when maybe Serious Crime or someone else has them in their sights".

"Very considerate of you, what's the real reason"?

"That is the reason; well one of them, I don't know if our suspects are at the top of this chain or just lower order villains. I am almost sure the children end up in France. I have a lead I am going to follow up there, that is if I can persuade the Super to let me contact our French friends".

"So you want me to find out if you go down that path you will not be digging a hole for yourself with the big boys upstairs".

"Do what you can to find out but keep it discreet. I don't want to blunder in where I'm not wanted; I don't want to have the case taken away either. Tell you what, fancy a drive and a pint in our favourite pub?"

"The '*Four Horseshoes*' eh. Love to, real ale and spicy chicken wings mmm. If I find out anything in time, I will text you and meet you there this evening".

"Doesn't your misses ever feed you? Bye, Colin and thanks".

Toni, Mike, and Adrian sat in the Folkstone Police station canteen, Adrian was looking pretty pleased having made the arrest and charged Bailey with three counts of abduction of a minor, in spite of what she'd said earlier he thought DCI Webb would pull rank and charge him herself, but no she was a woman of her word. Rare in the force these days. He was beginning to like this woman and was glad of his change of heart. Mike kept giving him sidelong glances, obviously confused, he'd not been very nice to her for a long time in fact downright obstructive. She wouldn't believe he had changed their strained relationship was too entrenched, he couldn't blame her but she would come around.

"Right sergeant give us a run-down of what you got from Alfred".

"I think you know most of it, just a few details to add to fill you in".

"No go through it all Mike it will refresh my memory and bring DI Finch up to speed".

Bloody Nora this is an all pals together party what is going on with these two? Mike was as perplexed as ever so reverted to the more formal address.

"Yes Ma'am. First Alfred Bailey admitted to picking up the girl from a small holding in Sidcup Kent, I have the address here. He collected her from a man and woman, he only knew the man's

Christian name, Joe; he did not speak to the woman and doesn't know her name, this was the only time he had been there. He said the girl had been drugged by Joe. Joe gave him the drink to give her later, he said he believed it was just a soft drink at first but thought differently when, after he gave her some, she fell asleep straight away. I don't believe him there; he is just trying to appear less involved than he was. He had been instructed to take her across the channel to a place in France an hour or so drive from Calais. He had booked the tunnel but when he got near he felt sorry for the girl, he'd never taken a girl before and didn't think it was right".

Adrian jumped in

"And he thought it okay if it was a boy and not a girl, what a nerve, sodding dickhead".

Mike continued ignoring her DI's interruption.

"Bailey said he thought the boys were to be adopted, or that's what his boss told him, but with the girl he was worried 'she might be exploited' his words not mine. He's naïve, shy sexually and easily embarrassed; he didn't want to talk about the possibility of them being used in the sex trade, he became flustered. I don't think he had any idea of the true purpose to which they were being used. Anyway he gave up the girl as someone he had found intending to tell his boss he'd been stopped at the checkpoint and had no alternative to pretend he had found her. He thought the security guys would take the girl, thank him and let him go".

"You know what, if he hadn't been on that watch list that is exactly what could have happened".

"You're right there, Ma'am good on the Dover customs guys. Now here's where he became edgy, he gave up the name of

Jake Snell and Henry Giles reluctant to write them down as 'writing made it official it was him who gave them up'; he said if they got to know it was him he would be a 'dead man walking' his words again. I pointed out we knew about them anyway and as it was all on tape writing it down was no different. His solicitor piped in then but it was just to support me so he carried on. After that it was easy it came pouring out, he was glad to get it over with. He admitted to taking two boys to the address in France on his previous trip. He described the men who took them but could only give a poor description of the house. He never collected the boys they were delivered to him at different meeting places by ambulance. He admitted to taking one boy on two other occasions several weeks before, he knows nothing of their names and can't remember the dates. I can find those dates from passport control as soon as we've finished here. He used a different camper then much older with room for only one kid. We need to look into the hire firm it seems odd, he never paid for the hire he said it was already taken care of. Each boy was transferred to another van at a rest point off the main road. The same van and the same place both times. He showed me where on the map, not significant I think a long way from the house of the last trip. He wouldn't admit to being paid, although I'm certain he was, he said he was threatened by Jake and Henry so had no choice. I will search his accounts and home, I'm sure there will be some unaccounted money on or near the dates in question. The CPS will need to show he accepted payment or his plea of duress my prove tricky to disprove. That's it Ma'am a little more work and we have him for sure".

"Good Mike, I agree but we need to safeguard him for he will be a vital witness when we apprehend Giles and Snell if we ever do. Now Adrian what have you been up to"?

"What do you mean, if we ever do"?

"Adrian I think there are other interests at stake, I will find out later, just let us have your report please and no more questions about them".

"That's crazy you should be taking in those two in for questioning at least, if you want to find those other kids they sound like they would be your best bet".

"I know, it may seem to be the way to go but I am sure Giles and Snell are not the ones calling the shots, there are bigger fish to fry here. I'm thinking if we act too soon we will lose those who are really running this show, so Adrian, like I said leave it for now and tell us what you have".

"So, we've opened a can of worms have we"?

Toni squinted and looked directly at him with pursed lips.

"I know, I know; sorry. I'll shut up. As I told you the girl Freda Spring is recovering and will be fine in a day or two, her parents will be taking her home as soon as the doctors release her, probably today. She remembers little at the moment as the drugs are still in her system, except her description of the cell confirms she was at the Reynolds place or somewhere like it and the house she was taken to later backs up what Bailey has told us. They live in Newbury much closer to your patch so perhaps your Detective Musgrove could question her later, I believe he knows the family. That's it. What's next"?

"For us we'll be going back to Basingstoke, I'm sure DIs Musgrove and Davis have found out a lot more. For you, just keep Bailey here and make sure he is well guarded. Strictly no visitors except his brief. You can let the CPS take him to court but make sure to have him remanded in custody here, no bail, explain the reprisal risk, if he goes anywhere else we cannot be sure of his safety. I'll keep you up to date with what I can but I suspect the whole caboodle may be taken out of our hands".

DC Andrews strode into the now busy canteen looking around for his boss surprised to see them all together at one table.

"Ah there you are Ma'am. I've been with SOCO, they are all done; have sealed the van and are on their way back now; are we finished here yet"?

"Yes we are Peter. I'll be ready to go in a few minutes, bring the car to the front if you will please I won't be long".

"Yes Ma'am. Goodbye Sir, Sergeant".

Peter nodded his farewells to DI Finch and DS MacManus, turned and left. Toni stepped forward and shook hands with the Folkestone officers.

"Well, goodbye you two it has been an experience. I will get SOCO to send you the results of the analysis and the hard evidence when they have finished, I'm sure the prosecution will hold up. Mike here has already given me copies of the tapes and his statement so I don't think there is anything else. I expect I'll see you again whilst you have Bailey in custody; I or someone will want him to give evidence against Giles and Snell we may do a deal to ensure his safety, that should be enough incentive for him to agree".

"No harm in us questioning him again to see if he has remembered anything more to help us, I'll keep you informed if there is. Do you want to speak to the Super before you go Ma'am"?

"No thanks Adrian he doesn't need to see me, probably be glad when we've gone he will have his station back; you tell him I said thanks for the cooperation, that will be enough. It is difficult working these cases without inter-force rivalry getting in the way, you did well for me both of you, and Adrian I like your new hat; keep it on straight eh. Goodbye".

Adrian knew his 'new hat' would be hard to wear but was determined not to go back to his old ways, the Super notwithstanding. Mike smiled was it possible the infamous DI Finch had changed, she hoped so. They walked Toni down the front steps and stood watching deep in their own thoughts as she and Peter pulled away.

"Good job Peter, a result and new friends".

"Yes boss for sure. You sit back and take it easy now, we'll be home soon".

Chapter 26

"Hey, Jake, I just had a message from France, they are really pissed off with us, Bailey never turned up. They waited two hours after the rendezvous time, then left. What's going on"?

Jake was miffed at Henry, why ask him; how was he supposed to know what had happened to Alf Bailey and that bloody girl? He should have gotten rid of her when he had the chance; damn Henry for thinking different; 'Greedy bastard'. He now had no way of contacting him as Alf had been told to ditch the burner phone. Then he remembered Alf had a personal mobile, nothing to do with this business, same problem, he didn't know the number.

"We could try and call him do you have his mobile number"?

"Don't be daft, even if I did; which I don't; I wouldn't ring him, what if he has been picked up. He could have been stopped by the police here or even in France".

"He could have had an accident or maybe there was a delay with the tunnel. Whatever, he is on his own now we can't do a sodding thing until he calls us. He still has my number; he should let us know what is going on".

"I wouldn't bank on it especially if he's been nicked, I just hope he keeps his mouth shut, he's a dead man if he doesn't".

Jake thought 'too right' anyway now this business with the kids had stopped he felt more comfortable; he could go back to just collecting from the clubs and girls as before with a bit from the local businesses too that should be enough for them, it was bloody Henry always wanting more. He didn't know why; he never went anywhere to spend it. He had a nice gaff and could pick from any of the girls. He drank in the clubs and local pubs, ate in the cafes and had the best take-aways, all without paying. Jake was blissfully unaware the loss of this income could mean the privileged life of crime he enjoyed might come to an abrupt and unhappy end.

Henry was worried not for Jake or Albert but for his own skin. The loss of income would mean his protective cover may dry up; one mistake was turning into a big headache. The other income from the girls, and clubs plus the pittance the local shops and businesses pay for their protection was small fry compared to the income from the kids. The money from the drug distribution never came to him anymore, not like in the early days when he was independent and could do as he liked. They must realize none of this was his fault and give him time to get things going again; bloody hell they've already had a fortune out of him what do they want, blood? This thought suddenly struck a fearful note within him, he shuddered. No matter what happened next he wasn't going to be around to find out, he'd put away a fair bit so could just disappear if he wanted. Jake was a bit of a liability now so he'd have to think about what to do there. He'd sleep on it; rash decisions were always a mistake. He could leave at any time.

Chapter 27

"The Four Horseshoes pub was an old inn in the middle of the village of Sherfield, a long walk or a short drive from where Toni lived and close to Mattingly where Colin used to live when he was a Detective Inspector at Basingstoke some years before.

Tonight she had taken a taxi and was sitting in the old public bar with her pint of Doombar ale already well tasted. There were two areas in this fourteenth century inn, the bar she was sitting in and a saloon which served as a restaurant. The food was plain home cooked fare, a necessary addition to the drinking for a modern public house. Toni often ate here to relieve the boredom of cooking for one. At this time of the evening it was quiet; the gap between those that had a swift half on their way home from work, and the later drinking and restaurant trade. There were a couple of regulars in, hanging on as long as they could, not wanting to go home to their perhaps less interesting homes just yet. Colin walked in ducking under the low doorway out of a habit instinctively remembered from regular use.

"I see you've started without me then".

A statement that stimulated the barman to pull the pint Colin always had. He leaned over and handed Colin his beer.

"Well, well if it isn't young Colin, a blast from the past fer sure, what brings ye back home Sergeant"?

DCI Colin Dale responded holding up the glass to the light in mock disapproval of its contents.

"Hello Jonesy, nice to see you too. Needed a fix of your buffalo wings and a pint of your best dishwater; and hey you cheeky bugger not so much of the Sergeant it was a long time ago".

"Okay, okay, keep yer hair on *'Siiir'*; how'dya want yer wings, spicy or barbequed"?

"Sweet and hot ta, and the tabs on that one over there".

"Tight bastard".

"I didn't hear that".

"You should have, only deaf when yer wanna be, I'll bring em over when they're ready, I'll do a few extra, she's bound ta pinch one or two, seeing as how she's paying".

Toni sat watching and listening to the banter between the landlord and an old drinking buddy. She smiled at their friendly exchange and beckoned for Colin to come and sit beside her.

"Got your text it didn't say much".

"Course not I needed an excuse to come down here besides what I have I couldn't put in a text".

"Well"?

"What do you mean 'Well' Give us a minute I haven't had a chance to have a sip yet".

Colin tipped his glass and drank slowly till it was two thirds empty, paused briefly then completed the task and licked his lips an obvious light of satisfaction in his eyes.

"I needed that. Right down to business".

"Do you want another before we start"?

"Not a bad idea".

He pretended to stand but turned to her and laughed instead.

"But I'll have it later. You, young lady have touched a nerve I can tell you, as soon as I started to dig below the surface, I was immediately blocked and had not only the Super knocking on my door but a phone call from the Assistant Commissioner telling me to expect a visit from above and to make sure I cooperate".

"Come on Colin tell me what is going on".

"Have patience I'm getting there. They came almost before I'd hung up and questioned me, the Super that is and some other guy I had never met before. They wanted to know as to how I was enquiring into something already being looked at by another team. They didn't say who but were applying pressure on me to tell what I knew. No, no don't worry I did not let on about you, I just said I'd heard something from one of my snouts and was just seeing if it would lead to anything".

"Did they accept that"?

"What do you think, they wanted to know it all. I had to say something plausible so told them my man had mentioned people trafficking of some kind, which I told them I took to mean asylum seekers. He had given me the names of Giles and Snell but wouldn't say any more. It seemed to quiet them down. They said it was all in hand and there was no need for me to pursue it further".

"Is that it"?

"Not quite, I tracked down the other character who was with the Super, he called himself Smith but I took a shot of them as they were leaving on my mobile. I don't know if Smith is his real name but found him through image recognition. He is IOPC, so probably more to this than even you suspect".

"Mmm. That is a turn up why would the police anti-corruption boys be doing looking at those two if it was just child abduction. Thanks Colin anyway don't stick your neck out any more will you, don't want you getting into trouble on my account".

"Oh, I told them If they liked I would question my source again to see if I could get more out of him. The Super liked the idea and asked me, on the quiet, to report anything I get direct to him and not to the Independent Office for Police Conduct; I don't think he liked being told what to do by that Smith bloke, it'll give me a chance to tap him for a bit more info when he's alone. Anyway tell me how did you get their names"?

Toni explained about the lucky break picked up by Compton. She told how she had been down to Folkstone to interview Bailey, and when Compton found out Bailey had been associated with Giles and Snell before it lead eventually to him giving them up as being part of a child abduction scheme. The girl Freda Spring had been returned to her family as had Michael Soper but according to Bailey there were still children in France she wanted to try and recover. The evidence found in the van by SOCO had confirmed Bailey's story.

"It'll be okay to press your Super for more information but don't go too far I don't want to upset anyone at this stage or they will shut me out completely. Now what about this other pint, you'll need it to wash down your snack, or a feast should I say". Spoken as she spotted the imminent arrival of a huge plate of sizzling chicken wings. "How much did you order"?

"Enough for the two of us I hope. Two more pints please Jonesy".

She sat back and smiled. "This is nice".

Chapter 28

Superintendent Munroe was in two minds, reluctant to let a potentially career enhancing case go to another force but fearful of those upstairs admonishing him for continuing with a task which he knew had moved outside his team's jurisdiction. His Chief Inspector was sitting opposite waiting for an answer.

"Look Toni I can't just let you send someone over to France just like that".

"I know Sir I will make contact with the French Police sound them out, see if they are aware of this trafficking. Try and wheedle an invitation, at least to see if there is anything at the drop off house to help us find where the boys have been taken or what has happened to them".

"Serious crime will be up in arms if we go much further without involving them, both our jobs could be on the line here you know that don't you"?

Toni didn't respond to the rhetorical question; she was wondering if she should tell him about her conversation with Colin but decided to bide her time it would probably scare Munroe into handing over immediately.

"Just let me try Sir, Jonny and Mel could handle the trip, Mel speaks French a fair bit, well I think at least good enough to find out what we want and Jonny is great at keeping things calm and to the point. A couple of phone calls at least to see where we stand".

"You are aware the 'Police National' and not the 'Gendarmerie' are likely to be the ones who will handle this type of case, there is a rivalry between the two forces in certain areas, not as bad now as it used to be but something to be avoided. Do you know anyone over there"?

"Yes Sir, I have one or two contacts".

A bit of a white lie; she'd met a French Brigadier (equivalent to a sergeant) and his side kick some years ago on a case when she was just a lowly WPC at Southampton nick. It was booze smuggling involving villains on both side of the channel. When they came over she had been allocated the task of ferrying them around. They had got on well during the ten days he was in England with arrests made on both sides, it was a good result for all. In the brief time spent together they'd built a kinship of a sort, one that years and distance did not diminish. He'd said to call him if ever she needed anything. It was a long time ago now, the old number she had may not even work, probable Jules Anquetil may have moved on.

"Okay, call them and see how they react, let me know before you do anything else".

"Yes Sir of course. Thanks".

Assembled around the old faithful squad-room table were the full team. The same white board now crammed with pictures, names and dates sitting at the end, with little room to add more. Toni as always opened the proceedings.

"Progress yes, that is for certain, but it has only pushed us into a more complicated position. If all else fails and it is taken out of our hands I have to say I am proud of what you have done so far. Two children have been returned to their families unharmed, so if we have to, you can all move on with that in mind, but it is not over yet, still more to do. Melanie do you speak

French as well as I think, or was it bull shit I heard you muttering last year"?

Mel responded embarrassed to say anything in French in front of everyone. She could speak the language quite well as she had attended school in France as a youngster when her Mother and Father had a home near Vannes. It started as just a holiday home but the family loved it so much the visits became longer and longer eventually she, her brother and her mother stayed for six months or more throughout the warm months with her Dad doing weekend commutes. The children became bi-lingual very quickly as all their classes were in French. She didn't speak the language much now, except on holidays, so much of her vocabulary had receded into some place out of reach. Unfortunately her Father died when she just was fifteen enforcing a return to England where her Mother needed to work; the small pension left to her was not enough to pay the bills and keep two homes going. The French home is still with the family, but now relegated to just a few visits each year as and when work allowed.

"Err yes a bit, I'm not completely fluent mind but I can get by".

"Good I want you to make some calls for me. Here is the number I have it is more than a little ancient but may still work. I want to find a Jules Anquetil he is a copper, or should I say was, stationed in Le Havre. If you find him get a number and tell him I will call him in private. He will understand".

"Do you want me to say who you are, I mean like Chief Inspector, or is it personal so just Toni Webb"?

"It's business, so my rank and name will do fine'.

Melanie left to attend to the task curious as to what was in her boss's mind.

"Right if Sergeant Frazer finds my contact I hope we can organise a visit to the house in France where the two boys John Digby and Anton Biggs were taken by Alfred Bailey, also the intended drop for young Freda Spring. That will be your task Jonny you and Mel will find what's there, if indeed there is something to be found. Get prepared take plenty of evidence bags and a forensics kit you know what you'll need. Now, DI Davis you have lots to do whilst those two are on their French holidays; you can follow up on the two places Bailey gave up at interview plus his home. Primarily the Sidcup small holding with the mysterious Joe and his misses, see if Compton can find out more before you go there; second the camper van hire company, get warrants for all three, I want proper recorded searches. Advise SOCO to be ready if anything looks promising at any or all of these sites use them to do a sweep. Harrold use your own team and DC Andrews too you have a lot of ground to cover. You decide who does what but use some uniform officers, don't go anywhere single handed. These guys are dangerous and we have no idea where we may come across them. Questions".

Harold was the first, but the other DI and all present round the table wanted an answer to the question.

"What about Giles and Snell Ma'am surely we are going to arrest them now, Bailey gave them up as the men who ordered the abductions as well as what we found out ourselves we can build a good case against them, an interview is warranted at least"?

"Sorry, not possible; we have to tread carefully there, confrontation with them is not permitted at the moment, we suspect there are others we don't want to lose; whatever you find out, by other means, if it leads back to them, that will be good, note it and let me know. None of you are to follow it up by contact with either men or delve into areas that may alert them to our presence at any time. I'll be in my office I want twice daily updates and more if you find anything crucial. Okay. Go to it".

She walked the stairs in thought wondering how long it would take for the content of these orders to filter back to Giles or Snell. She hated her thoughts at this time but the interest from anti-corruption made her fear police officers could be actively involved; she knew there was a loose tongue somewhere in her station, but a controlling presence from another force seemed a real possibility as well. Not good, terrible in fact, but not her problem either, well only her local 'toe-rag', whom she hoped Compton Busion had managed to track down; let me get to the office and go over the files again see if there is anything that has been missed. Toni's eyes were beginning to smart, flitting between sheets of print, computer screen and hand-written notes was taking its toll. She sat back and rubbed the tears of irritation away with the knuckles of her fingers. She'd have a short break soon, her concentration was slipping; there was nothing which stood out so far, just a few unanswered questions, but a rest was called for, as she did not want to miss a word or image to show her the way to move forward. The knock on her door was a welcome interruption.

"Come in Mel, you have something already, that was quick"?

Melanie thought her boss was being sarcastic but the look on her face told her she was quite serious.

"Sorry Ma'am, I have come to apologise for being so long; I've had trouble tracing the man you wanted. I'm almost there I think, just waiting on a call back for a number, a direct line to his office they said just need clearance from him to pass it on to us".

Toni looked in disbelief her watch displaying three thirty and some.

"Good God is that the time I didn't realize".

She'd been at it for hours. She put a marker in the page of the file at the point she had reached and closed it shut; the notebooks and tape machine likewise placing the whole lot in the large bottom drawer of her desk turning the key. She logged out of her computer and switched off. Her personal notebook with the days scribbles she put in her top pocket along with her pencil.

"There; I've had enough of that for today my eyes are killing me. So you've found him then"?

"Yes I think it is the man, has the right name anyway. There was another of the same name but just an ordinary policeman, I thought your officer must have been promoted by now so dismissed him as being your chap. The number you gave me was no longer in use, not enough digits apparently, although it was recognised as on old number used by the French police. Took a while and lots of calls to find him so I'm glad it's not my phone bill. The number I've been promised is for a Commandant Jules Anquetil of Le Bureau de Securité in Rouen, does that sound right"?

"I would think most likely, he was quite ambitious, a detective equivalent to a sergeant when I knew him, he has done well for himself, rank equivalent to our Chief Super or even an ACC no less, how long before you get his number"?

"They didn't say, they were quite hesitant, nervous l think, for them it's a bit like me asking the Chief Constable for his personal mobile number, if you know what I mean".

They both laughed, knowing what the CC would say.

"I do. Thanks Mel let me know when it comes through. Give them a nudge if you don't have it by close of play; it is quite important I get you two over there with some local help, I can't let you go in stone cold; I'm hoping it is the right Jules as he should be able to smooth the way".

Jules Anquetil spoke some English, a terrible accent he knew, but enough vocabulary for basic conversation. When the officer had approached him with the strange request he intended to dismiss it out of hand, but on hearing the name Chief Inspector Antonia Webb he was curious. Antonia rang a feint bell but the name of Webb meant nothing; Chief Inspector was a rank perhaps he should not ignore either, so he told his officer to call the English sergeant for more information, then changed his mind, asking for the number he said he would call himself.

"Who is speaking please"?

On hearing the strong accented French voice Mel Frazer responded slowly.

"Sir, I am detective sergeant Frazer, I can speak French if you like".

"No I will speak English, who ask my number please"?

"Sir it is my Chief Inspector Toni Webb".

Visions of his old English driver Toni instantly came back to him. 'Toni Aba'. Was it she?

"Ah you have name wrong it is Toni Aba, no"?

"Oh, yes oui, of course Abakoba was her name Sir, before she married; she now uses her married name of Webb".

"Now I remember good. I give my personal number you have pen yes, tell her call me now, I wait".

He read out the number twice to be sure.

"C'est bonne, oui Monsieur, merci au revoir".

Mel hung up, annoyed she had missed that Toni used a shortened version of her birth name when on the force as a young officer. It could easily have gone sour if the Commandant had not called back, anyway she had it now and almost ran up the stairs to Toni's office.

She pulled up sharp when she saw the boss was busy, she could see Compton through the glass. Although she would normally wait felt the boss would want the phone number right away so knocked. Toni waved her to come in.

"Sorry to interrupt Ma'am but thought you would want this now".

Mel handed Toni Jules Anquetil's phone number which had taken her half a day to acquire.

"That's okay thanks I'll find you later".

Mel left, it being obvious something was going on that was private for Toni normally included all her officers with whatever was current.

"So Compton you think you have found out who is leaking our information".

"I can't be sure who exactly, it could be one of three people, but I do know when and where. One terminal in particular has been used more than once with a unique password, when I know for a fact the officer who was allocated that password was not on site. Files were not modified, copied, printed or downloaded just read those times. I found other terminals where different passwords have been used, again files were just read. This is not normal; officers almost always enter the system to actively modify or add to their files, they don't have time to just sit and read them. Fortunately none have access to sensitive data except through me. One other thing makes me suspicious the access is nearly always during break or lunchtimes. This lot will not give up their breaks to do paperwork or read files, unless we have a flap on or something big is about to go down".

"Who do you think is doing this"?

"There are two constables, newly joined, and a civilian clerk who may fit the bill but it could be anyone, but how they have learned so may passwords worries me, we must tighten our security once we find out who is doing this. The desk sergeants keep a computer log of those on site and the timing of who comes and goes; IT has tapped into it and set a trap to warn me of activity using passwords when the officers allocated are not on site. I won't know who but I will see which terminal they are using so I could go and find who is sitting at a particular desk. As I said we could close the loophole by additional security measures, that will stop him but this way we have a good chance of catching this guy".

"Wow you have thought it through haven't you, sounds good but don't approach whoever it is, be discreet I don't want to tip them off, I could use this to our advantage".

Compton was buzzing with the thought of the developing intrigue and the part she was to play in it.

"Oh yes! I love it, shall I feed them false data like"?

"I hadn't thought of that, I would just have followed them to find out who they are giving our stuff to; your idea of introducing mis-information is a real possibility. Anyway let's find out who it is first, then we can talk tactics on how we deal with them".

Chapter 29

Superintendent Mitchell Vale, along with his friend and colleague Detective Inspector Frank Branch were friends from way back, back to early times on the force, times very different from today. Close to retirement now they had joined up the same week near to thirty years ago, meeting for the first time at the Police Training College course for new recruits at Hendon. Their progress through the ranks of the Metropolitan London Police had not been remarkable, however good results in court and a better than average clear up rate ensured their steady progress. Mitch was a little better at exams so made Sergeant and then Inspector a year before his friend Frankie. They were a good team and managed to stay together for several years. The split came when Mitch moved on to become a DCI and then two years later Superintendent of the station in Camberwell, leaving Frankie at the rank of Detective Inspector. Once Mitchell Vale had reached the rank of Superintendent they never worked directly on cases together but still remained friends, no resentment existed because of Mitch's progress to higher levels. There was a fundamental evil link that bound these two men for life. During their time together they were brutish in their dealings with the criminal element, in the days when the Police were less than straight they had learnt their trade from old hands who were not much better than the criminals they were supposed to be apprehending. They put away many murderers and rapists because there was nothing to be gained by letting them go with anything but the harshest penalty; it gave them a feeling of overwhelming power and a reputation of infallibility; through a network of informers and threats to known villains they were able to extort everything from free meals and booze to payments for turning a blind eye to their criminal activities.

They were not the only officers who bent the rules and took advantage of their power. They began slowly at first but through the years ended up controlling most of the crime in their district. They built up a 'dirt file' on everyone who worked at their station and on others in the Met. just in case one of them proved to be a future problem. They fed on the weak and vulnerable but controlled their leaders through intimidation, fear and by providing a measure of protection from the law, thriving on the feeling of power it gave them. Their original income was by taking a share from ongoing criminal activities but things had developed where they now had a say in what went down on their watch. The income from drugs had been fragmented, run by different gangs who were constantly at each other's throats, the same for those running the girls and clubs. Now what they ordered was obeyed, different groups ran the different activities, it was stable no inter-rival fighting and a steady income for all. Those who resisted were arrested and fitted up with one crime or another or if necessary disposed of. They never went near any of the criminals they controlled, contact was always through phone or texts by third parties, total fear was the motivation it worked well. These two didn't care they felt invincible, no one to question them. To the men in charge at Police headquarters it seemed Vale and Branch were doing a great job. The visible crime rate was down with the worst villains in jail serving their time.

"Mitch this Giles guy has fucked up proper the trade with Antoine has been compromised; I've heard from my source the police in Hampshire are searching for the missing kids all

211

because he had some idiot who let one of them peg it, what do think we should do"?

"Hey Frankie, don't get your knickers in a twist it's been taken care of. Snell has removed the bozo who killed the kid so there is no one left who will talk there. As far as I know the girl has gone over at least it's what Henry Giles was supposed to be doing yesterday".

"There's a report about a girl being found in Folkestone; the Hampshire police are on their way there so must have found out something. I can understand them being interested in the dead boy, after all the body was dumped on their turf, but why go to Kent; are you sure the girl has gone"?

"No, you are right I have not had it confirmed, call your snout at Basingstoke and find out what is going on. We don't need to do anything, even if they have caught up with her, the courier's name is Bailey he has no idea we exist. Henry and Jake are the weak link but they don't know who we really are either, they have never met either of us or don't have any phone numbers that can be traced back. We'll bide our time it will all fizzle out then we can start again".

"Maybe we should pull in Henry and Jake, we have enough on them to put them away for a long time, and it will look good for us to make a high profile arrest and will keep the Hampshire lot away from questioning them".

"Sounds good but we don't want to open a can of worms they won't give in easily and I don't want to draw attention to ourselves either. We don't even know if they have been sussed yet, we shouldn't waste a valuable asset by jumping the gun, they generate a good income for us even without the French trade, I don't want to lose that, let's wait and see".

Mitch always had the last word, not just because he was the senior officer more for his knack of always being right. Frank never argued beyond a certain point, he would present his ideas which were adopted, or not, depending upon how Mitch assessed them. In all the years they had been together it had worked well for him, he trusted Mitch's judgement. He would wait and see; he just didn't want to wait too long. Mitch and Frank had both married during their early years as lowly constables; the wives were friends blissfully unaware of their husband's corrupt life outside the home. Frank had salted away a nice nest egg, with accounts in Jersey and Spain he was close to retirement and wanted to leave with his pension to a life of luxury. Mitch had done the same although it was now more difficult to pay large sums into any account without good reason, so cash and valuables had been salted away in safety deposit boxes abroad; they kept nothing in England. From the beginning Mitch had given strict instructions to Frank that he keep a modest household in England living within the means of his police salary, any investigation into his bank accounts and lifestyle here would not look out of the ordinary. Their accounts abroad had been opened with cash whilst on vacation under an assumed name. The two had splashed out when on holiday, but it was the only time their ill-gotten gains were enjoyed, it was all about the retirement and the thrill of wielding the power. He'd send little Mary her instructions, that way they would know better what was going on.

Chapter 30

"Hello, Jules I..."

"Toni is that you, yes it is I remember your magnifique voice a la crème".

"One word and you remember me"?

"But of course, you in my heart, I not forget, it is too long time we no speak".

"True mon ami, but today I need your help".

"Oui, what it is , what I can do"?

"I will be quick then I give you my sergeant who speaks very good French she will explain the details to you. We have children missing who are being abducted and taken to France for the organ transplant trade. I want to send two officers over to investigate an address we have discovered that may have housed these kids".

"Stop, stop, you use words I not understand exact. Say again for me. I know children abduction to France and house here, but not more".

"Jules. C'est difficile. My sergeant will speak to you okay".

Toni handed the phone over to Melanie Frazer with instruction to explain fully in French what was needed.

After ten minutes of to and fro, between Jules and Mel she handed the phone back to Toni.

"Tres dessolet, Toni this very bad, I will arrange for officer to meet your detective Jonny and the Sergeant at police station in Calais tomorrow morning. Officer will take them to house, I get papers she need for search. You give me back sergeant I will pass to my assistant for arrange. I wish you bonne chance Toni, call me when all finish and you have men in gaol okay".

"Okay old friend I will".

Toni passed the phone back to Mel who immediately burst into French at a speed where Toni understood not a word. Her thoughts jumped from one item to another; 'things were moving at last; what an asset this girl is turning out to be; I must see the Super and let him know what is about to happen; I will call Colin again to see if he has come up with anything new; must finish reading the files; and whatever else there is to do. Calm yourself down, Toni Aba, take it easy, you're the detective with the "*voice a la crème*" remember, one thing at a time'. She switched off her racing mind, smiled to herself at his words, leaned back in her chair closed her eyes and remembered a long forgotten face; 'what a lovely man he is'.

Melanie interrupted her boss's reverie.

"There is something you should know Ma'am, the Commandant said to tell you he would enquire to see if any departments or officers were looking at cases involving illegal transplants, if so he was not sure if they would want to cooperate; some special forces are outside his control; he would let us know when we were over there".

"That shouldn't stop you in finding the house and doing a search, Jules will have all the necessary paperwork sent to the local officer in Calais. Go and put DI Musgrove in the picture, book the Tunnel for first thing in the morning, it will be quicker than the ferry; don't forget the forensic kit and your passports. I will arrange some Euros for expenses and a hotel if you need to stay over I'll leave them and a bank card for emergencies with the desk sergeant tonight. Call me with any results or if you have a problem. Take Jules' phone number too he may be able to help if you come unstuck. Good luck Mel and be careful, we don't know who we are up against".

"We'll be fine Ma'am, I'll go let the DI know what is happening, will you want to see him before the off"?

"I don't think so, unless he does, call me whenever, I'll be waiting. If you see DI Davies in the squad room tell him to come and see me".

"Ah Harrold thanks for coming, there's such a lot going on at the moment I have not had time to get everyone together for an up to date conflab. Anyway DI Musgrove and Sergeant Frazer are off to France to follow up on the possible house abduction site we got from Bailey; I want you and Peter to track down this Joe character at Sidcup".

"I've already started on that Ma'am, The name of the guy who owns the small holding is Ian Joseph Duden married, no previous not even a parking ticket, I presume the 'Joe' we want is him. The small business seems to be legit vegetable supplier to local hotels restaurants and the like. They run a stall at a market in the town centre car park every Sunday. Someone must have a serious hold over them if they are involved in this child abduction business".

"Good you seem to be ahead of me, get a search warrant I want you and Peter to go down there as soon as you can to bring them in for questioning, arrest them if you have to; take a couple of uniforms and a forensic kit. They may have a similar set up to Reynolds so be careful, don't tell anyone where you're going except the people you need, we don't want a repeat of what happened at the farm. If it looks like they have been holding children there call in SOCO. The murders and abductions are so interlinked you and Jonny Musgrove will work together on this now. A word of warning; be ready for it all to be taken away, the Super is very close to handing this over to the Serious Crime Squad but for now we'll keep at it eh".

"For sure Ma'am; what about Constable Owens shall I take her "?

"Not this time Harrold I have a job lined up for her this week with Constable Krane".

Harrold decided to stay at the station he had an idea he wanted to discuss with Compton. He had every confidence in DC Andrews so sent Peter to Sidcup with a uniformed officer and three CSIs. They found the couple working in the green house adjacent to the old house Peter walked in.

"Ian Duden"?

"Yes, what can I do for you"?

"I am Detective Constable Andrews; I must ask you to accompany me to the station".

"What's this all about"?

"I think you probably know already. I am arresting you on suspicion of abducting a minor. I must caution you. You do not have to say anything, but it may harm your defence if you do not mention when questioned something which you later rely on in court. Anything you do say may be given in evidence. Do you understand"?

"Yes, but you must know I had no choice".

"You can explain that later; officer take him to the car".

Peter moved towards Mrs. Duden intending to take her in also. She stood defiant looked him in the eye.

"You know he would have killed my brother and taken my daughter if we did not do as we were told".

"Tell me more, who threatened you"?

"My brother is in prison, two years for a robbery he did not do; fitted up by that bastard Franks from Camberwell. He came to us later and said John would have a nasty accident if we did not look after some kids. We refused and took no notice at first, then we received a finger in the post with a note saying it would be his throat next time".

Her eyes were full of tears her voice choking with the memory.

"We knew it was my brother John's finger. We knew it was wrong but what could we do, we couldn't go to the police, he was the bloody police".

"Where is your daughter now"?

"She is with her grandfather and has been for some time, it felt safer somehow".

Peter had intended to arrest her at the same time as her husband but his feeling her story was so awful it was probably true; he would treat them both easier than he had in mind. The police involvement angle, if true, worried him; these people were not safe.

"Good; I will do my best for your husband. If it checks out I will have him out on bail this afternoon and bring him back here myself. If not, then I will probably be back for you. I do have a search warrant and will leave these three officers here to conduct the search".

"Fine what choice do I have, if your copper friend finds out you are here my brother will be dead".

"Coppers like that are no friend of mine; If this story is no bullshit I will find out from Mr Duden where your brother is held and have him removed from danger at once".

"I'll believe that when I see it".

"Please believe it, I am on your side. Understand you must stay at home till I return".

"Where would I go. We did care for these kids you know; I have no idea what happened to them when they left us, I do hope they are okay".

Chapter 31

Force of habit kept Mary Newman alert, gathering information whenever the opportunity arose. As a civilian clerk in Basingstoke police station she processed old documents which needed transferring to the digital format. She had been employed, along with her colleague Samantha, for the last two months to carry out that arduous task. Unlike Samantha who did her work and then went home Mary became bored long before the day was done; she was not all she seemed to be; her password only allowed access to areas in the station computers for the task in hand. Largely unsupervised she was not always at her desk becoming a familiar and accepted sight around the station during lunch and coffee breaks as well as at times when she felt like it. She had become friendly with some of the younger constables offering to help them with their paperwork. Not thinking they were doing anything wrong they would often let her transcribe their notes into the appropriate crime files. She was accurate and fast, saving the officers, who were not too computer literate, hours of what to them was a time consuming chore. Over a period she had accumulated a list of passwords that allowed her access to all but the most secure sections. She knew which computer terminals were used by several different officers; they were the ones she always used when looking outside her allowed access. She never used her own terminal for anything other than for her designated task. It all started some six years before when she had been doing a clerk's job at Camberwell police station and had offered the same extra service to the young officers; the one mistake which changed her life was becoming involved with one particular detective who pretended to need her help, allowing her access to his password whilst he quietly watched her studying files and notes well outside her brief. At that time she only did this out of boredom relief from the mundane task of transcription, she enjoyed looking for details of cases to stimulate her naturally inquisitive mind. A week after she had first logged into Detective Frank Branch's server uninvited he came in closed the door behind him and pulled up a chair to sit next to Mary at her desk. Alone in the small room allocated to her she was a little perturbed by his close presence, but thinking he wanted to transcribe something private asked him what he wanted her to do. He put a hand on her knee and squeezed so hard she cried out in pain. He relaxed his grip a little but kept a tight hold.

"You're hurting me please let go".

"Mary Newman be quiet and listen to me very carefully. I know what you have been up to, snooping into places you are not allowed. I have watched where you go, poking into files not meant for you to see. If you fail to do what you are told I will have you up on charges that will put you away for a very long time".

Mary was petrified she had been found out doing what she knew was wrong but she was not a criminal he couldn't do that could he?

"I was only looking I didn't pass anything on I was just being nosey".

His face moved to within one inch of her ear, his hot breath peppered her temple as he spoke slowly and full of menace.

"Looking has put you into serious trouble, but I do have a way out for you; I'll let you know how soon, but for now just do your job and keep your damn nose out of other peoples' business, you hear".

She was afraid to stop him but stiffened as he moved his hand further up her leg to the top of her inner thigh; he suddenly squeezed so hard it took he breath away. Two seconds later he was gone, she sat unable to move, her leg throbbing with the pain and tears streaming down her face.

What had she gotten herself into, what did that bastard want, her body? She hoped not, he was too violent but what choice did she have, she had nothing else to give, or she would go to prison. She had a feeling it would not be too long before he came with his demands; she shook with fear at what he might do to her.

Mary's relief was tangible to the point of euphoria, all he wanted was information. He told her to apply for openings as a temporary clerk at various stations around the Met area and later to other stations in the south. She was good at the job and his recommendations ensured she was taken on each time a new position appeared. She stayed just a few weeks or so at each site doing her allotted tasks but collecting information in the same way as she had done before. She continued to rent her flat in Camberwell and returned there at weekends and on the days between transfers; when away she stayed at B&Bs near to whatever location she was working.

She was more than glad for after leaving the Camberwell station she never saw him again but received cash payments in the post along with instructions to secure information about specific officers or cases. She sent this information to a numbered post office box in Camberwell. She didn't ask for the money but had become used to the better lifestyle it gave her.

She had become expert at deception and more careful in her choice of candidates, no one realising what had gone on during her period with the different forces. Basingstoke was no different, the case file of the missing boys was not secured particularly well, in fact it was available for all officers to read, so she had no problems reading most of the file either but certain sections were closed and the printing of it was secured. She had to remember the important point and write them down later in her digs. Access to the detectives' passwords had not happened here, only the younger uniformed officers were susceptible, her offers to transcribe were not accepted by those who had reached a rank of significance as they were well capable of entering their own data and besides Compton Busion kept a tight rein on her staff. In addition to computerised information she kept her ears and eyes open to the gossip that always ran through the station.

Her official work was almost finished here but received an order to slow down from Frank Branch. He wanted her to delay long enough to obtain specific information about the Chief Inspector's instructions to her officers dealing with the murder and abduction cases; she had no choice but to comply. This time it was different he wanted the information in a hurry, she'd been told to deliver it by hand the next day, to a meeting place in Camberwell, she would do as he asked even though she did not relish meeting up with Branch after such a long time, the memory of his hand gripping her thigh and his fearful voice would remain with her always.

She would wait till the afternoon break when most officers were out of the station and those remaining went to the canteen. She wouldn't be able to access the murder file but had learnt the password of one of the SOCOs unaware she was watching his fingers on the keyboard as he logged in. She could get to see their reports and have a view of the abduction file. She didn't know if she could get what he'd asked but would give him what she found and hoped it would be enough.

Mary wished she could stop this; it was having a toll on her health, not sleeping well, moving from station to station, living in digs, constantly watching her back fearful of being caught, but more afraid of the man who controlled her every move. She would take the opportunity when she delivered the stuff to tell him she was sick and needed a break; he must listen or she would really become ill she knew she was on the brink of breaking down.

Compton Busion on was in the canteen just about to have a coffee when the intruder alarm caught her attention. She looked at the screen pleased to see her trap had been sprung.

"Hello someone's at it" She voiced out loud to no one special as she left the canteen and moved down the corridor to the doorway of the squad room, keeping well out of sight of anyone in the area. Not quite empty, she could see the occupant at the desk where the terminal that had triggered the alarm was in use; she wasn't surprised to see who was there. She silently moved away and went straight to Toni's office.

"She's clever that one she moves from one terminal to another matching passwords to the usual officer's workplace. Made a mistake this time though she has used a SOCO password but their terminals are not in the squad room area so had no option but to use a general terminal".

"Well come on who is it then"?

"Her name is Mary Newman a civilian temporary clerk been here over a month now supposedly transposing old files onto the computer system".

"Bloody hell, don't we vet these people, civilians having access to all our files is not on. How on Earth did she get the passwords"?

"I've no idea. Civilians are cleared by security at the Met before they are employed, we just get who they send. I looked her up she has a good record, been with the police for several years, worked all over with no complaints, in fact the opposite, several recommendations; what do you want me to do"?

"Maybe she's been doing this for years too. Do you mind looking into her finances and anything else that comes to light, like where she has worked and who thinks she is worth recommending, I don't want to involve other officers at this stage. By the way did she pick up on the false location you put in all the files"?

"She certainly saw it but she never prints anything, seems she just takes handwritten notes, it stood out well enough so there's a good chance she has written it down".

Toni had agreed with Compton concerning feeding the informer false information. She entered the address of an unused safe house into some of the files where Alfred Bailey was supposedly being held, it was worded in such a way that the security was of a low order as they considered Baily not worth worrying about. The idea being whoever was interested may attempt to get at him there, if they did they would be in for a surprise, for it was empty. It had been set up with several hidden motion sensitive CCTV cameras linked back to Compton's computers. Toni did not want confrontation only to find out who was receiving the information.

"Right we must close the door soon, get IT to change and reissue all the system passwords, tell them to wait till tomorrow and to issue a notice saying it is a head office routine security instruction. I don't want her to become suspicious as I want to follow this Mary to find where, how and to whom she is passing this data. Our current password system is not working I must have a serious talk with everyone here when this is all over. Please keep the trap you set up in place for now, it will help a bit in case she comes back for more, although I doubt if she will it is too dangerous for her. I know I don't need to tell you but don't mention this to anyone, there could be more than just this Mary; information has been leaking longer than the few weeks she has been here, I'm not sure who to trust so just you and me for now okay".

"You do realise the IT guys will be aware the alarm flag has been tripped, so may become inquisitive what do I say"?

"Never thought of that, things are never quite straightforward are they; say nothing for now, they won't know who it is, just that it happened right, I will have a word with them; this must remain covert until we have followed it to a conclusion. By the way Compton you did good there; we are making progress and this spy in our camp may be something we can turn to our advantage".

"Let's hope so Ma'am, let's hope so".

Toni returned to her office to find DC Andrews sitting inside waiting for her. He stood as she entered.

"I hope you don't mind Ma'am but I've been waiting a while".

She moved behind her desk and sat down.

"No of course not Peter, what can I do for you"?

"I have a problem with this guy Ian Duden and his wife. They have been keeping the children at their place alright but I don't think it fair to charge them. They have been forced to keep these kids by someone unknown; he said they would kill her brother, a very serious threat; and here is where I have a problem; they claim the threats come from the police".

"Serious indeed; do you believe them"?

"Yes I do Ma'am. I checked their story. They claim her brother was fitted up for a burglary he did not commit and sent to prison for two years. She says the arresting officer was a Detective Sergeant Franks working out of Camberwell station. I can't find an officer of that name there or anywhere nearby. She claims that soon after her brother was put away, she and her husband were told to accept looking after two boys. Apparently a human finger arrived in the post with a note saying worse would follow. When I checked at the prison I was told her brother had indeed had an accident in the kitchen and lost a finger. Threats against their daughter followed, so they sent her away to the grandparents. The wife is sure it was the arresting officer who was behind this and I am inclined to think the same. What do I do Ma'am"?

"Nothing for now except release them on police bail; I will look into it. It does back up something I have been suspecting. Thanks Peter".

"I only arrested Joe, I left his wife at home".

"Felt sorry for her I suppose"?

"Yes Ma'am I did believe her at the time, I thought they had probably gone through enough without my making it worse".

"Feelings should not come into it Peter you know that; she should have been brought in whilst you checked the story".

"Yes Ma'am. I'm sorry".

"Not to worry, go and send Joe or is it Ian home"?

"His name is Ian Joseph Duden but is known as Joe. What about the brother should he be protected in some way"?

"I'll deal with him, go write up your report, we will handle this internally no need to involve CPS".

Toni wondered who was this detective Franks; a false name maybe. She would find out from the trial records.

Chapter 32

"Where do we go from here"?

"Hang on a minute guv, I'll have the address in the satnav in a moment, it won't be far".

The sun had appeared above the buildings as they left the tunnel terminal and were moving very slowly creeping along the N16 just west of Calais.

"There you go all set, satellite acquired, stay on this road for a bit then take the second exit to the centre of the town".

Jonny sped up a little as he now knew he was on the correct road. He was not familiar with driving on the right so erred on the side of caution keeping well below the speed limit and constantly looking in his mirrors.

"I'm relying on you Mel to tell me where to turn in good time, I don't want to go whizzing by our exit".

"Don't fret Sir you have a couple of miles to go before we leave this road I'll give you plenty of warning".

In less than fifteen minutes they had pulled in under an ornate arched entrance into the Calais Police Station car park. There were plenty of spaces so Jonny chose a vacant spot hoping it was not allocated to some senior officer, oddly no one challenged them.

"Imagine trying to do that back home".

The station seemed to be back to front, there was no formal entrance into the building on the roadside just two fire escape exits closed tight. The main entrance was at the rear facing the wall surrounded car park; a dozen steps led to a grand covered porch and even grander doorway which was the only obvious way in. The pair walked up the steps having seen no one until they arrived at the large high ceiling foyer occupying most of the ground floor inside. A long counter to the left manned by three uniformed officers was their target, a queue of six or so people were at one officer's position, just one person taking in a loud voice at the second and the other officer was occupied on the telephone; they chose him. They approached with their badges held out for his perusal. He held up his finger to halt their interrupting his call, whilst leaning forward to examine their ID. The call finished he used the same finger to call then towards the counter.

"Good morning, officers follow me please we expect you".

He said nothing else, stepped out from behind his position and walked towards the back wall without looking back. Jonny and Mel exchanged glances smiled and followed the man to a bank of four lifts. He pressed the button at the first lift the door opened at once.

"Please entre, Commandant Hergeot is on etage three merci".

They entered and pressed the third floor button. Again a smile to each other as the lift ascended.

A short, black haired middle aged man in a dark suit, white shirt and wide red tie, was revealed as the door slid back.

"Welcome Detective Musgrove and Sergeant Frazer my name is Maurice Hergeot, I am to be your guide here. Please come to my bureau".

Mel walked next to him speaking in French whilst Jonny followed, she was explaining what they wanted to do as they traversed the long corridor to an office about halfway down. She asked if they could speak English for Jonny's sake.

"Your French is very good but I find your words a little different".

"Vannes is where I grew up we lived there for many years".

"Ah Breton, now I understand the accent. Let me tell you what we do okay. The address for the house you have told us has been put under a watch by my officer, we have not made in deep enquiries of the owner if we not want warn them before we go in".

Jonny interjected here eager to get on.

"Have you a warrant to enter and search"?

"Oh yes we have Mandat de Perquisition can go very soon, remember you have not authority, only observation yes"?

"Of course, when you have finished is it possible to collect forensics if it is the place where children have been kept"?

"Not official but I too busy to look at you all time, I think you comprend no"?

Jonny nodded and smiled, he liked this guy, he was going to be a big help. Toni's friend in high places has come through alright.

"I wait for my Brigadier Manne to bring car and we leave; your car stay here you come with me, good"?

Jonny nodded his agreement and whispered to Mel.

"What's a brigadier"?

"Something like a sergeant, the French have more ranks than us, our Commandant is similar to a DCI but there are four different levels of Commandant, you only know which when they are in dress uniform. Don't worry about it I'll tell you if any top rank brass arrives".

"Our guy seems very accommodating".

"He may be, but that is just the polite French way, if we do anything outside what he wants, you will certainly find out soon enough, just be polite and very patient. I'll go ahead and get the forensic kit out of our car, meet you by Chief Hergeot's car".

The journey to the house near to of the village of Crécy-en-Ponthieu was quicker than expected. The A16 Motorway was uncrowded, unlike British M roads, with a legal speed limit over eighty miles per hour; what little traffic there was, moved along at a good pace. The police driver ignored this 130 kmph, often exceeding 150. They left the fast road went straight through the toll gate which opened automatically as the police car approached. The brigadier, their driver, had obviously studied the route as he followed the now winding and much slower minor roads turning left and right at various junctions and crossroads without referring to any map or sat nav. He stopped a few yards short of an almost hidden lane.

"Voila we are arriving, the house is down this lane on its own, very quiet no neighbours, big land and many trees. We think it is not occupied now, my officer is there on his feet watching, he radio me no one comes or goes in many hours. We will drive down okay".

The car moved slowly down the narrow lane to a widening driveway as they came into sight of the rather imposing property. It looked a little run down in need of some care. Paint was flaking from the window frames and shutters and the weeds were beginning to take over a once well-tended front lawn. It certainly looked deserted. A tired looking man stepped out from behind some trees on the left part of the driveway and walked towards them. Commandant Hergeot exited the vehicle and spoke to him.

"He is sure no one inside, he look round the back too no one he sees, we have a key" he said, pointing to a large powerful ram that Brigadier Manne was lifting out of the boot.

All five walked towards the porch. Hergeot banged on the door and pulled the large brass handle with a chain that disappeared inside. There was no ring from the chain bell so he banged again shouting loudly in French, obviously demanding entry. No one came.

Two whacks with the ram splintered the fairly substantial frame like matchwood, the door swung fully open with great force bouncing back only to be stopped by the big boot of officer Manne. All five peered through the doorway into the central hall; stairs to the left next to a closed door two more doors to the right, one of which was wide open, the hall doglegged to the left behind the stairway towards the rear. Manne returned the ram to the car and came back armed with a box full of plastic shoe covers and gloves which he distributed to everyone.

"Please wait here we go in make search first, we be sure safe for you".

Jonny and Mel complied as the three French officers entered. Jonny could see they had split up immediately on entry one to the left one to the right and the other up the stairs. He could hear shouting from inside.

"What's he saying Mel"?

"They're calling all clear to each other as they enter each room, they are being thorough don't you think, won't be long".

"Putting on a performance for us perhaps".

"Cynical thinking, but probably true; It's their show for now we have to be patient".

"I suppose".

233

Chief Hergeot appeared from behind the stairs and came to the front door.

"No person here now, so please to go inside, I look only quick but I think we have a bad place here, I go to car to call équipe médico-légale for special examination of house; remember you look but take nothing".

They move in together and enter the first room on the left finding it empty except for a small bed in the corner with a soiled flock mattress no covers. The two rooms opposite and to the right were similar except one had a broken chair. The windows were shuttered but unexpectedly the lights were working, although only a dim single lamp illuminated each room, it was enough to see there was little here except the beds. Beds that may reveal who had used them.

"Mel I'm assuming that 'medico whatsit' are their CSIs"

"Yes same as our SOCO; not much here let's move on, upstairs or out the back first, eh"?

"I think our friend is giving us the run of the house for a short while, I saw the other two go down the hall and are now out in the rear garden. Let's make the most of it and split up; You look at the rest of the rooms down here I will go up, we'll call out if either of us finds anything".

The first two rooms to the left on the first floor were completely empty, no furniture rugs or curtains. The shutters were open and the room was dusty to the point where they looked like they had been empty for a long time. So far there was no evidence that this house had been used recently; then what did the chief mean that this was a bad place and why bring in forensics, there must be more.

The first room on the right revealed the first signs of what he was looking for. It was clean in the extreme, he thought he could smell bleach, no more like the clinical smell you get in hospital. The bed in this room was akin to that from a hospital, not so elaborate as the modern all electric ones of toady but still it could be raised and lowered with a foot pedal and had an adjustable back support. There was no mattress. A bedside locker, again of an older design, stood next to the bed with a plastic chair in the corner. Two short gas cylinders and some plastic tubing lay under the bed. He moved on eagerly, his earlier despondency that they would find nothing dispelled but the thought of what had been happening here rapidly returned him to his sombre mood. The next room confirmed their original fears but it pleased him in one way they were at least on the right track towards stopping these bastards, this place couldn't be used again. The room was completely clean, pristine white walls and ceiling, the window taped off with plastic sheeting; air-tight and germ free. A clinical sink in the corner with hands free taps. Four large gas cylinders were mounted on the back wall, devoid of tubing. Two large tables, purpose built to perform medical procedures stood side by side in the centre. Finally above each table fully adjustable overhead light clusters. This room was obviously used as an operating theatre. A trolley made to carry the instruments of surgery lay on its side by the far wall, now empty. The room had been cleared in a hurry, everything that could be easily removed had been taken away only the heavy items remained. This suggested to Jonny that perhaps only one or maybe two people had been here when an order to evacuate had been received; also more disturbing was the fact that they knew we were coming. The good news in all this is in their rush they are sure to have left evidence behind. The room at the rear was in chaos, mattresses, soiled linen, boxes of different sizes some closed and some with various medical toiletries spilling out, but what caught his attention were the various articles of worn and crumpled clothing amongst all this debris. 'DNA from these should tell us a lot' he thought hoping to find matches to the missing children. 'Not good news for the families even so closure of some kind he supposed, better than not knowing although that was a doubtful assumption'.

Jonny went back down the stairs to find Mel sitting on the bottom step head in hands.

"What's up Mel are you ill or something"?

She raised her head looked at him with eyes full of tears unable to speak straight away.

"What is it love what has happened"?

She just pointed to the rear.

"Outside, Jonny its outside".

Reluctant to leave her in such a state but needing to see what had upset her so much he moved towards the rear door.

"Stay there love I'll be back in a minute".

Once outside he could see he was in a large garden surrounded by trees, once well cared for but now overgrown; overgrown all except for a patch of ground to one side, where the two officers and Commandant Hergeot were standing. Jonny moved over and immediately saw what had moved his sergeant to tears. A makeshift unfinished shallow grave with the hair, knees and toes of a child showing through soil hurriedly scattered over the remains. A gasp of breath, missed heartbeat, despair shook his large frame on seeing the tight curled hair and the dark skin of his knees and feet. 'Anton I am so sorry, too late, too bloody late'.

"Detective Musgrove we must vacate this place for our men of medicine science to study, they arrive in five minutes. We go back to Calais find you hotel, we return tomorrow there will be good evidence here for you and for we also. We have some people in sight for this terrible crime we can discuss with you later".

"Yes Sir that will be good I will fetch Sergeant Frazer".

Melanie had regained her composure somewhat and was waiting by the car not wishing to go back in the house, well not today anyway. Jonny walked over and put his arm round her shoulder giving her a brief hug.

"I'm sorry Jonny showing us up like that in front of those French coppers, they must think we are a load of pansies".

"I've seen enough dead bodies in my time but the whole thing in that house and that lad in the garden would move the devil to tears, yours wasn't the only wet cheek in there so don't worry, it shows you have some empathy. Look we're going back to Calais soon, once the lab boys arrive, pick up our car and check into a hotel. The French CSIs will be here all night and tomorrow too I imagine; we'll came back first thing by then they may know something. Where's the forensic kit box"?

"Oh, I left it in the hall shall I get….."

"No, no, I'll go".

Jonny opened the now redundant forensic kit box, removed the fingerprint and DNA data he had brought with him to give to their CSI technicians, there was no chance he would be taking samples now it had become too complex. He would rely on the French police to give him the results. He had no idea how they stood legally if he had to present French results to the CPS, would they be valid or not. He would get Mel to explain and ask that extra samples be taken for the English scientists to analyse independently just in case their DNA evidence was inadmissible in an English court. On returning to the car two white vans had turned up and half a dozen men were donning protective clothing. Hergeot was talking to Mel; he handed the comparison data to him who passed it onto one of the suited technicians. Before he had a chance to ask Mel to translate his thoughts concerning samples for them, Hergeot spoke.

"We look for match to these prints today the DNA take longer. We duplicate all samples for you to take back for you analyse at home, okay, we go now yes".

The ride back was uneventful and in silence each with their own thoughts, all wondering who was responsible for the half buried young soul. Jonny was composing his report in his mind he would write it up in his notebook a soon as he got to the hotel, he wanted to get everything straight in his mind before he phoned Chief Webb.

Chapter 33

The Hotel recommended by Hergeot was just what Jonny and Mel needed. Comfortable rooms with large double beds and bathrooms with both bath and separate walk in shower.

"See you in the restaurant at seven Mel is that alright with you"?

"Yes Sir, I want a soak right now followed by a large G and T. Seven is fine".

Mel went straight to the mini bar and opened the only two miniature Gordons in there, topped up with one small Schweppes, there were no lemons or ice but the can and bottles were cold enough, it was gone long before it had time to become even a little bit warm or her bath had time to fill.

Jonny sat at the desk, come dressing table, with his notebook spread ready. Where to start? He wrote about the welcome and the route to the house; naming the officers and their role in the events of the morning. He paused not wishing to recall the harrowing discovery of Anton just yet. They had missed lunch, he was hungry too late now, but too early for dinner; he raided the mini bar, a bag of nuts some weird crisps, a bar of unknown chocolate and a coke did the trick. Half an hour saw the notebook updated and checked. He would call the boss now.

"Hello, Jonny how are we doing".

"Okay Ma'am, the Commandant Hergeot has been very cooperative. We visited the house and are going back tomorrow".

"Good did you find anything of interest"?

"More than that Ma'am a great deal more".

Jonny went on to explain how they entered and the search he'd made. Confirmation signs that surgery had taken place supported their theory of forced organ donor trading. Telling about the discovery of the partially buried body of a youngster he thought was probably Anton Biggs, again caused the same emotional response he'd felt at the time. He paused for an over long period not able to continue.

"You all right Jonny"?

"Err, yes Ma'am just looking through my notes, lost my place don't want to miss anything. Oh yes it looks like whoever was there left in a hurry, only a short while before we arrived. Someone is warning them for sure. It could be from our side or here even; the Commandant hinted they are aware of these abductions and have someone in the frame already. I'm not sure if that is true or just false bait set to tempt us to open up on where we stand. If they have a leak I don't want to give anything away".

"Quite right but I think the leak is with us , I'm sure we are close to tracking it down, and have plugged the hole anyway. I suppose you don't have any definitive ID for the body yet"?

"No chance, we only found it a couple of hours ago and couldn't see the face, only the hair and skin colour made me think of Anton, it could of course, be another coloured boy. French SOCO are there now although their pathologist had not arrived before we left; it will take them some time to extract the remains, we'll be able to at least have a view of him tomorrow so if it is our boy I have prints and Photos for a first check, plus DNA for confirmation later. I would like to have stayed but were forced to leave with the Commandant. I don't want to overstep the mark at this stage so I am going with the flow. I'll let you know as soon as I do".

"Thanks, Jonny, have a glass on me, and Mel too okay".

"Will do ta. Bye".

Jonny took a long hot shower followed by a cold burst at the end. Dried and naked he lay on the bed and immediately fell asleep.

His phone woke him with a start, he was unsure where he was for a few seconds.

"Where are you Jonny it's quarter past seven"?

"Oh dear; sorry Mel I dropped right off; I'll be with you in ten have a drink".

"I'm already on my second hurry up".

Mel was sitting at the dining table a half a glass of red in her hand with a nearly empty bottle beside her.

"About time too, what happened"?

"I don't know must be all this foreign travel, jet lag I expect makes you tired they tell me".

"You daft sod have a drink".

He liked the way she fell into friendly banter when away from the job and only used the formal 'Sir' and 'boss' when they were working.

"What a day eh. You know I phoned the Chief earlier; she is aware of the information leak and has a good idea who it is. I'm glad I called before we got stuck into dinner and this stuff, it's very nice, what is it"?

"A Bordeaux of special vintage, the waiter tells me it is well under priced for the quality, so I ordered two bottles, one each, we've nearly drunk yours. What do you fancy to eat"?

241

"I don't know what all this means; pick something for me, but not snails okay".

The 'moules marinéres a la creme' and the 'canard du maison' was consumed with gusto the second bottle of red had disappeared too.

"Do you want a pud"?

"No thanks just a coffee and a cognac please Mel that was a great choice".

Two coffees and two brandies later they were ready for bed. No mention of what was really on their minds.

"The Commandant is picking us up at eight so see you here for breakfast at seven, don't be late this time".

"I won't, goodnight Mel"

"Night".

The morning brought them together again. A silent journey to the place none of them wanted to see again. Four officers from two different Countries with the same thought 'why do I do this'? They knew in their hearts it was the excitement of uncertainty during the chase, the feeling of elation when a hunch panned out, the satisfaction of bringing to justice those that defied humanity and followed the path of evil; in the end closure for the families and for themselves. They all knew there was a limit to what could be tolerated, to some it came quickly, others died or left the force before that fateful moment was reached. All four here had some way to go before their time came to quit. This scene would take them all one big step closer.

The arrival approached; the self-questioning faded. Three detectives exited the car and moved towards the house; the brigadier driver remained with the vehicle. One of the science guys came out the front door to greet them. He spoke rapidly in French for several minutes to Commandant Hergeot loud enough for all to hear. Jonny looked at Mel for information. She spoke to Hergeot who nodded; then began to translate what had been said in a clinical unemotional voice.

"It seems, Sir, they have found two bodies in that grave one on top of the other. The pathologist has made a brief examination of both. The body on the top is a male of dark skin approximately twelve years old, he has had both kidneys removed, not necessarily the cause of death; autopsy will provide that. His body has been in the grave for only a couple of days at most. The second child is a white male again about twelve years of age. This body has been in the ground for a much longer time, a week or more maybe; difficult to be sure of the exact time. Actual cause of death will be hard to determine for he has had several body parts removed surgically; both kidneys, heart, liver, and ..."

At this point Mel choked and couldn't finish her sentence. The pause left a void that could almost be tasted. Mel grabbed her Inspectors arm put her mouth to his ear and whispered.

"They took his eyes Jonny these monsters took his fucking eyes".

Jonny took her hand from his arm and squeezed it reassuringly.

"Take it easy Melanie let's just calm down a bit, I know this is bloody awful and what you're feeling pulls at your guts but what we find here may enable us to save some other poor kids and put these bastards away for a very long time. If we're going to do that I need you to be the best at what you do".

"I'm sorry Sir, I find it difficult sometimes, they are just children how can anyone do this to them"?

"Would it be any better if they were adults"?

"No of course not, what are you trying to say"?

"I don't really know Mel only that it's affecting me too, so remember you're not alone that's all".

The initial shock was fading now, her making the verbal translation for Jonny had released so much pent up emotion; his empathy had partially settled her troubled mind; she was now ready to go to work.

"Shall we go in Sir, there is more evidence we should see in the rooms, not just what has been found in the garden".

Commandant Hergeot recognised the stress reaction he had just witnessed, controlling his own response to the discovery sapped his ever dwindling mental energy. An over stressed muscle would produce lactic acid and pain, the oxygen debt produced would quickly be repaid by the body's rapid breathing. An overstressed mind did not so easily recover it required a long process of rest and often never did. When the limit is reached breakdown ensues, he hoped he would be aware of the time when he needed to stop. Not yet though, these boys deserved more from him. He moved towards the door indicating the others follow.

"Please let us see what science has found for us inside".

Hergeot and Melanie moved from room to room where the various CSIs had been working. Many fingerprints, fabric and fluid samples had been taken all logged with photographs of the positions of their discovery. Some of the prints corresponded to those that the English detectives had brought with them some were new. The small size of some prints indicated they belonged to children. The identification of Anton Biggs was confirmed. The other boy was as yet unknown, his prints did not match any they had for now. Prints matching John Digby were found in one of the rooms but no sign that surgery had been performed on him in the makeshift operating theatre although many blood samples had been found there. The room where there were boxes of medical supplies and soiled lined provided blood and skin samples. All of this was being transported back to the laboratory for analysis. The DNA profiles would be compared to those Jonny had brought with them, a frustrating slow process but one that brought certainty as to who had been here.

"Detective Musgrove équipe médico-légale have look in the garden with the dog they find one body, this time a female of sixteen years. She be here for long time three months more. She be French we identify from missing person. We make autopsy of three here after we arrange transport of boy Anton to home. If other boy English too he will be sent to you. Soon we go to mon bureau we discuss our cooperation. Must close these persons from new abductions, we look find your boy John Digby before more killing ".

Jonny did not need Melanie to translate, the Commandant made it clear enough, there was little he and Melanie could do here. He was promised that any and all information relevant would be sent to them at Basingstoke. He also knew that this had grown into an international crime that would almost certainly be taken over by a Serious Crime Squad from the Met. Basingstoke didn't have the resources to handle this alone.

"Sir, they have found another body at the rear of the garden under the trees, she's a French kid they said she has been missing for a long time, just sixteen years old, her kidneys and liver are missing nothing else though".

"I know Hergeot has just told me. We are going back to his office in a minute for a debrief, then I'll call the Chief; we will go home later today nothing we can do here".

"What about the bodies"?

"They'll do all three autopsies here and then send Anton home. We don't know the nationality of the other boy yet so he will stay here until a positive ID can be made".

"What if they arrest who ever killed Anton will they not need to keep his body here until after the trial"?

"I have no idea Mel but considering the way things are going it will be out of our hands soon enough".

"Please detective Musgrove I have many things to tell you, I speak to Sergeant Melanie first she translate for you later, is okay"?

The three climbed into Hergeot's car and returned to his office at the Rouen police station.

Commandant Hergeot had a large file opened in front of him with Jonny and Mel sitting the other side. Brigadier Manne stood slightly to one side. Four coffees were standing untouched in front of them. Ten minutes later he had finished as was the coffee.

"Well where to begin. I'll keep it brief, give you details when I write it up if that's alright with you Sir. The Commandant and his men have been having the same problem as us, children missing, not quite the same methods but still the same result. They have tracked some of the kids alive who reported being held captive, they have also found others dead, organs missing. They have not been able to track these people down, that is not

246

until our contact. This address was the first real lead they have. The owners have been traced and are currently being interviewed. They are denying all knowledge of what had gone on their, saying the property has been rented out for the last year. They have traced other properties these people own, and coincidentally they raided one yesterday to find a similar set up as at our place here. Locked rooms and medical equipment, no bodies though. There are two more houses under scrutiny, they are out of the jurisdiction of this district so are waiting for search warrants and the go ahead before they raid these. It should happen anytime now. One house appears to be empty but there is activity at the other, cars in the drive and people seen inside through the windows. They have cordoned off both properties. I would like to hang around till after the raids but he said he will send us anything they find and it's not necessary for us to wait".

"I want to know what happens here, how will he take it if I ask to stay, I don't want to alienate him"?

"Not sure, he seemed quite insistent that we need not remain. A polite request will let you know".

"Commandant Hergeot Sir, we return to our hotel now to collect our things and will go to the tunnel and home after. We will come by here to say goodbye before we leave; it would be nice to know the result of your raids on these two houses if we may".

"Hmm. It not necessary you come back, can speak goodbye now. If you wish you can know what is in houses before you go. But not stay long okay, I have officer more senior to me who not want you here, understand".

"Thank you Sir, we will take your kind offer and come back here later to say aurevoir".

Chapter 34

Mary was surprised at how easy it was to access the SOCO files, almost too much information, some stuff she didn't understand. She concentrated on any new data she could find, entering a note for each item in her little book. Some forensic stuff from a van at Folkstone, fingerprints of kids and something about a guy Bailey who had matching prints too. She found some interview report on the missing person file with his name and the mention of a safe house where he would be sent. The name Giles and Snell came up in the interview report but no detail. She was looking for something special to give to Branch to put him in a good mood, but nothing stood out other than what she had noted so far. Little did she realise she already had the very thing he was after. A quick glance through the other files, where she had access, revealed little change except for one, the constable in question was assigned to the address of the safe house, she included that extra bit of confirmation in her book. What she had now would have to do, any longer on the terminal was dangerous; someone may come in and question her or try to log into a file whilst she was using it. She shut down and left the squad room whilst it was still empty. She went to the canteen to find most of the staff were lingering before returning to their desks. She grabbed a coke from the vending machine chiller and a packet of biscuits, sat next to one of the new constables who's reports she had helped enter into the system. He smiled and they exchanged hellos.

"Sorry Mary, love to stay and chat but my tea breaks over, I have to go or the Sarge would be on my back".

"Don't worry we'll catch up another time".

She quickly finished her drink and snack, remained seated, waiting for the few minutes it took for the canteen to start emptying, then left with a group of uniformed officers, and returned to her workstation. Once back at her desk, she read through her sketchy notes making a much neater hand-written copy to be given to Branch, she embellished it a bit, with as much extra detail as she could remember, for there was very little real new information; she was sure she had not missed anything important, it would have to be enough. Normally she would have posted it to the PO box but he had told her to bring it to Camberwell as soon as she finished work. She didn't mind, a night in her own bed rather than the digs would be very nice, she would drive to her flat first and walk to the pub where he said they should meet, that way she could have a few drinks after. The General Abercrombie was not far away, she often used it at weekends as the food was good and the students from the local art college, who used it daily, gave the place a lively atmosphere. He said to keep her mobile phone charged so he could contact her if anything changed. Five o'clock was a long time coming, ever cautious she did not want to leave early as it may be noticed, but on the hour she was up and gone.

June Owen and Keith Krane were waiting outside the station. They were out of uniform in one of the unmarked cars. Their quarry was the informer Mary Neman. They had been briefed fully by Toni and had gathered as much information about her as they could from her personnel file; their task was to follow her over the next few days and report everything she did. Chief Inspector Webb's instructions were very clear.

"If it goes on for too long I will relieve you but in the mean-time take turns to sleep in the car if you have to, I want at least one of you to be watching all the time; don't lose sight of her. I want eyes on that woman twenty four hours a day. What I'm really after is the people she meets; a good description is essential and take pictures if you can. Under no circumstances approach her or anyone she meets. Keep well out of sight at all times, call me anytime day or night if you get anything suspicious, and yes, in answer to your imminent question Keith, you will be on overtime".

Seemed easy enough, lots of hanging around Keith thought and the overtime will come in very handy.

"Here she comes, give her a chance to get underway".

"PC Krane I have done this before you know".

"Alright, keep your hair on, just trying to help".

They drove out slowly giving Mary a chance to move well ahead, at the junction she turned right when they were expecting her to be going to her lodgings north of town which would have meant a left turn.

"Where is she going I wonder, maybe she will be doing the hand over tonight"?

"If she stays on this road she's going to join the M3 so probably her flat in Camberwell, we'll see. I'll hang back a bit I don't want her to see us following".

June was right Mary slid into the queue of traffic that led to the motorway slip road, she joined the same queue a half dozen cars back. The traffic was heavy but Mary was a careful driver so easy to follow, it may be more difficult when they hit the M25 and eventually the South circular and Camberwell Green. Assuming her flat was her destination June had a good idea of the route she would take which would make following her a little easier.

Sure enough the M25 turned into a bit of a crawl but eventually they followed Mary a few cars behind as she turned off heading for Bromley, then Lewisham, through Peckham to Camberwell. Confident she had not been seen June held back for the final couple of miles certain her flat was where she was headed. Mary was lucky and pulled into a space fifty yards from her house; for June parking near was going to be a nightmare.

"Keith look, I'll drop you off so you can see where she is going, her flat is number 37 right, make sure she goes in, I'll try and find somewhere, call me if here is a change".

"Okay, but what if she stays in all night"?

"Just keep her in sight for now we'll figure something out when I've parked ".

"Keith Krane was glad he'd brought his coat as he stepped out. He turned his back to Mary as she arrived at her door, she had seen him at the station on occasions so may recognise him if she were to look directly at him, but a figure on the other side of the road walking away would not be of interest. He turned to see the door close behind her so turned back and moved closer looking for somewhere to watch without being seen. Cars were parked both sides nose to tail with the occasional small gap. The flats were converted old Victorian five storey houses occupying both side of the road, their front doors just a few feet from the pavement, no gardens to speak of, nowhere to hide for Keith there. Every so often there was a more modern block which had been built with a drive and parking to the front, one of these about a hundred yards from Mary's place gave Keith a good viewing point off the pavement out of sight even if it was a little further than he would have liked. Some fifteen minutes passed when June came along the road scarf around her face head down. She would have walked right by where Keith had hidden except he stepped out just before she arrived.

"Hey, you startled me".

"Sorry, didn't mean to make you jump but there's nowhere else we can see her flat without standing out in the street".

"Hmm. Not too good here either, I must find a place to park where we can see her door. For now we'll wait a while, someone may go out and you can guard the space whilst I get the car, if not we can't stay out all night like this. We'll have to take it in turns to go back to the car have a warm-up and have a rest, one hour each maybe, let's see".

"It may not come to that someone is bound go out for a drink or some food, we'll get a space. You know what I can't understand why so many people want to live here, it's so crowded and dismal. Hardly a tree in sight and hell to park; did you know you even have to pay to park outside your own house how crazy is that".

"Hold up we may not need to do anything, someone's coming out of her house can't see who it is though. Get back out of sight whoever it is they're coming this way".

Mary closed her door having showered and dressed ready to enjoy an evening out planned for after the drop with DCI Branch. She was early enough not needing to hurry, the walk to the pub was not far. The meeting made her nervous but the way she had worded her report made the information seem more substantial than it was, he had never criticised her information before but then there had been no face to face meeting, anyway he would just probably take the envelope and leave he wouldn't risk reading it in a public place like a pub.

June followed behind as Mary walked at a leisurely pace to the end of her street she turned left into the main road heading towards the Green. Keith stayed back having crossed to the other side both women in his sight. As she approached the next junction Mary looked round, not suspecting she was being followed but to check the traffic as she wanted to cross over, a few cars and a bus went by, Mary trotted smartly across at a short break in the oncoming vehicles.

Keith was now well behind but on the same side as Mary. June continued on her original side parallel to and almost level with her quarry; she stopped to look into a store window letting Mary gain a few yards.

The General Abercrombie was on the corner of the next junction on the same side of the road as Mary and Keith. Mary arrived at a door facing the main road it was wide and permanently open, she could see it was busy inside, a few punters were sitting on the benches outside drinks well demolished chatting loudly above the hubbub coming from inside. Mary wondered how she would find Branch amongst all this lot, she walked in and disappeared from sight.

Keith caught up quickly walked past the door and round the corner to find another doorway facing the side street. He was fearful she may have slipped out but had not really had enough time to do that, the street was clear, she was still inside. He walked across the street to the corner opposite the side door, seeing June move across the main road covering the front entrance. June's phone rang.

"Do you want to go in to see if you can spot who she is meeting. I'll wait here I can guard both doors from here".

"Okay, it is quite noisy in there so I doubt if we can talk on the phone. I'll do a quick recky and let you know".

Three or four minutes went by, June appeared at the front door.

"She's sitting alone at a table in the restaurant section at the rear, only a few people in there. The front bar is massive and jammed packed with youngsters mostly. I don't know if there is a back door I can't get there as I would have to go right past her. We can't cover all the exits from outside so I'll go back in and observe, if she goes anywhere other than out of the two exits we know about I'll follow and call. You should be able to hear me even if I can't hear you".

"Sounds good I'll wait here".

When June returned Mary was not alone, an older man slightly out of place in this environment was sat opposite Mary his back to June. Heads close together in order to be heard through the continuous din from the bar. June took a picture with her phone camera whilst pretending to text.

"Did you get it"?

"Yes Sir, it is all written down here in my bag. There is an address where they are hiding someone and lots of names, well a couple of new ones, here".

Mary went to remove the package to give to him. Branch put his hand on her arm. She froze remembering the power of that grip.

"Not here. I will leave by the rear door wait a minute then you go out the side and come round the alley at the back you can give it to me there. You have done very well Mary you can finish up down there, I'll let you know where to go next. Don't look so glum I have a bonus for you too".

Mary's fear subsided he seemed to be pleasant and a bonus, she wondered how much. She wanted to ask him if she could stop altogether but did not quite have the courage.

The man got up to leave and in doing so turned to look into the bar, June took several shots as he rose and turned noticing him moving to the back of the restaurant. 'A back way out' she thought. Mary sat for a while and then moved back into the bar, made her way to the side exit lost from site in the crowd. June headed for the front calling Keith as she went.

"She met this guy he is on his way out the back, she's heading for the side door, should be with you any second".

"Okay I'm watching".

Mary was almost at the door when she had the sudden urge to pee, the toilets were just to the rear of the side entrance she couldn't wait till after she had given Branch the envelope so nipped into the ladies, she'd only be a moment. Being familiar with the pub's layout, rather than push her way through the throng to the side door, Mary used the bar push fire door next to the toilets, an exit which led to the alley where she knew Branch would be. She left with the envelope in her hand looking into the dark passage wondering where he was, was she too long in the toilet had he gone back in to look for her. She strained in the dark to see if he was further down the narrow passage. The sudden pain in her back was intense and numbing, her body tensed rigid for the briefest of moments, she had no time to scream falling face down in the gravel and dirt, the second strike pierced her heart everything ended in that moment for Mary Newman. Branch bent down snatched the envelope from her now clenched fist, grabbed her handbag and moved to the far end of the alley. Pushed through the bushes, over the low wall into a passage leading to the next street. He took her purse and phone discarding the bag. All over in thirty seconds. He'd send one of his officers to investigate the mugging.

"June where are you"?

"At the front has she come out yet"?

"No sign of her, where did she go"?

"She was on her way to the side door where you are. Wait there I'm going back in, there must be another exit through the restaurant section".

June hurried inside the still crowded bar pushing her way to the rear of the restaurant, the fire door was shut but not locked she pushed it open and stepped into the dark alley behind the pub. The lighting from the bar only lit a small area near the door and her eyes had not yet adjusted to the darkness. She looked left to see the road where Keith was waiting no sign of Mary or the man, then right into the darkness her night vision gradually improved as she proceeded slowly along the passage. She saw the body of Mary only a yard in front of her, using the flashlight of her phone June knelt to check for a pulse; not a murmur. She rose nervously looking with the aid of her temporary light to see she was alone in this dangerous place relieved the man had long gone.

"Keith there is an alley behind the pub come here now we have a big problem".

"What's up, are you okay; I'm coming".

The pair stood over the body of the dead girl looking at each other. Their first thought was to call the local police but that would reveal their clandestine operation, which would go down like a lead balloon.

"We can't just leave her there".

"Yes we can, and we must do just that, remember our instructions. Come on Keith we should go, leave it to the locals; we'll try to find a pay phone and call it in, we can't use our mobiles they will be traced, if not someone else will find her soon enough. I have pictures of the guy who did this, we cannot change what has happened and will not reveal our presence here".

"Let's go then, there's a rail station at the end of the main road we may find a phone there".

The side road off the alley had a few people who were outside the pub door smoking. June went first walking at a casual pace, no one took any notice they were too busy chatting, Keith followed a discreet distance behind. Once round the corner they joined up with interlinked arms and walked slowly along the main road till they were out of sight of anyone near the pub who may have been looking.

"Safe enough now where did you leave the car June".

"On the other side a couple of streets down from here, let's cross over".

Once seated in the car they sat in silence for several minutes, bemused by their situation.

"I didn't expect what just happened Keith, how could we have known. She may have been leaking information but she didn't deserved to be killed. Did he spot me in the pub and guessed what we were doing, was it my fault"?

"Stop rambling June, there is no way you are to blame, even if he saw you why would he think you were special, there were so many people in that place he wouldn't have known you from Adam. Come on let's find that phone".

June parked outside Loughborough station under one of the iron bridges that crossed over the junction of roads. The station was above street level with stairs to the different platforms. Keith searched two deserted platforms with payphones to find them either out of order or vandalised, no one was on duty to ask, the ticket office was closed, ticket by vending machine only. 'What a place' he thought as he descended the dark stairway, he wasn't going to waste time searching any longer certain there wouldn't be one phone anywhere here that worked, he just wanted to go; it couldn't be soon enough.

"Nothing doing, all the phones are buggered we will just have to leave it; get going young lady, shortest way back home will do me fine. I'll call the boss".

Chapter35

It had finally come to this, an over whelming desire to unload everything, a desire she must resist until she knew whom to trust. She felt like a juggler with too many balls in the air where the slightest lapse in concentration would see the whole caboodle collapse around her.

The news from Jonny and Mel will spur her bosses to take the case away. Serious Crime would be the obvious group to take over. Then came the devastating events in Camberwell. The fact Keith and June hadn't reported it to the local police was good as she did not feel secure with anyone from that location. The meeting in Camberwell was obviously instigated by whoever was controlling Mary someone who was very familiar with the area. When Colin had been warned off investigating Giles and Snell by anti-corruption it nagged at her for those two villains operated nearby, a feeling the Camberwell police were possibly the real IOPC target, she dismissed that idea at once surely corruption at that level was not possible today. Compton Busion still hadn't identified the man, thought to have killed Mary although June's phone shots were very clear. The Camberwell police had conveniently deemed Mary's death to have occurred during a mugging; the lack of intent to follow it up made her think again. Toni decided to withhold the fact her officers were present at the time and was not going to show anyone her suspect's picture at the moment, she wanted to see who, if indeed anyone, would turn up at the false address. The guys from anti-corruption were the last ones she wanted to be involved with yet. Her feelings that someone from Camberwell was involved made her a little paranoiac; she would speak with Colin before going down that sticky road.

Politics was not her best forte; she had no doubt powerful and dangerous people were involved here and would attempt to shut down anything that may expose them, she would do the same and play the covert game, determined to have some control over what happened next.

She knocked on Superintendent Walter Munroe's door having decided to put her trust in the man she had known the longest; if she was wrong she would soon find out before a complete commitment.

"Come to put me in the picture Toni, I was wondering what's going on, plenty of activity but no communication, I do not like that as you well know. I've given you free reign till now for I'm sure you have your reasons".

The controlled anger in his voice was clear and understandable, it was now or never for Toni.

"Sorry Sir, It was not my intention to keep you in the dark for so long but much has happened in such a short time I was unclear where it was leading. I now have a good idea where we stand and have reached a point where you may need to call in outside help or even hand it over all together".

"So that's it you are reluctant to let this one go and you think telling me would have made me run scared and hand it over".

"To be honest Sir, perhaps a little of that was in my mind but when you hear what I have here I have no idea who to trust, I even had doubts about the people in this station".

"Including me!"

"I hoped not you Sir, but it has held me back for a while, this goes deep. IOPC may have an idea what is going on but we have ruffled some feathers in London that is for sure, we may be getting some flack over this".

"By we, you mean me"?

"I suppose".

"Let's have it then what has gotten you so jumpy"?

"We have an informer in our midst, or should I say had, she was a civilian looking at files she should not have had access to. I believe whilst passing on her information she was murdered, the locals at Camberwell have put it down to just a mugging gone wrong. I don't know if they were aware she was stealing information from us and I don't intend to tell them, well not yet anyway".

Toni withheld the fact that they had almost witnessed the killing and had a photo of the killer, she knew Munroe would freak out that she had kept that little gem quiet.

"Why the subterfuge Toni what is wrong"?

"I'll come back to that Sir, the main story here is one you already know something about except the child abductions have now for certain been traced to France, with two men here, Henry Giles and Jake Snell, organising the entrapment and transport abroad. We have viable forensic evidence that these kids are being used in the illegal transplant trade. Children taken in England were being sent to France where the operations were being carried out. The French police have discovered temporary clinics where the operations were conducted. Young dead bodies have been discovered in the grounds some identified some not yet; they have also arrested several people they believe to be involved".

"Have Giles and Snell been arrested yet"?

"This is where we met a problem Sir, when I contacted a friendly officer in London to find out about these two much earlier in my investigations; that is before we had any idea what they were up to; he was warned off by IOPC so I have held back as much as possible, not wishing to reveal my interest; IOPC could have an officer under cover, I don't know. By the way all of this is not on file yet; if you want all the details Sir I can go through everything with you".

"That won't be necessary I have enough information to make a decision; I think now is the time to bring in the Serious Crime Squad don't you"?

"They will think it a bit late but better now, we don't have the manpower or authority to deal with all the fall out especially with the overseas involvement, best keep IOPC out of it for now though, they may spoil something I have ongoing".

"If that's what you want, leave it with me then Toni, I'll get things rolling and put out a warrant for the arrest of Giles and Snell after all I have not been warned off and can feign ignorance as nothing is on record. Can you trust your man in London"?

"With my life Sir".

"That's good enough for me; just keep me in the loop with any new developments; now we are exposed I don't want to be caught out missing something I should know, okay".

Walter Munroe picked up the phone and set in motion the apprehension of Giles and Snell then dialled the Assistant Chief Constable, this was going to be a tough day, about time he earned his keep.

It appears her trusting Munroe was not such a bad idea, he hadn't pressed her about anything trusting her to provide him with all the information he needed; still she would wait and see if anyone took the bait Compton had placed in the files about Bailey's safe house, before she asked him to contact the IOPC.

Chapter 36

"Are you sure this is the right place"?

"Yes she wrote it down twice in her report. It said Bailey would be transferred to a safe house and one of the coppers was sent orders to report to the same address".

"Well it seems deserted to me perhaps they changed their mind; let's just sit in the car for a while see if anyone comes or goes".

"That's hardly likely, if they want him safe they will have at least two coppers with him, they won't be going anywhere this time of night; I'm going to have a look round the back, you wait here Frank".

Frank Branch wondered if the death of Mary had been noticed by the Basingstoke station. She would have been missed when she did not turn up for work, but the agency would have sent a replacement so maybe not a problem.

Mitch Vale hated exposing himself like this, he should have listened to Frank and got rid of the kid and Bailey earlier, trying to get at him here was a last resort effort to cover their tracks. He left the car and approached the house from the alley that ran at the rear of all the houses in the block that side of the road. The garden was backed by a high fence with a gate which led to the alley. This gate was not locked. Mitch opened it slowly, peered down the garden into the rear windows; all was in darkness, he thought even if the curtains were drawn some glimmer of light would show. He decided to move in for a closer inspection. The rear window to the small extension looked into a kitchen, dark and deserted. A small crack in the curtains of the room next to the kitchen showed it to be completely empty not a stick if furniture, nothing. He moved down the side entrance towards the front convinced this house was deserted, had their source fed them false information or had Bailey been sent somewhere else as a precaution. He peered through the front window to see another completely empty room; this place was never intended to be a safe house. Annoyed he had wasted his time he walked out the front gate and down the street back to his car.

"Let's get out of here Frank, we've been led on a bit of a sodding wild goose chase".

"Where do you think Bailey is being kept"?

"I don't know and don't care, if Bailey has given up Giles and Snell it's too late for them now anyway. Those two won't talk even if they get arrested".

"I'm aware they don't know who we are but if Giles let's on he's not top man it could set them looking further. We should warn them in time to disappear before they are questioned".

"Sounds good to me Frank, it may be too late but when we get back send a message to Henry and Jake to make themselves scarce. Come on now let's get home".

Compton was sitting at home in the middle of dinner when the alarm signal flashed up on her mobile. She put her knife and fork down looked at the screen, to see the man approach the back door of the house. The image was not too clear but she knew the recording being transmitted to her terminal at the police station would be much better quality. Once one camera had been activated then all the others would be recording. The front and two indoor cameras were sending their signals to her office along with the two street mounted units watching along the road for vehicles. She stood leaving her unfinished meal on the table, unable to take her eyes off the screen walking to the front door of her apartment. It took twenty five minutes to arrive at her desk, beating Toni by five minutes, whom she had called on the way.

"Compton what have we got"?

"Just loading it up Ma'am won't be a moment".

They both hovered over the console as the image she had seen before appeared much clearer. Full body image and a clear face. The low light sensing cameras had done a fine job. The man moved to the front where he was again seen with a clear image of his face. Toni had an inkling that this man's face was familiar, she didn't know where from but she would bide her time it would come back to her if she left it alone for a while. One street cam saw him walking along the road which he passed to be out of view. The opposite camera saw him pass the first where he entered a car over a hundred yards from the house. The image of the car was poor almost out of range but significantly she noted that he entered the car by the passenger door, he was not alone. The car was pointing away so when it drove off they lost contact altogether. At that range the number plate was not visible, but immediately Compton was on to traffic control to look for images of cars passing through adjacent roads to try and identify it.

"Compton bring up the image of the man from June's camera".

"Yes Ma'am it's not the same man, I've been looking at that face trying to match it for ages".

"I know but I want to look at them together".

The two faces stared out at Toni side by side; she knew these two men from somewhere but frustrated and annoyed for recognition to elude her.

Chapter 37

Peter Andrews was not sure if what he had discovered was of any significance. His interview with the camper hire company manager showed it to be a genuine concern. The lettings to Bailey on the surface seemed quite normal. The underfloor compartment in that particular van was news to them. They do not directly own all of the hire vehicles but borrow them from various sources as needed. This van was privately owned and was made available by its owner when he wasn't using it, the company effectively acting as an agent. Bailey had rented other older vans before; this was a new one for the hire company having only let it out four times this year; twice to Bailey. It was the owner's name that struck a chord with Peter; James Vale. Bailey paid the owner direct, with the company claiming a commission. He knew the name from somewhere but couldn't place it. He wanted to know more about this man but decided to see the boss first.

"Hello, Peter what can I do for you"?

"I have come across something that on the surface seems legit but I have a niggling doubt".

He went on to discuss his interview with the hire company manager, when he mentioned the name of James Vale Toni raised her hand for him to stop.

"Well, well I don't believe it, it can't be him".

"It's true Ma'am that's what he said his name was".

"Sorry Peter I don't mean you; look I think you have hit on a significant piece of the puzzle. If what I think is true there is going to be a big shake up soon. Right now, discreetly have a look into James Vale, where he lives, what he does for a living, any relatives anything you can find without alerting him".

"What is it, who is he you seem to know the name"?

"I do, I do but all in good time Peter, just check him out for now you'll know soon enough'.

Peter left her office to pursue his task not sure what to make of it, that name certainly shook her up he couldn't wait to find out more.

Toni's mind was racing as it does when she is on to a lead as significant as this. She pulled out the two photos Compton had printed off for her. This time recognition was not so elusive. Mitchel Vale and Frank Branch, older now but still the same. Two detectives she had met before briefly when she worked in Southampton. She'd been asked to deliver a package containing evidence by hand in order to maintain an unbroken chain. She'd been told, on arrival at the Camberwell station, to hand it to Detective Inspector Vale. The desk sergeant there directed her to his office. She knocked and waited, the door opened and the two men, whose pictures she was looking at now, stood before her. She introduced herself and offered the package asking which one of them was Detective inspector Vale. They both laughed asking her to guess. Being a young inexperienced constable she was tongue-tied and a little afraid, not knowing what to say. They passed lewd comments to each other about her as if she wasn't there. One of them grabbed the package from her hand and scrawled his signature on her transfer docket, telling her to '*get her black arse out of his office*'. She ran from that station, not crying although she wanted to do so, her anger prevented the tears from forming, she would remember those two and stay away.

The incident had gone from her mind until just now, it was insignificant as over the years she had come across much worse bullying. Her rank prevented personal incidents like that from occurring now and the force had grown intolerant of such behaviour, although she was sure some of the younger officers suffered still.

These two were 'old school' and had probably not learned the lesson; their seniority a shield against any who may complain; she doubted if any did, she certainly hadn't back then.

It was becoming clear that anti-corruption were more than interested in these officers and it wasn't for minor bullying offences. Her video of Vale surveying the false safe house was ammunition the IOPC would love to have and she would certainly hand it over but all in good time. This level of corruption ran very deep, whom to trust was a serious question in her mind.

Although she had confided in Munroe, and he had passed the case to Serious Crime just as she wanted Toni still wasn't sure of her own Superintendent's motives, his earlier request to keep him informed whilst keeping the IOPC out of the loop, worried her; DI Davis was a concern too; he hailed from Camberwell, she was not sure if he had seen the photo June had taken when Mary was killed; he must know Vale and Branch and would have said something if so. Was her suspicious mind going too far; it could be but better to err on the side of caution; a difficult decision was soon going to be hers to make.

"Colin, it's me again, can we talk"?

"Not on this phone Toni, meet you later usual place okay with you"?

"You're just after a free pint you bugger, but yes seven tonight will be fine".

"Good job, you are right about the pint and spicy wings of course. Are you alright"?

"I think so, I'll tell you later, I might need your help".

As usual Toni was in the Four Horseshoes bar first, her pint well on its way to being empty when Colin Dale arrived walked to her table and sat opposite.

"Just as I thought you are using me as an excuse to come here and drink all night, how many have you had"?

"Cheeky bugger always late, but glad you're here though".

The pub landlord appeared from nowhere with Colin's usual pint placing it on the beermat beside him.

"Is it wings fer ye again young Colin"?

"I'd love to but not tonight Jonesy, I won't be staying long, and I'm paying for the beer tonight so no comments eh"?

"Pay for the beer are ye, must be feeling sick or summint"?

Jones moved away a chuckle emanating through his broad Hampshire grin.

"Well Toni what's up more about those two characters you were on about last time"?

"Not quite Colin, well yes maybe but much more, I need your advice really. I know what I want to do but I would like you to see if I am going about it the right way".

"Tell me what has happened since I saw you last".

"Where to begin…"

Toni went on to describe the events of the past days. He already knew of her fears concerning the abductions. It all came out nothing held back. The killing of Reynolds and finding

Michael, Alfred Bailey and the girl Freda, the names of Giles and Snell, the murder of Mary and the photographs of the two Camberwell policeman and their probable involvement. The fact that she had held back on telling Serious Crime and the IOPC about the murder of Mary by Branch worried Colin the most. Having also kept that little piece of information from Munroe including the visit of Vale to the set up safe house left Toni Webb so exposed and liable to severe censure and possible dismissal.

"Oh my, you have put your head on the block haven't you. What made you think you could keep all this to yourself".

"I have no idea whom to trust Colin, almost everyone I know could be under the influence of Vale and Branch. These two guys have power over many people in the criminal world and God knows how many in the force itself. The new Inspector, DI Davies comes from their nick, maybe he is a plant, even Munroe was at Hendon the same time as them, did I make a mistake in telling him, I see gremlins everywhere what should I do Colin".

"Keep calm to start with; although I agree Vale and Branch are corrupt as hell and need to be stopped your idea those around you are part of their band of informers does not hold water. Munroe would have pulled the plug on you and warned them off long ago if he was in their pocket. DI Davies may not be all he seems but so far he has been a great help, you said so yourself. He must know them and if he had seen the photo of Branch he would either have told you or warned them off before they went to that false house to look for Bailey; neither happened so I don't think he knows about the picture or Busion's ruse. I tell you what you can do to check Davies out, it's easy just show him the pictures, you'll know straight away if he is strait".

"You're right it's simple and I want to make it complicated, if Davis is kosher he will identify them and ask me what it's all about, if not what will he say, whatever, I will know won't I"?

Look as soon as you have DI Davies sorted you must go back to Munroe with all the information concerning the identification of Vale and Branch as corrupt officers in a special file. Date everything as it happened but insert your fears of there being an informant in Basingstoke station, and be specific how you routed her out. Also mention again fears that reporting it too soon would then give the offenders time to retaliate and worse cover up by eliminating witnesses. Again express doubts how you wanted to be sure of your facts before accusing such senior officers by passing this information to the IOPC. Give him the file and tell him you think IOPC should be informed. I know it's passing the buck but Munroe has the seniority to ride out the backlash you don't".

"He will never forgive me I should have gone to him sooner and he will know it".

"Tell him you thought he was in on it because of the leaks especially the one where the raid on Reynolds farm was compromised. He will be so upset about your doubting him that he will forget to bollock you for not telling him sooner and especially for leaving him holding the hot potato. Say you are sorry but had to hold back until you were really sure of him".

"You know what, Colin that is almost true and stating the truth should be the way for me to go. Thanks mate I feel much better; tomorrow I'll do exactly that. Now drink up and get yourself home to the family".

They left the Horseshoes together and parted their ways at the roadside, one happier than when they arrived the other very concerned for their friend.

Chapter 38

The morning began early at Basingstoke station. There was an atmosphere charged with expectation. The officers were at their desks shuffling through files, looking at screens, busy but not taking in what they were seeing; all waiting for something to happen. Chief Inspector Webb walked into the squad-room immediately feeling the tension. A disturbing quiet filled the air as heads turned to look at their boss; it lasted only a moment before they returned to their business. Toni was ready to test DI Davies and in public too, then she could move on.

DI Jonny Musgrove stood up and moved over to Toni.

"Good morning Ma'am what is happening, there's a buzz going round, are we off the case"?

"All is fine Jonny, not entirely; well not yet, I need to update you all with some new information".

She raised her voice enough to gain her officers attention, walked over to the white board posting enlarged pictures of Vale and Branch. Her eyes were on Harrold Davies as she stepped back for all to see. His reaction was obvious, his mouth fell open as he stood.

"Where the hell did they come from, what have they got to do with this"?

She moved over to where he stood staring.

"You have something to say Harrold"?

"You're damned right I do Ma'am; I know these bastards from old".

"Tell me about it, but not here let's move to my office; Jonny you come too".

"Well Harrold what has you so upset"?

Those two ran the Camberwell nick when I was there, you needed eyes in the back of your head to avoid their shit. That DCI Vale was; how can I put it, 'very demanding' his side kick Frank Branch was no better. I was only a sergeant back then so had to tow the line. They caught a lot of villains I'll give them that, the Commander thought the sun shone, if you know what I mean the figures made him look good. Their methods were effective alright but more than a little suspect, evidence appeared from nowhere or disappeared if that is what suited them. Some of the villains seemed to get away with almost anything. If one of us outside their team made an arrest we almost never got to do the interviews, they would take over; often when we had someone bang to rights they'd let them go, telling us to keep away as they were using them to get at bigger fish. I can go on if you like, but you either joined them or they made sure you only got the crap jobs and ended up on the worst shifts. In the end I'd had enough so applied to move away, lots of officers either fell in with them or were severely intimidated and forced out. I was lucky I transferred to the fraud squad at New Cross. I'd put that nick out of my mind for years now. Those pictures were quite a shock".

"Why didn't you complain to the IOPC"?

"You're kidding, one thing IOPC didn't exist back then the former police complaints commission were a joke, anyone who did complain ended up at the wrong end of any investigation usually leaving under a cloud. These guys were all powerful and to be avoided. You never answered my question why are their pictures on our case board where do they fit in "?

Toni then explained to Harrold and Jonny about the covert operation set up by Compton Busion that secured the photo of Vale and what officers Krane and Owen had done, during the murder of Mary Newman in obtaining the picture of Branch.

"I know I kept this tight and sorry to have left it until now for you to be included, but I was very afraid of these two men and their ability to place an informer such as Mary in our midst. Information has been leaking from here before she joined us I still have no idea who is responsible for that. As it stands Superintendent Munroe has decided Serious Crime will be taking over our abduction investigation, no doubt IOPC will want all our evidence concerning these cases and will probably interview all of us here. You must cooperate with both parties and answer all questions. Let's hope they do right by us and the lost children".

"Ma'am did you think I was an informer"?
"Yes Harrold I did, I'm sorry but your connection to Camberwell and the leaks starting so soon after you joined were too much of a coincidence for me to ignore".

"Good, I would have suspected me too; am I cleared now"?

Toni laughed relieving the tension between them and winked at him. "I'll let you know".

Chapter 39

Jake Snell had been preparing for this day a long time. He may appear to be the less intelligent of the pair but his street wise nature for survival was strong, instinctively so.. Three years had passed since he put his escape route in place, he'd urged Henry to do the same; Henry Giles ignored his advice as usual; this did not stop Jake making his own preparations.

First was the money, he rented a safe deposit box in town where he put all the cash he could skim off from his collections. He converted much it into Euros, it had mounted to a sizable sum by now enough to retire on for a while anyway. He had his bank account in France under his other name which he could access once he was over there. The money in Jersey was probably out of his reach for now anyway, never mind what he had was plenty.

His next task was to prepare a new identity. Jake's friend Lenny, who lived next door when they were kids, was the same age and looked just like him, they were often mistaken for brothers and had remained friends ever since; the difference being Lenny suffered a heart condition from birth so was more or less housebound now. Jake took the opportunity to use his friend a little by borrowing his identity and using it to obtain a genuine passport under his name, Leonard Bartram. Jake told him about the passport and why he wanted it, Lenny didn't mind he was never going anywhere abroad and Jake was always good to him; gave him money all the time and some weed now and then; he liked Jake.

His third item of preparation was to have transport untraceable to him and an exit route planned. He bought a van with his new false name, registered it at his friend's address and left it parked on his drive except for the odd occasion when he took it for a run. It was equipped with a bed and a portable toilet and most important an 'Eberspaecher' heater for it could be very cold during the first week or so of his chosen route. Not quite to the standard of a camper van but close enough to afford Jake a bit of comfort during his planned escape.

On the morning of the text from their boss to get out fast, Jake didn't hesitate; he took his car round to a car dealer friend, a pre-arranged cash exchange for his BMW; then collected his van and the money from his safe deposit box. He chose a sea exit least likely to attract attention. The freight ferry from Immingham to Esbjerg in Demark cost him the best part of a grand; booked on-line with his friend's credit card. He'd taken his identity but didn't have the heart to take his money too so had paid the cash back into Lenny's account with a little extra for old times' sake.

Jake Snell said a cursory farewell to Henry and left straight away not telling him where he was going or even that he was leaving for good; Henry Giles hardly noticed his departure. By early evening Lenny Bartram, as he now become, was on his way north on the A1 towards Grimsby. His idea was to drive down Denmark through Germany to the south of France, beyond that he had not planned but knew he had to get away now.

Henry said cheerio to his long-time colleague without thinking, his mind was elsewhere. On reflection later that day, he wondered where Jake had go to, his sudden goodbye and out of character departure worried him, so much so that he thought the warning in the text was something he perhaps should take more seriously. He had intended to ignore the message as there was no sign that the police were interested in him but the consequences of them finding out what they had been up to made him think again. He could go abroad for a while to let things cool down a bit and come back later, a holiday in Spain wouldn't go amiss. He had a bundle of euros stashed away he would take some of that and book a flight. Flights to Alicante and his favourite hotel were fully booked for the following day so ended up on an early morning plane to Malaga. He was not familiar with that part of Spain but was sure he'd find a nice hotel when he got there. He decided to take a taxi to Gatwick, he did not like to be parted from his beloved Jaguar but detested airport parking even more especially that early in the morning. Booked in at the Gatwick Hilton for the night as the check in was ridiculously early, he quickly packed and was on his way by six that evening.

The partnership of many years was over, neither man thought about the other nor regretted the separation.

Jake parked in line behind a few smaller trucks, the heavy duty lorries were in a separate queue. His lane was for empty vehicles, those carrying goods went through another process. No one looked to see if he was really empty, 'a lot of trust there' he thought but then wondered what could you take that would be of interest or worth smuggling, he could think of nothing. Check in was simple an officer logged his registration number on screen against the booking reference, looked at his passport scanned it on his machine, said his 'good evening' and 'have a nice trip' all done. He stuck his boarding label in the window and moved on to park up ready for loading. Once on board he followed the signs to his cabin which he was to share with another driver. He opened the door the other guy wasn't there yet; dumping his bag on the left hand bunk he went up to the restaurant deck and bar. All these years of ducking and diving led to this moment; he was going to enjoy himself from now on no more being told what to do by Henry; three beers later and a plate of steak and chips in his belly found Jake tired, happy and ready for bed. The next few days saw Jake Snell, now Leonard Bartram, disappear into Europe never to be seen again.

Getting to check in was slow even though he only had a small handbag, the queues at security were the usual nightmare, removing coats, belts and shoes taking the pocket change and putting it in the tray, the alarm of the scanning machine detecting his mobile forgotten in his shirt pocket was winding up Henry to a point he wished he'd never left home. He eventually arrived at an ever open bar in the departure lounge with an hour to spare before take-off plenty of time for a drink. A pint of lager and a dark rum chaser was his desired tipple even at this early hour. He sipped the beer downed the rum and relaxed a little from the trauma airports threw at him every time he travelled. He continued to sip the beer but added a second rum, by then thinking what he was going to do following this rush to escape. He wondered what he was escaping from and if it was even necessary. Why had his unknown controller panicked Jake and him to leave the Country, he had a sudden thought that they were going to take over the business whilst they were away, put someone else in their place. Was it all because of a fuck up with the kids that was not his fault anyway? He had a sudden urge to cancel this trip and go back. He stopped and remembered what had happened to those that had not followed orders. He was glad to be out of it for a while; he'd promised himself a holiday sometime soon, so why not now? He finished his beer and looked on the overhead screen to identify his departure gate. He trudged down the long walkway with others on the same treadmill, like sheep to the holding pen waiting for the chop. Most of the passengers on his flight had already arrived at the departure lounge. This flight was all the same class he'd been allocated a seat near the middle of the plane, he was not relishing the scramble when the flight was called. He approached the desk with his boarding pass and passport.

"Mister Giles sir would you mind stepping this way please".

The desk steward indicated for Henry to follow him. He was reluctant to move.

"What's going on is there something wrong with my passport"?

"Oh no sir nothing like that we are obliged to do a random check on some passengers for security reasons, we look in your hand luggage and ask a few questions it's just routine it won't take a moment if you just follow me".

"Why did I get picked eh"?

"It just comes up on the screen sir it could be anyone of the passengers; pot-luck really".

Henry was not sure, another stupid airport inconvenience to put up with, but it seemed genuine enough so he followed the steward into the small annex room at the side of the check in desk and placed his bag on the table as he had been asked. At that point the door opened and two uniformed police and another in plain clothes entered.

Before he had time to react one officer had hold of his arm snapping a handcuff on his wrist as the plain clothes officer spoke.

"Henry Giles, I am Detective Inspector Paul Fortune, you are under arrest for conspiracy to murder Martin and June Reynolds. You do not have to say anything, but it may harm your defence if you do not mention when questioned something which you later rely on in court. Anything you do say may be given in evidence. Do you understand"?

"You can't do this. It's got nothing to do with me".

Henry was so angry that bastard air steward telling him it was a random search; give him half a chance he'd break his bloody legs.

"Mr. Giles do you understand the caution"?

It suddenly sunk in someone had dobbed him in, he wondered if Jake had got caught too or if he had got away, funny he hadn't asked and Jake hadn't told him, so had no idea where he had gone.

"Of course I bloody do, I was nowhere near Reynolds when he was killed, I have a dozen witnesses to prove it".

"I'm sure you do but that makes no difference to the charge. You will be taken into custody for questioning, if you require a solicitor to be present and cannot afford one a duty solicitor will be provided for you. Take him away sergeant".

"Where are you taking me'?

"You'll find out soon enough".

The Serious Crime Squad was run by senior officers from London Met at The Yard; DI Paul Fortune being one of six detectives operating out of a building in Wandsworth which is where they were headed now. Kent's Assistant Chief Constable had called them in following the discussion with Monroe whose request to apprehend Giles and Snell was sent out to all ports and airports luckily just in time to spot Giles impending departure from Gatwick. There was no sign Snell had made any attempt to leave the Country through the ports or airports, even before the warning was issued. They thought he was laying low somewhere in England and would surface some time later. Maybe when they questioned Giles he would give up Snell's whereabouts. It didn't matter they were after a bigger target. The serious crime unit along with IOPC had others in mind and they were getting close.

Henry Giles sat on the thin not too clean mattress of the iron framed bunk. He was unable to take in what was happening to him his rambling thoughts trying to make sense of his situation. 'Arrested for a murder, no that's not right conspiracy was what that copper had said. The fact that he did not actually do the deed and was miles away at the time would not matter. If that cunt Jake had sold him out he was up shit creek. He would get a good lawyer argue his case to get him out on bail; they couldn't prove anything he hadn't told Jake to kill Reynolds he would say he told him to just to get rid of the problem by paying him off. The trouble with that was they would want to know what problem was big enough for Jake to have killed him. He would have to think of something else. "Bugger! bugger! bugger! You stupid bastard, should have gone sooner".

Henry lay back on the bunk and drifted off into a fitful sleep; he didn't sleep for long.

"Henry Giles what have you got to say for yourself. You and your pal Jake have had it all your own way for too long. How come you were involved with Reynolds"?

"No comment".

"Now come on Henry that's going to do you no good. We have Jake doing this for certain; his fingerprints, his DNA and the shells he left in his house are a perfect match to those that killed Reynolds and his mother. Bike tyre tracks and soil samples are a match to the ones found on the bike in his garage. We have text messages between them; the lot. He has no way out but you do. Give us something so we can make it easier for you".

"If you've got all that what do you want me for I had nothing to do with it. Another thing where is the recording tape, the caution and stuff you usually do at an interview"?

"We can do all that if you want, at the moment this is all unofficial, no record, no witness, just you and me no one will know what you say has come from you".

"How can I know you won't stitch me up"?

"Look I'm not after you for the murder, Snell is going to have to take that rap on his own. The conspiracy charge will stick if we present all the evidence especially the stuff Bailey has revealed. What I'm after are the ones who forced you into this".

Henry did not know this DI Fortune; he was breaking the rules with this unofficial interview and coppers who break the rules shouldn't be trusted. They must have caught Jake, the stupid bugger leaving those shells in his gaff and that bloody bike. God knows what he has told them, probably blaming me for everything. As for Alfred he had no idea if he knew anything that would implicate him; although he could have given up Joe. Did they know who was his boss already? He didn't; well he certainly wasn't sure. Was Fortune fishing? He'd have to give him something if he wanted to get out of here.

"Forced is right enough". Henry held up his left hand to show his little finger was just a stump. "This was just a warning, insisting my life belonged to them or it would be my head next".

DI fortune remembered the report concerning a severed finger of a prisoner used to threaten an innocent family. The same man maybe.

"Nasty; you should choose your friends more carefully. If you tell me who they are I'll cut their balls off for you".

"That would be nice but I have never actually seen them, my head was in a black bag when they did this".

"How did they communicate with you after"?

"Text on pay-as-you-go phones which were dumped after then new ones arrived".

"Hm, by post I suppose"?

"Yes as it happens. So what".

"After all this time you must have developed some idea who it was leading the way".

"One of your lot was my gut but I wasn't going to be nosey was I"? Holding up his damaged digit.

"Camberwell was your nearest nick; do you think it might be someone from there"?

"Could be I suppose; I don't know".

"Give us a name, you must have one in mind".

"If this gets out I'm dead; these blokes have more power than you can imagine, they will sweep you aside; being a DI doesn't make you immune".

"I'll take my chances. Listen Henry I'll do a deal, tell me who you think it might be and I'll drop the conspiracy charge.

Another thing, at formal interview I will word the questions so you are not seen to be the one who gave up the name".

Henry couldn't believe he was going to get away with this, he'd no faith in the word of DI Fortune but had little option. He wondered what deal Jake had done, if any.

"Look I can't be sure so don't hold me to this but a DI Vale was one copper at Camberwell I had dealings with a long time ago, I've had a feeling he may be behind this, he was a scary bloke back then".

"Good enough. Do you know any other detective at Camberwell"?

"I've met some but don't remember their names. Look I'm done; that's all you get from me".

"Okay Henry, I'll be back this time it will be for real".

Paul let Henry rest for a while; he would keep his word concerning the conspiracy accusation however Mr Giles would face another more sinister charge.

"Interview with Mr Henry Giles. Present, his solicitor Lucian Philips, Detective Sergeant Norris Brown, stenographer Constable Faye Tenison and myself Detective Inspector Paul Fortune. Timed at 21:10. Henry Giles you are still under caution for the tape a reminder; you do not have to say anything, but it may harm your defence if you do not mention when questioned something which you later rely on in court. Anything you do say may be given in evidence. Do you understand"?

"Yes".

"I must inform you that Mr Jacob Snell is facing charges on two counts of murder. A Martin Reynolds and his mother June

Reynolds. I believe you were involved when you ordered Mr Snell to carry out these killings".

"I had no idea he was going to do that; I did tell him to pay them for a transport job they did for an acquaintance of mine, I even gave him the money".

"It seems Jacob kept the money, he probably had an argument and killed them. In view of this statement the charge against you will be reconsidered".

"Is that it can I go now"?

"Not just now Mr Giles, you have been illegally transporting children; the job that Reynolds was doing for you and your acquaintance. Who is this person instructing you to do this"?

"I have no idea I was threatened with my life if I did not obey, I never met him".

"Not a problem we already have a good idea who it is, would it surprise you to know it may be a police officer"?

"Not really, half the coppers in Camberwell are bent".

"I doubt that, maybe one or two have overstepped the mark. Whom do you know at Camberwell that might fit the bill"?

"That's funny 'Old Bill' fitting the bill. I was arrested once by a Detective Vale, nice guy he let me off with a caution, not exactly a rogue I would think".

Henry was pleased with himself the detective had been as good as his word the conspiracy charge was gone and the name of Vale had been dropped in with no indication he was grassing anyone.

"You didn't take much notice did you"?

"What notice"?

"The warning given by detective Vale. Since then you have been running prostitution, providing protection or extortion by another name and your latest venture abducting children, transporting them overseas for use as donors in the illegal transplant trade. Several of the children have since been found dead and I can lay all that on you and Jake Snell".

"You said you would drop the charge; what's going on"?

"I did this is different. Henry Snell, you are under arrest for the abduction of children for the purpose of removing their organs to be used in illegal transplants. In addition you are charged as an accomplice in the murder of several of these children. You will be held in custody until such time as you appear in court. By the way I thought you'd like to know we haven't found Jake yet. Sergeant; take him to the cells".

Paul was pleased with the outcome Giles would get what he deserved and Vale could bear looking at, he'd pass a copy of the tape on to Smith at IOPC. Now comes the sweat; collating evidence and paperwork with his Basingstoke colleagues in preparation for the CPS.

Chapter 40

"Sir, there have been some developments you should know about".

"Come in Toni what has happened so soon after I saw you last"?

"I don't know how to put it but I have to be honest, I had no idea who was leaking information and when Reynolds was killed I went through everyone who had prior knowledge in time to warn his killer and I came up with three people. Unfortunately one of them was you Sir. I hoped it wasn't and eventually was sure it wasn't, in the meantime I kept certain things from you I'm sorry".

"You mean after all these years you didn't trust me".

"I'm afraid so, I trusted the evidence I had no choice, when I tell you what I have you will understand my reticence".

"You'd better tell me then before I kick your arse out of here".

"We knew we had a leak so set a trap and laid out some false information. Mary Neman was a civilian clerk here, employed to carry out basic transcription work. We found out she had obtained officers passwords somehow and used them to download information concerning the abduction cases and passing them on to someone outside, we didn't know who at that point. We followed her to a meeting place in Camberwell and obtained photos of a meeting between her and at that time an unknown man. We were unprepared for what happened next".

"You still haven't explained why you suspected me. Carry on".

"She was murdered immediately after the meeting; my officers were out of sight and had no idea what had happened. They were following orders to try and discover whom she was meeting and not intervene, so left the scene undisturbed".

"Why on earth did they not call it in"?

"We thought that it was possible people from Camberwell could be involved and did not want to give them warning of what we were doing. It proved right as it happened. The man Mary met has since been identified as Detective Inspector Frank Branch working out of Camberwell".

"Bloody hell, you still haven't told me why I was on your radar".

"To continue Sir, the false address we had fed to Mary was the supposed location of a witness that knew who ordered these abductions, we wanted to see if anyone would try and get to our witness, so set up CCTV to record anyone who happened along. Here is the cruncher, we have clear shots of Superintendent Mitchell Vale approaching the house and checking through the windows, when he discovered it was empty he left by car with a driver. We picked up the car on traffic cameras late, it had false plates. Vale is the Super at Camberwell nick and the long-time associate of Branch. The death of Mary Newman was investigated by a detective from Camberwell and was passed off as a mugging gone wrong and filed as unsolved within a week. Once I had identified these two I still had doubts as how far their influence reached as information had been leaking well before Mary Newman arrived".

"And you thought that it was me"?

Toni did not respond, letting Munroe digest the facts; he sat saying nothing obviously waiting for her to explain why she decided he was clean.

"I came to you the other day because I instinctively knew you were not involved but I hadn't yet identified these two bastards, so held back about Mary and the safe house until I was completely sure. It is all in this file here Sir everything I have told you all the details and more; I think now is the time you should hand it over to IOPC, I haven't mentioned I kept you out of the loop I didn't think you would like anyone to know. I am sorry I didn't trust you Sir; I was perhaps a little paranoiac".

"Indeed you were; quite a story and an investigation that should have been passed to Complaints well before it reached this stage. I understand why you delayed so long but am sad you had no faith in me, but I suppose that is the burden of being a policeman trust nothing or no one until proven. You have handed me a pretty loaded parcel to deal with here. I will go through it all in detail, you will stay around, be ready for some questions you hear; I am not going into the 'Lion's Den' unless I am sure it is watertight and I am fully armed".

Toni left the office sad her suspicious mind took so long to resolve the dilemma.

There was still the outstanding problem that someone here at the very least had spoken out of turn leading to the death of Reynolds and his Mother. She had eliminated DI Davies and Walter Munroe, that left one other but seemingly impossible candidate who fitted the bill.

Chapter 41

Thursday afternoon, standing by his desk buttoning his overcoat about ready to leave for home, when DI Norman Cox received a written notice through the internal mail to report to IOPC at nine am the following day. He'd opened the envelope not knowing what was inside; when he read the instruction where to report and not to speak to anyone before the meeting, he froze. His heart rate doubled in seconds sweat broke out soaking the under arms of his shirt already soiled from the long day. He slumped back in his chair, what did they want? In his heart he knew, the day had come at last. He couldn't speak to the Super, he didn't trust him anyway, and Branch made him very afraid after all it could be him that has dropped him in it. He stood slowly weak at the knees looked round the room nobody had noticed his reaction. He stuffed the dreaded note into his coat pocket and left, omitting his usual parting 'goodnight'.

"Detective Inspector Branch thank you for coming in, I am Chief Superintendent Smith and this is Detective Sergeant Bonington, he will take notes. You have been summoned here to answer a few questions about certain incidents that have occurred concerning personnel working at Camberwell Police station. You are not under caution the enquiry is informal at the moment however it will be recorded. You may have a representative of your choice present at this interview if you wish".

"No I'm fine how can I help"?

"That's good Frank, the right attitude, you don't mind if I call you Frank do you, better to keep this as informal as we can, eh"?

Frank recognised the technique the friendly approach before the axe falls, he'd used it himself often enough. He would go along for now sus out what they were after.

"Fine by me Sir".

"Do you know DI Cox"?

"Of course he works at our station, we cross paths occasionally at work but I don't know him personally we don't socialise or anything".

"When did you last see or speak to him"?

"I don't really know exactly a few days ago two maybe; he was dealing with a mugging, a girl got killed; he wanted to know if I had heard anything on the vine, I told him I would sound out my snouts".

"Did you"?

"Did I what"?

"Sound out your informants"?

"Err, no, I'd forgotten about it till you just reminded me".

"A bit slack of you Frank, a fellow officer asks for help and you forgot".

"It wasn't a serious request like, just see if anything was about when I next spoke to one of my guys, I just hadn't got around to it that's all".

"Did DI Cox seem different in any way"?

"What do you mean"?

"Was he agitated or angry, did the murder of this girl upset him in any way"?

"I have no idea I didn't notice anything. What is this all about, what has DI Cox supposed to have done"?

"I'm sorry to inform you that DI Cox took his own life last night. We are trying to establish his state of mind and look for any reason that may have caused him to take such a course".

"Well ,well, poor sod. What can I say; I know he was divorced and now lived alone, but it was a long time ago, I would've thought he'd gotten over her by now; I don't know maybe he was lonely or something; sorry Sir I don't think I can help much".

"That's alright Frank, please keep this to yourself, he has a daughter who has not been informed yet; we don't want her finding out except through us, you understand. We may need to speak again. Interview terminated 0945".

"Of course Sir, sad business".

Frank Branch held back a smile of relief as he left the room; he was expecting to be grilled about his own activities and was shitting himself when he was in there. Now he knew how his victims felt, it wasn't nice; no wonder they caved in quickly his methods were much more direct than these guys. As soon as he found out Coxy had topped himself he knew they weren't after him. He'd find Mitch when he got back and tell him what had gone on. On arriving at Camberwell he found Mitch had also been summoned by the IOPC. 'Not unexpected' he thought Mitch would find out soon enough. They could have a chat when he got back.

"Superintendent Vale thank you for coming in, I am Chief Superintendent Smith and this is Detective Sergeant Bonington. You have been summoned here to answer a few questions about certain incidents that have occurred concerning personnel working at Camberwell Police station. You are not under caution the enquiry is informal at the moment however it will be recorded. You may have a representative of your choice present at this interview if you wish".

"Why would I need a representative Chief Superintendent Sir, if this is informal there is no need is there"?

"New protocol Vale we have to offer a rep to comply, it's up to you".

Mitch noticed the use of his surname alone and no recognition of his rank, better be wary of this fellow was his thought, sit tight listen and say as little as possible.

"I'll pass, what do you want".

"We have reason to believe that certain officers at Camberwell and other stations nearby have been subject to undue stress and wish to find out who is responsible and why. As senior officer you must be aware of what is taking place in your area or you should be. Can you bring to mind any recent incidents which may have caused someone to suffer such pressure"?

"About time someone took notice, I been asking for more officers for a long time, lack of manpower means long hours at work and little sleep for most officers. The nature of the work itself is stress enough without all the extra hours".

"Superintendent Vale I do not need your opinion concerning the under manning debate. Please answer my question".

"Well I admit I apply pressure to my Inspectors and they in turn to the sergeants and so on down to the constables, that's my job. Everyone wants results from us and we do very well with the fellows we have, and better than most. I can't think of any specific example of undue stress applied to one of my men".

"Then how do you explain the suicide last night of your man, Detective Inspector Cox"?

"What the hell are you saying, Cox killed himself, how, why"?

"That is what I am trying to find out; so what do you think may be the reason".

"It's a bit of a shock, I need a minute".

Mitchell Vale thought he was to be quizzed about Giles and Snell, so was a little relieved in one way but this Cox business was going to be a nuisance; he would have to be careful the investigation did not go further.

"I'm sorry he has done this it can't be work related. His case load wasn't any heavier than anyone else. In fact he had been investigating the stabbing of a young girl behind a local pub, a mugging he said. Very little to go on, no forensics, no witnesses. I had told him to wind it up if no further evidence came to light by the end of the week. Lack of manpower means we cannot give time to unsolvable cases".

"So it was your judgement that this was an unsolvable murder".

"Is that a question".

"No an observation. You make decisions every day that affect those around you. Very quick to close this case it seems, did it not upset DI Cox, did he not ask for more time"?

"No he did not, he was probably relieved to move on to a case he could do something about".

"Well I can tell you now he was upset, very very upset to the point where he took a pistol to his head and blew his brains all over the wall".

"Well I can't be held responsible; he was obviously deranged".

"That's as may be but the note he left was much more specific. This poor officer was so scared of you he'd rather die than do his duty, God forgive him".

"What can I say I had no idea he felt this way".

"Superintendent Vale, we will continue this later, in the light of your possible contribution to officer Cox's untimely death, you will be interviewed again sometime soon. You will make yourself available and return here when required, I suggest, with a representative of your choice. I remind you not to discuss this current conversation with anyone other than your chosen representative. This interview is terminated at 14.20".

He wasn't going to let these two off the hook but would have to be sure they had no way to wriggle out of this. He wasn't even sure if they were the end of the line or was someone more senior pulling their strings, he hoped not for the sake of the force. He shuddered to think what harm they had done over the years; how many officers had been turned. Getting rid of this cancerous pair in the public view was his aim but expected pressure to keep it under wraps from above was most likely, he would resist and persist.

Smith looked again at the note found next to the body of Norman Cox; to have brought a young man to do this and not to care in the least was evil.

'I have done terrible things for these two, I now have no choice I cannot continue cowering to their bidding here or anywhere. Vale is a shit Branch even worse. Mary Newman died, stabbed behind a pub a terrible way to die. It was up to me to find her killer and bring closure to her family. I failed. I am corrupt. I hid the facts. She was not mugged; I kept the money I found in her bag. Witnesses to her killer were ignored. I lied. They lied. They destroyed my life made me worthless. I am so sorry'.

Chapter42

"My oh my Walter Munroe to what do I owe the pleasure"?

"Can't I visit an old friend now and again"?

"Old maybe, but friend is stretching it a bit don't you think".

"Not today Smithy, I have something that will curl your toes and make me your best pal forever".

He opened his briefcase and withdrew the file Toni had given him, placed it on the desk. Smith ignored the file.

"Tell me more Munroe, you would not be here unless you were forced".

"I heard you have a little problem around the Camberwell area, this will help solve it big time. We would like to have pursued it ourselves but it is probably more your responsibility so here you are. You have two bent coppers there needing your special treatment, we unearthed them during an investigation into child abduction. There are most likely more; it is up to you now".

Walter stood up ready to leave.

"Where are you going"?

"Back to my office, where do you think. You read those files and study the pictures. Speak to my officers they have been told to cooperate but tread carefully they don't trust you lot; memories of the old days when anti-corruption was crap"?

"Just tell me who".

"Read the dam file, what's in there will make you cry, or it should do if you have any empathy left; just put them away; forever, Vernon".

Vernon Smith and Walter Munroe had served together as PCs in Brighton many years before; not exactly friends but knew each other well enough. There had been a period when Brighton had been investigated by anti-corruption where, to put it mildly, several senior officers had been found wanting. The two PCs were not involved but learnt how corruption had crept into their station and they were lucky to have not been swept up in the aftermath of dismissals.

The next three hours saw Chief Superintendent Vernon Smith hold back on his emotions more than once. This file handed him was the ammunition he needed to arrest Vale and Branch right now but that would be too easy, they would clam up and seek legal protection. He would then have to prove every little complaint. Knowing his bosses they would look for ways to cover the worst of this enormous slur on the force, every conviction made on evidence given by either men would be brought into question, a legal nightmare. The CPS would throw out everything he gave them that was even remotely questionable. He couldn't let that happen he feared a whitewash and those bastards just being put out to pasture with a slapped wrist, they might even keep their bloody pensions. His thoughts were running away with him; that should never happen, he'd better make sure it didn't.

Sergeant I want you to make a call for me; I want Branch back here pronto but I want to frighten him a little too. It would be fine if he decided to make a break for it and run, life would be much easier for us if he did.

Vernon toyed with the idea to do what he never did, involve the press. Not yet though, he would wait to see the reaction of his superiors, but once in the public domain they would find it hard to cover up, especially when kids were involved.

Chapter 43

Branch had been sat in his office for best part of the day waiting for Mitch to return. 'Where the hell was he, had they kept him there'?

Mitchell Vale was wise to Smith, he was worried he had someone under cover at the station watching their every move. If he went back there Frank was sure to question him and that would be good enough reason to haul them back, having been told not to talk to anyone. The further away from Frank he could stay the better for him.

He'd send Charlotte and the kids to the villa in Deja and join them later when it was clear. They had bought it a few years ago from the inheritance when his mother in law died. He always kept his finances in England clean. A bit of cash in a safety deposit in his cousin's name, was the only dirty money here, easy to get at any time should he need it. He'd stay at home for a day or two they could call him on his mobile if they wanted.

Frank answered his phone expecting it to be Mitch but was caught out by the voice of Sergeant Bonington requesting he return to The IOPC building at once, some new evidence had come to light he was needed to clear up a few disturbing anomalies. Bonington was very respectful used his full title with please could you come now, a sorry if you are busy, it won't take long and thank you for your cooperation a rehearsed speech leaving no doubt about what was expected.

'What the fuck did they want now, what evidence, they're doing this to put me on edge, if so it was bloody well working'?

He tried Mitches phone again; no answer. Mitch gave him an almighty bollocking and told him to keep his head down after he told him what he'd done to Mary. Frank thought Mitch would be pleased getting rid of another loose end but he was clearly mad called him a 'fucking idiot' and 'you don't bring shit like that to your own doorstep; means I have to clear up the mess you made'. Frank felt deflated but did as he was told so had no recent dealings with Coxy.

Mitch through Cox had been covering the Newman case so it is possible the IOPC were wondering why the investigation had been cut so short. He'd be okay if that was the only reason he had been called back but it could be something else entirely. His choice was limited run or brave it out there were so many things he had done in the past that were way out of order it could be any one of them. Running was not an option at this stage, it was an admission of guilt and he hadn't prepared a safe escape or any escape for that matter, he didn't need one; he didn't feel like that now. He'd said he would be over at once and that is what he would do. If it got hot in there he would shut up and ask for a rep. He did not know who that would be, so would ask for time to consider, delay things a little, give him time think.

"Ah Frank thanks for coming back so quickly it's just we have found a suicide note that shed some light why DI Cox took such drastic action. I think you may be able to clear up some of the questions it has raised".

"I'll do my best Sir, but I had little dealings with DI Cox he was working under Superintendent Vale's instructions".

"Quite so, but the note is very specific concerning the murder of Mary Newman and it mentions you by name. It seems we also have a detailed description of the suspect killer. Can you think why he would mention you in the note"?

Frank was struck dumb. 'What had Coxy said in the note about him. Who had seen him in the pub with Mary, he was well out of the way of the main bar and kept his back to the crowd, what details could they have he was dressed all in black and kept his head down'?

"I have no idea what did it say"?

Smith opened the file and read from the copy of the note.

" *'Vale is a shit Branch even worse'.* Just the one sentence".

"Is that it? He was obviously depressed and was fed up with the job so expressed his anger at me and Mitch".

"Possibly that was all it was but I think not. He also complained he had been forced to close the murder enquiry and was threatened when he hinted he knew who was responsible. Was it you who threatened him"?

"Now look here this is going too far. I told you I hardly spoke to him, let alone threaten him. I had nothing to do with the case and you know I have no authority to close an enquiry anyway".

"That is true but you are great friends with someone who can. Let's move on to the identity of the suspect killer. Did you see the written descriptions issued by DI Cox before they were destroyed"?

"I had no idea there were any".

"I can assure you there were; the originals were found in DI Cox's notebook. We also re-interviewed the witnesses to verify their descriptions. We will leave it there for now Frank. One more question, what can you tell me about Henry Giles and Jacob Snell"?

"That a big leap; what is going on here this is like a witch hunt, I think I need a rep. You know I'm just an ordinary copper, I'm feeling a bit out of my depth here with you now".

"Not so ordinary it seems. That is your right of course, whom do you have in mind"?

"I don't know, you must give me time to seek advice".

"Fine, interview terminated 16:42".

The sergeant turned off the tape.

"You will have access to a phone in the outer office call whomever you like, I will give you half an hour or a little more if you need it. You will not be permitted to leave the office".

Frank was trying to think who would help him, he had almost no friends on the force just enemies. He needed a good lawyer, there was one they had used as duty solicitor a few times he was quite competent and he had been cooperative in helping them secure convictions; the guy's number was in his office he called the station to find it for him. Whilst he waited for the call back he had time to reflect on what had happened today, his situation seemed dire. He felt cold; the sweat of fear that had oozed from every pore during the interview had wet his shirt and underclothes chilling him physically; mentally he was far from chilled; the memory of his hands round her throat and those eyes looking at him in disbelief, came roaring back.

'My God I should have run when I had the chance, they are going to charge me with that cow Mary's murder'.

Even though he was her killer he felt like he was being fitted up, he was no longer in control of his destiny. Things looked bleak. The clerk he'd asked to find the number was quick to respond and he had Richard Marchant on the phone within minutes. A brief explanation of his predicament achieved the desired result Marchant would be with him in under an hour. He asked if Smith was available of the uniformed sergeant who was obviously his guard. He used his radio sent the single word "Done".

"Officer Smith will be with you shortly Sir".

Richard Marchant spent twenty minutes with Branch who put him in the picture. He did not tell him everything.

"Look Frank it is difficult to judge what is going on here, I suggest you listen to the questions and answer them if you feel comfortable with what you want to say, if not refer to me. Tell the truth they probably already know the answers you should be giving; lies won't help you here. When in doubt or if the truth will incriminate you just say no comment, but if you do that for everything it can work against you. You've been a copper for a long time you know how it works".

"I do that and it doesn't look good; let's get it over".

"Interview with Detective Chief Inspector Frank Branch. Present his representative Mr. Richard Marchant, Detective Sergeant Simon Bonington, stenographer Constable Lucy Marakes and myself Chief Superintendent Vernon Smith. Timed at 20:08. Detective Branch I must caution you before we continue. You do not have to say anything, but it may harm your defence if you do not mention when questioned something which you later rely on in court. Anything you do say may be given in evidence. Do you understand"?

"Yes Sir".

Under caution; things were getting serious, Branch hoped Marchant was up to the task he did not want to be held in custody he really wanted to get away.

"Let us resume where we left off. What can you tell me about Giles and Snell"?

Frank was glad they were going after those two it took the pressure off him as Mary's killer.

"They are two minor criminals who work in our area, low level really, they act as informants from time to time. They are useful to us in keeping an eye on what is happening. We have put away several villains using their information".

"Is that all, low level you say, let me see. We have them running among other things extortion, prostitution, and last but not least child abduction. What do you say about that"?

He looked at Marchant who put his index finger to his lips.

"No comment".

"Giles is under arrest charged with offences relating to Child abduction. Snell is in hiding; a warrant is out for his arrest on two count of murder and you consider them to be low level; you are either incompetent or are lying which is it"?

"No comment".

"I think you at the very least have turned a blind eye to the activities of these criminals in exchange for monetary gain, or you are the perpetrators of these crimes and they are in your employment. I accept you may not personally be running the show but may have been coerced by another, you tell me".

There it was, he had been waiting for it, a sprat being offered. In order to get out of this he had to give up the mackerel in the form of Mitchell Vale. He had used the same technique himself many times before and knew the chances of going free were slim even if he turned against his old mate. What to do?

"Can I get back to you with that one, I need to consult you know".

"Fine we will wait outside".

"Look they want me to give up my boss for me to face a lesser charge".

"You told me they were investigating a suicide of a fellow officer and were trying to blame you, and now we have come up against a whole new set of charges nothing to do with the suicide; what do you want me to say"?

"Just tell me what is best".

"Leave it to me, say nothing".

Marchant knocked on the door indicating they were ready.

"Chief Superintendent Smith, my client made me aware of the facts surrounding the unfortunate suicide of a colleague, but now a whole new line is being presented. It would be unfair to continue until I have had more time with my client. It seems complex so I will need more than a short while to understand what is at stake, in view of the late hour I suggest we terminate this interview and return here tomorrow".

"I take and accept your comments as valid and will delay this new line of questioning, however before we conclude tonight I would like to go back to my earlier investigation concerning the death of DI Cox. DCI Branch please can you explain the fact that we have photographic and witness evidence showing you were with Mary Newman just before she was murdered".

His stomach knotted; he felt sick and his vision tunnelled almost feinting. It took a moment for him to speak.

"No comment".

"You were also seen entering the alley where she was found dead a few minutes later. Further to that DI Cox left a note to the effect that you and Superintendent Vale forced him to dispose of evidence concerning his investigation into her death. Can you explain or contradict any of this"?

He was fucked, no matter what deal he could conjure up by giving up Vale they would not negotiate with a murderer.

"No comment".

"Frank Branch you are under arrest charged that on the night of October the 16th last you did murder Mary Newman contrary to common law. You are still under caution and will be held in custody until such time as you will appear in court. This interview is terminated at 21:05. Officer take him away".

Vernon turned to Richard Marchant, what he was about to say would determine whether he could secure a good case against Vale; the evidence so far was at best circumstantial, even the photographs of him at the so called safe house could be explained away. Vale was clever, he kept a buffer between him and the villains he used. He needed Branch to confess and give up Mitchell Vale. If the incentive was strong enough it could happen.

"Mr Marchant you may accompany your client to the cells. Off the record I suggest you give him some good advice as there are other charges pending of a more disturbing nature; he knows what these will be so don't let him fool you into thinking he is innocent. If he cooperates fully we may be able to help with regard to sentencing and much more in his interest where he may be placed after his conviction. A policeman in an ordinary prison on a murder conviction commands some sort of twisted respect but one who has abused kids will be lucky to keep his balls attached. Let him know we are prepared to negotiate, but he has to be with us one hundred percent".

"Look Smith, I am just a duty solicitor not a criminal defence lawyer; however I am not stupid, I know what you are trying to do. I will pass on your comments and advise him to instruct suitable legal counsel before he speaks to anyone again; however I will not advise him to confess. I don't like bent coppers any more than you do so I hope you get what you want. I doubt if I will be involved after today. Goodbye Chief Superintendent and good luck".

Smith waited for the room to clear turned to Sergeant Bonington smiling, knowing they had achieved a reasonable result today.

"Not bad so far Simon. We have a straight solicitor no less, still Branch will get the message at least. Let him stew for a few days. Our next effort is on following the money they both must have stashed it away somewhere. I tell you what sergeant, contact that detective from Basingstoke, DCI Webb, I think she seems to have her head screwed and her super network ferret Busion may be able to help. Give them a call perhaps you can go down there, see what they have apart from what is in the file. I want more arrows for my bow before I tackle Vale".

Sergeant Simon Bonington was up very early, hoping his VW Golf would not be held up on the 'sometimes parking lot' of the M25. Traffic jams were the bane of his life, the old girl tended to overheat. Today he was lucky, the run was trouble free, turning off the M3 motorway sooner than expected arriving at Basingstoke police station an hour before his scheduled meeting with DCI Toni Webb. He parked in what seemed to be an available place, he left a note in the windscreen to say where he would be just in case it was an allocated slot.

Smith had educated him well, the role of the Independent Office of Police Complaints, still known as anti-corruption by most old hands, had its problems in the past. It was feared and not without cause. Many good officers were questioned to the point of distraction and had their reputations tainted by the mere fact they had been called. Results were poor and unsatisfactory in many cases; hence the creation of the IOPC.

The new department staff were finding it hard to put the past behind them. Show a friendly and a considerate approach to all, was Smith's advice; the only officers who received less were the ones who had crossed the line and even then you stayed nice until you had the evidence and were really sure.

Soon it would be the turn of Superintendent Mitchell Vale to receive that friendly consideration, but before then Simon Bonington was here to find the evidence needed to make his boss really sure.

"Come in young fellow sit down how was your journey"?
"Fine Ma'am thank you".

"Good. I expect you have guessed already I'm Chief Inspector Webb we spoke earlier; I am happy to help you nail this officer to the wall, so ask what you like, look where you want and use my guys to ferret out anything and everything you can okay. Constable Compton Busion is the one you want, she will introduce you to her team, if you need more time than today, stay over, it's too far to commute; Compton or one of us will sort out somewhere for you to stay".

Toni stood when she saw Mel by her door, Simon followed.

"Ah. This is Detective Sergeant Frazer; thanks Mel, Sergeant Bonington wants Compton's den, show him where to go. Let me know how you get on Simon; door's always open here".

She went back to her desk and buried her head in a file leaving Simon and Mel walking away side by side towards the stairs.

"Quite a shock eh"?

"Err yes I was expecting ... I don't know what I was expecting".

"Someone different I think. She's a woman of ideals and dogged determination. Do your job well and she will back you to the end; follow me and we will go and meet another one who is different".

"That would be Constable Busion I think, what's so different there"?

"Another workaholic plus she thinks off the wall at times, if you want anything to be found online our little 'hacker extraordinaire' will find it; her office is two flights down".

Although down in the basement Busion's domain was large and well-lit, four desks each equipped with the latest terminals; Unix based systems, on a hard wired LAN; connection to the outside was through a special terminal with firewalls a match for anyone who would try and breach them. The one-man IT department two doors along had less equipment but he was often involved with Compton and her team in developing their own unique software. He was responsible for all the station officers terminals, not connected to Compton's machines.

"Hi there Mel, who's your friend"?

"This is detective Sergeant Simon Bonington, he's from the IOPC".

"Bloody hell what have you done Mel? Oh my God is it for me what have I done? Whatever it is, it wasn't me and if it was I didn't mean it, please don't take me away"?

"Don't fret Compy he not after us".

"Thank goodness for that, what are you here for handsome?"

"He turned to Mel you dead right there, she is different".

"I'm not different, you are! And don't talk about me behind my back; come on Simon tell Compy, what can I do you for"?

"I've been told you are the one to come to if I want information not normally easy to get at".

"Of course you have, all legal and above board, me"?

"I don't know or care about that I just want to put away bad coppers, if we have to play their game a little to catch them out that's okay by me".

"Who are we after today Simon, someone nasty I hope"?

"Very much so, the guy we think is running the child abduction racket".

"Ah that would be Vale or Branch or is it both"?

"We already have Branch for the Murder of Mary Newman, thanks to you lot I believe, but Vale is of a different order. He has kept his hands clean delegating in secret using Branch to do all the dirty stuff ".

"Can't you turn Branch to give him up you must have enough on him to do that".

"Oh yes we have but all the evidence is circumstantial; Branch is not a credible witness it will be the word of a murderer against an officer of high rank with an exceptional arrest record. His superiors will be busting a gut for it not to be true; some pretty powerful people will be on his side; we don't even know if he is the top dog here. Vale can refute our questions, especially those based on Branch's statement, easily enough".

"What about the photos of him at the safe house"?

"On their own they mean nothing he can have prepared a legitimate reason to be there. What we need is the money. No way has he done this without payment, there has to be a substantial nest egg or two that he won't be able to explain. That is what I would like you to find".

"Love to, young man; you know we have just the chap here who does that kind of research in his sleep. Together we will find this pot of illicit gold and spirit it away. Are you married Simon"?

Simon felt his cheeks redden and saw Melanie give a chuckle.

"My, you are direct aren't you; you're the clever one, if you really want to know you can find out without my help".

Melanie shot a dagger like look at her friend but couldn't hide her smile whilst rescuing the visiting officer from his embarrassment.

"Thanks Compton we will be back, let you get started eh. Follow me Sergeant we can go and speak to DI Davies he has been working the case and is the fellow Constable Busion was talking about, he is a fraud expert. What can be better for you than a computer whizz and a master seeker of illegal money".

"That Compton is really something, I hope DI Davies is less up front".

"Take no notice of her she was just winding you up, Harrold Davies is very down to earth, he's not my direct boss I work with DI Jonny Musgrove, but has been a big help on this case, more your type, straight as they come".

They arrived at the squad room at a busy time, a get-together meeting where the day's work was being allocated. Now they were officially off the abduction cases, there had been a vacuum for a day or so but that was quickly filling, catching up with the more usual work of a country town force. Mel walked over to Harrold's desk where he had been issuing Peter and June their task to check on a burglary from the day before. Mel held back waiting for Harrold to finish and the officers to leave.

"Sir, this is Sergeant Simon Bonington of the IOPC".

Harrold offered his hand which Simon took. A firm handshake and a smile to go with it, made him relax.

"DI Harrold Davies, welcome to Basingstoke sergeant. The Chief has briefed me on what you need, between us we should find what you want. Villains are basically greedy, they always lie, especially to preserve their ill-gotten wealth and they feel invincible when they have been undetected for so long. These are their main weaknesses in that order; greed, lying and invincibility. Thanks Mel we will be fine from now".

"I will see you later Sergeant, good luck, find me if you need to stay over, I have a decent place in mind".

"Thanks".

Melanie wandered over to the other side of the room where Jonny was sitting.

"Morning Mel who's that"?

"Sergeant from IOPC, name of Simon Bonington, chasing up dirt on Vale before the interview, he thinks Vale could get off without more evidence".

"I bloody hope not is there anything we can do"?

"No, I don't think so, not yet anyway. Compton and Harrold will follow the money, best way to flush him out".

"Good, keep an eye won't you".

"Of course".

Mel looked over to see Harrold and Simon leave. Spoke aloud to fall on deaf ears as Jonny was immersed in his computer screen.

"Going downstairs I expect, they have a long day ahead, I'd better book the Hotel he won't be going home tonight"

"What was that Mel"?

"Nothing Sir, do you need me for anything"?

"Not at the moment".

His attention immediately returning to the Desktop screen. Mel moved over to her desk and computer, she was going to poke around into Vale's background herself for a while; the cousin interested her.

Two hours in had produced little results, It seemed Vale lived within his means. Vale's salary of a Chief Inspector was around fifty five thousand a year after tax. His home cars and lifestyle reflected that income. His joint bank account was always in credit by a couple of grand give or take, with a savings account of ten. He used the savings for his twice yearly holidays and Christmas nothing out of the ordinary. They checked the camper van that his cousin owned and found it was in fact purchased when money was transferred from Mitchell Vales joint account; a sum of thirty two thousand. They thought this was the breakthrough but further investigation found that Mrs. Charlotte Vale had inherited a little over seventy thousand pounds when her widowed Mother died a few weeks earlier. The fact that the van had been used by Bailey with a dubious hire agreement was a link to Vale but a weak and coincidental one in tying him to the actual abduction. The balance of the inheritance was transferred to a euro account in Majorca Spain, again in his wife's name. Most of this was used last year to purchase a small villa near Deja, Majorca. All seemed in order, Harrold thought it looked too good too perfect. Most people lived well up to the limit of their income, even the very well off indulged, this man was too good to be true. A sudden splash out of Thirty odd thousand on a camper van the family never used, was out of character if he was as careful as he seemed. Perhaps it was his wife who instigated that purchase after all it was her money; the same may be true of the villa. Harrold wanted to dig deeper.

"Compton, can you check to see how much that villa cost for me and see who actually is the registered owner".

"Sure what are you thinking".

"Vale has not put a foot wrong in his own name, maybe the wife is where we can find a weak link".

"Okay Harrold give me an hour I'll see what I can do".

Whilst he was waiting Harrold decided to go through the joint account in detail, sometime the most innocuous thing would trigger an idea he could work on. His sole income was his salary after tax, some small payments such as refunds on returned purchases and one when he sold his car, and his wife's inheritance. The house was paid for, the mortgage finished after twenty five years of regular payments, no abnormalities there, no sudden big injections of cash. The household bills were mostly by direct debit. His children were at state school, the eldest about to leave and go to university. They both had small bank accounts into which he paid a regular fair sum. All of this was too clean there must be some oddity; he gave up it was not to be found in his everyday dealings. If he was receiving cash in the UK he was not banking it here. He must have a deposit box for paper currency; other money will be in overseas accounts, but none could be found in his name in the obvious European countries, that left Swiss accounts, but there was no indication he had been there in twenty years. Spain and France were the places he went on holiday and the odd time to Jersey he must look at these again.

"Harrold, Simon, come here, I have discovered where it is or some of it at least".

"The villa in Spain belongs to his wife, she paid for it from her Spanish bank account. She paid thirty thousand euros leaving her just over ten thousand euros in that account. Here is where it goes wrong, I thought it would be a crap sort of a villa for thirty K so had a look at the original property advertisement literature, luckily it was still online. It has four bedrooms all with en suite, large everything, with a sea view terrace, and pool. It was on offer for three hundred and twenty thousand euros. There is no mortgage or outstanding loan against this property that I could find, there is no way she got that piece of real estate for thirty grand".

Simon did a little dance, took Compton's face in his palms and gave her a big kiss full on the lips.

"Gotcha, you beauty gotcha".

"Hold your horses Simon it is not that simple".

"What do you mean Harrold that's a lot of unaccounted for cash he won't be able to explain that much away"?

"He doesn't have to; he wasn't the purchaser his wife was and she is not under investigation. It is possible that she had a private arrangement with the vendor to pay the balance by instalments or deferred till a later date. She may be registered as the owner but she may only have a shared use of the property in line with what she has paid. We have no access to the contract so your case against him is not remotely watertight; you will have to take your kiss back".

"I'll keep digging I don't want to give my kiss back".

Harrold laughed.

"Compton you old tart go on then, it's a good start early days yet".

Simon blushed again although not sorry for his exuberance or the kiss.

"How can we get to see the contract Harrold"?

"I'm sorry Simon we can't, not from here anyway. You could search Vale's house; you may find some paperwork relating to the sale but I doubt she keeps her contract there; there is a downside though, by trying to get a warrant he would be alerted before you were ready, you need solid evidence when you bring him in; you must not give him time to cover his tracks. We will see what comes up when we search for the agent who sold the property, and we'll investigate the previous owner as far as we can from here. If you use what we have found as it stands it will backfire, he can deny all knowledge of the arrangement; the wife has only to offer a reasonable explanation even if unproven, and your efforts will be regarded as out of well out of bounds, your Commander will force you to call a halt. Let's keep going you may yet have an excuse to give her another kiss".

"I heard that; can't wait".

She winked at Simon then asked Harrold

"Do you know the wife's maiden name"?

"Hang on it should be in his personnel file. Yes here she was Charlotte Katherine Crundle before they married".

Compton then spent the next hour trawling the accounts of banks in France Spain and the Channel Islands for the name and all combinations. Simon sat behind her marvelling at the speed of her fingers and programmes she was using to whittle down the massive search. She'd had several hits in Jersey and Guernsey two in France and four in Spain.

Two stood out from the possible combinations both with the name of Mitchelle Charlot. A sterling investment account in Guernsey of more than six hundred thousand pounds and a Euro savings account with BNP Paribas at Rouen France of just under one million euros. These two showed no activity and all details were blocked. All other accounts flagged up were current accounts and had much smaller sums they were in regular use; seemingly genuine. She was unable to obtain an account holder address from either and her request direct to the bank in France for the dates and nature of the deposits was refused. No accounts used any combination with the names Katherine, Crundle or Vale. The only certain overseas Vale family account was the joint Spanish account found earlier. If one or both of these were Vale's corrupt money he had hidden it well.

"Ma'am we have a small problem I need your help. I want details of an account in France, Rouen to be precise; your friend over there may be able to do something. Another in the Channel Islands; I can handle that one".

She went on to explain their search and how they were getting closer. Toni left Compton with her promise to do what she could and hung up.

"Hello Jules, I hear your officers have made arrests".

"Ah oui Toni, we have more to do, the suspects tell us much, we will follow the route for other clinics. I ask Commandant Hergeot send report for you okay"?

"Thank you that will be good. I have a favour please; we need details of bank account for Mitchelle Charlot, BNP Paribas Rouen. We have no way to see this, can you help?"

"Of course mon amiss for you it is done; I will send information par email yes"?

"Yes, merci, I will come to see you when we have finished this business".

"Oh yes, that be very good; any more for you I do today"?

"No thanks Jules, bye".

Toni called Compton with the news. Harrold had been busy and returned to the Busion den with a list of Vales leave dates over the last seven years, and his holiday destinations.

"If we can tie the dates of his visits to France and the Channel Islands with the dates of deposits it will add to the strength of our claim these accounts are his. Any chance you can do that"?

"I expect so but not yet the boss is trying to get the French account details and I have a friend at the Bank of England who tracks money laundering schemes to free up the information from Guernsey. We have to do this covertly so will have to wait a while for either to happen through official channels".

"I noticed there were no hits in Spain and Vale has been there quite a few times, don't you think this is odd".

"Not at all. Many Spanish institutions are not available to us; several of the smaller banks are closed off from our search engine".

"The Vales often go to Deja on Majorca; can you make a specific search to see if there is a match to a bank in that area".

"Possible; I can try but to search through private accounts without authority or a warrant is hardly legal. I doubt I can do that without leaving a trace. If I am spotted then anything I gather will be inadmissible and will open me and by that I mean us, to prosecution; what is worse he will find out".

"Do it in the afternoon the Spanish will be at siesta and by the time they go back to work you will be long gone".

"It doesn't work like that Harrold but you have given me an idea; now buzz off you two go for a coffee or something, I have some heavy hacking to do".

Harrold and Simon left knowing that Compton would not give up till she had an answer.

Hola, a small bank a few miles from the luxury resort of Deja in Majorca had two interesting accounts. One in the name of Mitchelle Charlot and another Charlotte Vale. The former had deposits of over four hundred thousand Euros, the latter less than four thousand. At the moment she was certain her interception of the data was undetected but downloading a complete history could not be done without ringing some serious alarm bells at the bank. She set up the hack ready to download the Charlot and Vale accounts and at the same time a second programme to run a search of every fifth account in the bank's archives. When the alarm was triggered in the afternoon, no one would be ready and by the time it was being looked into a hundred or more accounts would be affected. No money would be missing and at the end of Compton's intervention all would return to normal. Access to the two accounts would be hidden in the chaos; it would be put down to a computer software glitch. When it turned out all was fine the Hola Bank manager would breathe a sigh of relief and he certainly would not be telling their customers of such a 'little problem'.

It was all coming together nicely, deposits into all accounts were found to coincide with the Vale's holiday visits. Jules had fulfilled his promise and sent a complete dossier via Busion's email. The Guernsey bank responded without delay once the Bank of England fraud unit asked for cooperation. The French and Guernsey accounts showed only deposits and no withdrawals. Still not proof the account holder was a member of the Vale family. The Spanish account in Deja, was much more promising as there had been internal transfers from the Charlot account to the Vale account, not large sums but enough to show they were run by one and the same person a Mrs Charlotte Vale. Compton wondered if Mitch vale was aware his wife had foolishly made these transfers; she thought not. Another arrow for Smith to use. The final clincher was the address of all the accounts; the same PO box in Rouen which was registered in the name of Mitchell Vale. Vale had been clever but no match for Compton. She left her desk and took the stairs up to Toni's office, calling in at the canteen on the way guessing correctly Harrold and Simon would be there. Harrold knocked on Toni's door. They left fifteen minutes later all four with smiles on their faces.

"Well do I get another kiss or not"?

"You deserve one for sure, but I'm sorry for my earlier spur of the moment reaction, I don't normally do that sort of thing".

"That's okay Simon I was only pulling your leg; I hope what we have gathered here will do the trick. Harrold and I will keep digging we'll let you know if we find more".

"Thank you both and thank DCI Webb for me too, I'll keep in touch with what happens".

They made their way to the exit Harrold shook Simon's hand as he bade him farewell. Compton accompanied Simon to his car.

"Where are you going now"?

"Home why"?

"You know it's after midnight and Sergeant Frazer has already booked you in at the local Holiday Inn".

"Oh I didn't realise; it is a bit later than I thought; where has the time gone?"

"Look follow me, I pass your hotel on the way home it's not far, much safer to drive back tomorrow, don't want you falling asleep at the wheel do we"?

"Okay I am feeling tired, thanks".

Compton and Simon left the station car park, one behind the other, each feeling satisfied with the day's result.

Chapter 44

Simon was up at the crack of daylight, he skipped breakfast to be ahead of the daily rush; anxious to be at his desk when Smith came in. He was excited by the information he had gleaned at Basingstoke and knew his boss would be more than pleased. He wondered if his Super had learnt anything new from Giles and if they had traced the whereabouts' of Snell.

"Let us form a plan of action, sergeant. I will have to take the lead, he won't allow a junior officer question him, but I will want you to make a comment so that he will object. I would like to expose his lack of willingness to cooperate fully; his objection to your intervention will stand out when we play back the tape. I want to make sure we have enough to hold him here before we bring him in. No wriggle outs for this slippery bastard".

Chief Superintendent Vernon Smith and Sergeant Simon Bonington spent the next three hours formulating the sequence of questions which they hoped would lead Superintendent Mitchel Vale down a cul-de-sac he would fill with his lies. Lies blocking his way out. By lunch they were as ready as they could be. Simon had called Busion to see if she had anything new; she hadn't but promised to call at once if she found even the smallest item of interest.

"Simon please find out Superintendent Vale's whereabouts and request his presence at once. If he doesn't respond go and bring him in under caution".

His enquiry at the Camberwell station informed Sergeant Bonington Superintendent Vale was at home. When he called his wife answered.

"This is sergeant Bonington of the IOPC ma'am, please may I speak with Superintendent Vale".

"Wait a moment sergeant".

"Yes Vale here, what do you want"?

"Please Sir, it is requested that you come to the IOPC office today to help with our continuing enquiries".

"What time"?

"As soon as you are able Sir, Chief Superintendent Smith will be waiting".

"Fine, I'll be along".

Vale hung up. He was hoping this Cox business would go away but in his heart he knew IOPC wouldn't let it lie. He now had to think whom he could have as his rep. It would be good to have someone more senior that Smith at his side but when he told them what it was about they would want to steer well clear; his reputation did not help in this situation. A good brief would be better someone with a bit of guts who would put this Smith in his place if he was even an inch out of order. Gregory Fairbanks would be good and as he was owed a favour now would be the right time to cash it in.

"Ah Superintendent Vale, thank you for coming in I assume Mr. Fairbanks is your representative, we have met before. Good morning Sir"?

"Good morning, before we proceed it would have been more in keeping with my client's rank that he be summoned here by a senior officer".

"My sergeant was instructed by me, I can assure you Superintendent Vale was accorded all respect, his attendance here is voluntary and was a request not a summons. Shall we go through".

Five persons were in the room Vale and Fairbanks took seats on one side of a long table, Smith and Bonington the opposite, A female stenographer sat at a small table to the rear. A twin recorder to the far end. When everyone was seated Smith began the preliminaries; the recording was started, time and date were stated along with the names of all present; the young stenographer began typing verbatim all that was said. Chief Superintendent Smith was in his element.

"Superintendent Vale I have to inform you Detective Inspector Frank Branch has been charged with the murder of Mary Newman; in view of the fact you are his senior officer and long-time friend it is necessary for me to caution you before we proceed with this interview. You do not have to say anything, but it may harm your defence if you do not mention when questioned something which you later rely on in court. Anything you do say may be given in evidence. Do you understand"?

"Yes".

"It has been established Mary Newman was an informant who has be working at several police stations as a transcribe clerk. She has been providing information for a long time to DI Branch for illegal purposes of his own. He says Detective Inspector Cox was forced by you to hide the evidence; this is what caused him to have a breakdown resulting in his suicide. This is supported by the note Cox left. Did you know Mary Newman"?

"Not that I recall".

"Let me refresh your memory; she was employed at your station two years ago, since then you have endorsed her employment by other stations on no less than five occasions".

"If she worked for our station I would not have come in with her contact on a daily basis. If her work was considered to be of a good standard my staff would have written a report to that effect, I would then have signed off that report along with many other documents brought in front of me. This endorsement would have carried over from job to job providing her work remained satisfactory. I have no memory of this girl".

"Why do you think DI Branch killed this girl"?

At this point Gregory Fairbanks intervened.

"I understand Branch has been accused, but your question to Superintendent Vale assumes Branch is guilty. That fact is unproven therefore he cannot have an opinion and will not answer".

"I will rephrase the question; do you have any idea why Branch would want to kill Mary Newman"?

"No, I was unaware DI Branch even knew her".

"Did Branch come to you after the death and ask you to cover up his involvement"?

"No he did not".

"When you learned of the death you passed the investigation to DI Cox is that correct"?

"Yes".

"Can you explain why DI Cox, in his suicide note, would accuse you and DI Branch of forcing him to hide evidence implicating DI Branch"?

"I have not seen this note so cannot comment, he was obviously not in his right mind, so whatever he said there is not to be taken seriously".

Sergeant Busion now spoke up loud and angrily as Smith had planned he should ; this was a very suitable moment.

"What do you mean not to be taken seriously, the man killed himself when working on a case you had given him and when he opens his heart confessing to committing a crime forced upon him by you it is not serious"?

"I will not answer you; I do not expect to be questioned by a junior officer; I expect to be treated with the respect my rank deserves and demand I be questioned by an officer of equal or senior rank".

Smith knew Vale was rattled as his aggressive tone; a tone that would be as clear on the playback as it was now.

"I'm sorry about that Vale, my sergeant is obviously much more upset than yourself by the loss of a fellow officer; he will desist from further comments. Let us move on. We have discovered around the time of her death Mary Newman had passed on to DI Branch the whereabouts of an Alfred Bailey who was caught recently abducting young children. We have cctv of you surveying that very house; will you please explain what you were doing there"?

Vale was shaken, this was too close for comfort he needed time to think a no comment at this stage would be damming; he needed to provide a good reason. He asked to consult with Fairbanks.

"Gregory I don't know how they got those pictures I was following a tip off what shall I say".

Gregory Fairbanks knew that was a lie his long experience told him that Vale was corrupt and although he had agreed to be his advisor he was not going to become involved beyond the minimum. He would find a reason to walk away as soon as he could.

"Look Mitchell I don't know what is going on here, if you were there through a tip off then say so, if not tell them what really happened, but do not offer a no comment, remember they are asking questions where they most likely already know the answer; you've been a copper long enough you know how it goes".

"I went there after DI Branch told me he'd had a tip off, he suspected there would be drugs".

"Very odd for you to go there personally, it wasn't even on your patch; why didn't Branch pass it on to the Drug Squad"?

"I don't know, Branch wanted to make the bust himself but was unsure before he called in a large force, I helped him out".

"As a friend"?

"Yes".

"Do you often do things for your friend DI Branch outside your expected normal duties"?

"He's a friend and long-time colleague, It was not illegal".

"Do you know this Alfred Bailey the man who was supposed to be at the house you visited".

"Of course not".

"Then how do you explain he had free use of a camper van belonging to you".

"I don't have a camper van".

"We have a van in our forensic laboratory registered to your cousin but originally purchased by you. Your cousin is the keeper but you are still registered as its owner, we even found your fingerprints inside. Explain your statement that you don't have a camper van"?

"That van was bought by my wife as a present for my cousin, its only in my name because he did not bother to do the paperwork. I had forgotten all about it".

"Strange; because the hire company, who keep the van at their yard, gave us a mobile number of the person they contact when anyone wishes to use the van. It seems that Bailey had free use permitted by the person at that phone number".

"So what".

"Well it is either you or your cousin who would do that and the record of calls for that number were found by interpolating the masts shows they were made in the area in or around Camberwell Police station. How do you explain that unbelievable coincidence"?

"No comment".

Mitchell Vale was not easily broken he felt cornered by this new turn of events, he'd had no option but to 'no comment' for he had no reasonable answer; they were calls made by him but never expected the unregistered pay as you go phone to be identified. He felt a cold shiver when he remembered it was sitting in his desk drawer at the office. He must hide it before they do a search; shit maybe they had already done so whilst he was sitting here. So what; it was all circumstantial there was no real proof but not good all the same. This bloody Smith was very thorough; he'd have to brave it out.

"Have we finished; I'd like to discuss my options with my representative. There does not seem to be a charge of any kind here all you have is the note of a deranged man, the word of a possible killer and some circumstances you have interpreted in completely the wrong way. I have work to do and need to return to my office".

"No we have not finished by a long way, you my consult with Mr. Fairbanks of course. I will arrange for some refreshments however you will not be permitted to leave this room, you have fifteen minutes. Sergeant Bonington, CS Smith and stenographer Marakes leaving the room at sixteen eleven".

"You have gotten yourself in a bind Vale I don't know how I can help; you are going to need someone better than me if this comes to an arrest. You'd better tell me if they are going to come out with anything more, I'm at a loss without some prior knowledge, thinking on your feet against this lot is a tightrope, one slip and they will can hang you".

"Gregory I've done a lot of things in my time but no different to many others just wanted to keep the villains at bay. They may find some old skeletons I don't know what. Just get me out of here today. I can come back tomorrow I have to protect my family".

"I'll do my best what they have so far is serious but not enough to lock you up unless they go for an arrest which I think is unlikely. We'll see what else they have then I will pull out all the stops this one time. You understand I'm not the best man for this, I'll not be here tomorrow".

The room was again ready with juice and coffee untouched on the table tape started at sixteen thirty one; preliminaries complete.

"We have investigated your finances in order to be sure there have been no transactions considered out of the norm for an officer of your rank. This was conducted with discretion in accordance with current police regulations. We have found no trace of any untoward dealings here. However we did wonder how you were able to buy a house in Majorca. There was no transaction from your account here".

"That's easy to explain; my wife had an inheritance which we used to buy in Spain, and the van was also bought from the same money".

"Who owns the Spanish house"?

"We both do I think, I'm not sure it could be in Charlotte's name, I left all that business to my wife; I'll have to ask her to be sure".

"Do you have a mortgage"?

"No it was paid up years ago".

"I meant on the Spanish property".

"No, well I haven't taken out one and I doubt if Charlotte would have done without asking me".

"So you own the whole thing no partners or anything"?

"No its all ours for when I retire".

"Good enough, now do you have a bank account there"?

"Yes my wife has a euro account its easier when on holiday to have a euro card less charges or mucking about with exchange rates; we use it a lot when on holiday".

"Sounds reasonable where did the money come from"?
Vale thought this guy is fishing trying to make out we had bent funds there. He knew there was an acceptable sum of euros in that account so he was feeling okay to continue.

"The balance of the inheritance plus a thousand or so euros she transfers from home from time to time; we use it when on holiday and top it up when we can. I don't know how much is in there at the moment, I can find out if you like".

"That won't be necessary. Remind me how much did you say your wife inherited"?

"I didn't say; but if you must know it was a little over seventy thousand".

"And you spent it on a camper for your cousin and a place in Majorca is that right"?

"Yes most of it, or rather, my wife did; it was her inheritance not mine".

"You had no say in where it was spent then"?

"No I didn't mean that; it was a family decision".

"Of course that's as it should be, I'm sorry I made the wrong assumption it's just you keep mentioning your wife had the accounts in her name and the inheritance was hers and not yours. I see now you decide financial things together, is that right"?

"I already said didn't I"?

"Yes you did , now let us clear this up once and for all. Your wife bought a camper for how much"?

"Thirty two thousand give or take"?

"And the house in Majorca"?

"Thirty I think".

"The balance about ten thousand was put in her holiday account, is that correct"?

"Yes I believe so".

"Good that settles my mind where you were able to spend what seemed to be beyond your income. The Hola bank confirms the account in the name of Charlotte Vale has a balance of a three thousand nine hundred and eighty eight euros, just as you might expect. The problem I have is another account, at Hola bank under the name of Michelle Charlot, has a balance in excess of four hundred thousand euros. How do you explain that"?

Vale went cold; how the fuck did they get to that account; it was locked solid or so he thought; the Hola Bank Manager had promised him anonymity nothing had ever come out of that account he would deny it was anything to do with them; he hoped to Christ he wasn't going to lose it.

"I can't it's not my account"?

"Or your wife's"?

"No of course not".

"Then how do you explain she transferred money on several occasions from the Michelle Charlot account to the Charlotte Vale account, small sums just a few hundred or so each time"?

He couldn't believe his ears, what had she done, the stupid bitch I'll kill her, his mind was now in turmoil. His throat was dry so much so he couldn't speak. He reached for the glass of juice, which had remained untouched until now. He swallowed slowly attempting to calm the anger directed at his wife, his voice returned but not knowing what to say he sat in silence for a full minute.

"For the tape Officer Vale has failed to answer. Do you wish to comment"?

Smith waited for ten seconds which to Vale felt like forever; the words would not come. He turned to Fairbanks who looked him in the eye and shook his head indicating he should keep quiet.

"I take your silence as a 'no comment'. We will move on"?

"I believe you said your house in Deja cost thirty thousand euros and it is all yours with no mortgage or loan outstanding; is that correct".

Vale nodded his composure returning, he would brave this out.

"Yes that is what I believe".

"We have looked at the advertising literature for your house it was on offer for three hundred and twenty thousand at the time you purchased it. Do you expect us to believe you only paid thirty thousand for a four bedroom luxury villa with a swimming pool for such a paltry sum"?

"I don't care what you believe that is what I was told".

"By you wife I presume".

"Presume what you like you can't prove any different".

"I won't have to the fraud squad is in contact with the Spanish police who are actively securing the contract details from the vendor and the notaria who handled the sale. We will soon know the truth of the matter. We will move on. What can you tell us concerning another two accounts we have discovered one in France and one in Guernsey both in the name of Michelle Charlot"?

His world was falling apart he had no idea how to answer; he just wanted this Smith to stop tearing his life to pieces. Becoming lightheaded like he'd had a skin full; vision closing in looking through an ever narrowing tube; unable to breathe without gasping.

"Shut up, shut up, leave me alone"!

Fairbanks stood and moved over to Vale who was now slumped in his chair eyes closed.

"Please get some help at once; Superintendent Vale is obviously unwell".

Was this an act or was he really sick? Smith had no alternative he picked up the phone and called for the doctor in attendance who was used by the local police. He knew he should have called for an ambulance but did not want Vale to pull the wool over the eyes of an inexperienced paramedic and have himself carted off to hospital. Fortunately for Smith he had met the doctor a few times before, who agreed to come at once or he would have had to resort to an ambulance. In the meantime he loosened Vale's collar and tie. Felt his forehead, which was clammy then checked his pulse which was racing above a hundred. Not faking then; the bad news had caused this attack; proof in Smith's mind the man was so guilty his body reacted to the overwhelming thought of what was to come. He hoped he wasn't having a heart attack he did not want this bugger to die before he'd spent twenty years in prison.

The doctor was attending Vale within fifteen minutes of the call; he listened to the heart took temperature and blood pressure. Vale opened his eyes and was able to sit up.

"Nothing untoward here his pressure was low but recovering, temperature was normal, pulse was a little high but reducing. The heart seems sound".

Fairbanks was concerned for his client even though he knew he was not happy to be representing him.

"What was the cause doctor"?

"A panic attack most likely, a check up with his GP in the next week or so would be advised.

"Is it urgent, should he go to the hospital now"?

337

Vale had recovered sufficiently to be aware he was being talked about.

"What's that you said about hospital; what happened am I alright"?

"You are fine; a feinting attack brought on by stress you will be okay in a few minutes, you won't need to go to hospital and you don't need me anymore either. I must go, I have surgery soon".

Smith stepped in he did not want Vale or Fairbanks to start demanding hospital treatment.

"Thank you for coming so promptly Doctor, officer Bonington will walk you out. Mr Fairbanks, Superintendent Vale in the circumstances I will call a halt to the proceedings for the time being. Superintendent you will be escorted to a secure room with a couch and all facilities so you may rest and recover fully; you may ask for refreshment as you wish, an officer will be at the door which we will leave unlocked in case you feel unwell again. We will reconvene in an hour".

"I think it would be much better if Superintendent Vale were allowed home for the night, I am sure he will give you an assurance he will return tomorrow in fact I will fetch him here myself".

"Nice try Fairbanks but that is not going to happen he stays here. Officers please accompany the Superintendent to the rest room".

Vale rose and walked out listlessly head bowed between two burly uniforms.

"Gregory, how come you are representing this scumbag"?

"He called me; said he was being harassed by IOPC about officer Cox's suicide he did not tell me more. I think he was unaware what you were about to reveal; if I knew he was bent I would not have offered my help".

"Now you are stuck with him but it won't be for long, we have more, much more when we reveal what he has been up to it will make you sick".

Smith allowed Vale an hour to think and sweat. He may have used the respite to gather his thoughts and make up some story or other; it mattered not; he was going down.

"I hope you are feeling better Superintendent".

"A little, can't we do this tomorrow"?

"We won't be much longer I assure you. Now concerning the Michelle Charlot bank accounts. What do you have to say"?

"They have nothing to do with me".

"Would it surprise you to know the French account has a balance of near one million euros and the Guernsey account six hundred thousand euros, along with the four hundred in Majorca that makes a cool two million, Michelle Charlot is pretty well off".

"Still nothing to do with me".

"So it is all down to your wife, it is all her money; is that what you are saying"?

"Of course not the names are just a coincidence".

"I don't think so; have you forgotten she transferred funds from the one in Majorca to her personal account, for which you hold a debit card"?

"It's a mistake, I've no idea why that happened".

"How do you explain that all four accounts have statements sent to a post office box in Rouen registered to you"?

"No comment".

He thought he was safe, he had prepared those accounts so well; untouchable; everyone always did as he told them but that stupid bitch had fucked it all up, wanting to spend money beyond what he'd allowed her; and on what? Bloody women's rubbish no doubt. Now it was never going to be the same, he faced prison unless the powers above were not prepared to bring shame on their beloved force. He may not have the good life he craved but they may want to sweep it under the carpet; a cover up was not out of the question; he'd make a special call when he got the chance. Little did he know Smith was about to squash even that small ray of hope.

"Our French friends have some interesting news too; it transpires your account there has deposits that come from the proceeds of illegal organ transplants. Grimes and Snell have been abducting children on your orders, shipping them to France for your murderous French masters to butcher".

Smith paused, letting the gravity of the situation sink in, he held back on the smile of satisfaction.

"Please stand. Mitchell Vale I am arresting you on a charge of conspiracy to murder Mary Newman. Other charges relating to the abduction and murder of children will follow. I remind you, that you are still under caution. Your representative will make arrangements for you to consult with a solicitor. Officers take him away. Sergeant please switch off the tape and secure the two spools. Constable Marakes, thank you for your time; please have the transcript printed and placed in the appropriate evidence file".

The two uniforms marched him out of the room; not so gently this time and not to the comfortable room as before but to a cell in the basement.

"Wow what was that"?

"Sorry Gregory, I suggest you organise a brief for him and step well away; you haven't heard the half of it".

"Don't worry I'm off now; not sure if anyone will want to take him on, it will have to be a duty solicitor for now and a court appointed lawyer; I don't envy them that task".

Gregory Fairbanks left never to return.

"I don't normally do this Sergeant but I'm going to buy you a drink. That was magic, even though I say so myself and your contribution was brilliant. What's your poison"?

"A pint of bitter would be great Sir".

"Come on Simon, I'm thirsty".

" Just a quick call Sir and I'll be with you".

"Toni Webb"?

Simon smiled and nodded.

"Good job; let's go".

Chapter 45

Toni Webb was at a loss, many unanswered questions where whirling around in her head, not least the still unknown leak. Almost everything had been taken away from her, even though her teams were following up with tracing those who were involved in some minor way. The case against the child abductors was now with serious crime, the corrupt police officers were in custody being dealt with by IOPC. Her French counterparts were in process of rounding up their own suspects and recovering children who may be still be missing. Her evidence and files had been sent to both parties; she should really be able to sit back and relax; however it was not in her nature to leave questions unanswered. She picked up the phone.

"Jules, bonjour".

"Ah Toni mon amis; how are you"?

"I am good my friend, please I would like to come and visit; not just about the investigation, although I would like to know how your officers are progressing, I need to get away and to see you would be wonderful".

"I will ask detective Hergeot to send you a full report, he has done good I comprend; sorry for English some words difficult".

"Don't you worry I know what you mean; you are well ahead of me I have almost no French; perhaps you can teach me a little when I see you. Reports from Maurice are fine we have some already but I want to see for myself where these children have been taken. I want to try and understand how Doctors who vow to preserve life can do such dreadful things; it can't be just greed".

"So, are you coming to see me as a friend or is it official? I will have a room for you at my house".

"As a friend first, business second and Jules don't make yourself trouble I can stay in a hotel".

"Monique happy to see you; she be very upset if you no stay at our home".

"You are too kind, please text me your address I will come in my own car. I have one maybe two days to clear my desk, I will call you before I depart. Aurevoir Jules".

"I am joying to see you soon. Goodbye Toni Aba".

Toni smiled at his reference to her old name which brought back pleasant memories. Quite a few things to do; it would be great if she could clear her desk by close tomorrow and set off the morning after. She spoke first to Munroe to tell him all was quiet at the moment so she was taking a few days leave not telling him, or anyone else, where she was going. Her detectives were quite capable to deal with anything in her absence. She booked the tunnel for a morning departure anyway; nothing like a deadline to concentrate the mind.

Chief Superintendent Smith was in a unique position he did not have to answer to anyone outside his independent department. If he suspected officers more senior to him he had the power to question them. In real life however pressure from above was difficult to resist. The most senior officer in the Met was Commander Newton Blakewood; when he called you answered; and call he did.

"I understand your position Vernon but you do realise that pursuing a case against Branch and even more so against Vale would bring into question all the cases they had ever dealt with; we would have lawyers crawling all over us demanding retrials and release of their clients for a dozen reasons. It would be a nightmare".

"But Sir these two committed murder and instigated the stripping of organs from children for money. They salted away thousands of pounds over many years and abused their position as police officers to demand others bend to their will. They deserve life imprison".

"I know, I know I feel the same as you but we must look at the larger picture. I can arrange to quickly dismiss them at once for abusing their position of trust and make sure they do not get their hands on any of their ill gotten money. We will keep an eye on them to make sure they do not start up anything illegal again. What we don't want is to be forced into releasing a multitude of villains from prison or face lawsuits for compensation just because those two fucked up".

There it was, the not unexpected cover up to protect his arse and the money he may be forced to concede in lawsuits or was it more than that; maybe Vale and Branch were not the top dogs; had influence from elsewhere prompted the Commander to follow this path. Vernon was senior officer in this case he would resist, but in his own way. The Commander needed some reassurance so he would pretend to go along with what he was suggesting, for now anyway.

"I understand the difficulties it will bring but the nature of their offences will make it difficult to hide, too many people know about what they have done. If they are seen to go free someone is bound to kick up a fuss, what do you suggest"?

"For now we can bide our time if anyone asks what is going on say you are still gathering evidence. We will keep as low a profile as we can for as long as we can then release them quietly under the protection of their lawyers to return to us on completion of enquiries. That could last for anything up to a year. It will have all died down by then; we report their dismissal for unacceptable conduct and they slip quietly into retirement".

"Hm. It could work what about their pensions"?

"If we withheld payment, someone may ask questions concerning the nature and seriousness of the offence, best let sleeping dogs lie, eh Vernon".

"I'll think about it Sir I may have a better way; I'll get back to you. Is that all Sir"?

"Yes I think so, nasty business; well done, by the way, for wheedling them out we don't need people like that in the force now do we".

Vernon Smith wanted to smack the Commander in the teeth, 'we don't need people like you either' he was thinking. There was no way he'd let them get away with what had just been suggested. He would quietly investigate this man Newton Blakewood and his associates, he would be very careful these men were powerful and dangerous. What he was about to do next was a little underhand, it went against his normal behaviour but he wanted to strike at the heart of this corrupt pair with no get out clause.

"Sergeant Bonington we have a problem".

"The Commander"?

"Of course, it is what I feared; pressure is being applied from above, they want to bury this. Vale may have friends in high places; I suspect more likely our leaders are worried the fall out will affect their lofty positions. I don't know how high this reaches but must find out if Vale has someone in his camp pulling Blakewood's strings. I want you to be very discreet, by that I mean don't get caught snooping under any circumstances, find out who he has been talking to recently, see who his friends are, any communication from anyone outside his normal contacts. Perhaps you can use our friend in Basingstoke".

"I can't believe they want to cover up child murders and a level of corruption that defies belief".

"They will put all the blame on Giles and Snell. They will use Serious Crime's concentration on the search for Snell as the prime news story; their aim being to divert attention away from the IOPC. We have strict non-disclosure rules so can't be seen to show bias by promoting our case in public. I have an idea where our friends in the country may be able to leak this to the press without any comeback; leaving us clear to proceed with our case against these two corrupt police officers unhindered".

Whilst Simon left to call on Compton Busion, Vernon Smith made a similar call to DCI Webb.

"Detective Webb, this is CS Vernon Smith of the IOPC, I have a need to speak to you about our position regarding certain doubtful evidence supplied by your station".

"What evidence have we supplied that you now find has a problem"?

"Not something I am prepared to discuss over the phone I will be down to see you today, please make yourself available".

" I am due to go to France in the morning".

"Don't be concerned I only need an hour to put you in the picture, you will not miss your trip; the fact you're travelling abroad is fortunate"

"I'll be here".

"Simon did you make contact".

"Yes Sir".

"Good we will be leaving now".

"Chief Inspector Webb I need your help".

"What is this about questionable evidence"?

"Forget all that; it was said to satisfy another problem I have; I will explain and then perhaps you will want to help".

"Go on I'm all ears".

"I had a visit today from Commander Blakewood, he persuaded me to downgrade the charges against Vale and Branch, or so he thinks. This is not going to happen. I believe they may have bugged my phone hence my cryptic call to you. I need them to think I am going down the route suggested, so if they think I am calling into question the evidence it will keep them sweet. They will think I am here to persuade you to cooperate".

"You know I have thought someone other than Mary Newman was an informer; I had a feeling it went much higher; do you think it is Blakewood"?

Not sure; possible he is just bending with the wind looking for an easy way out of trouble; could be someone else is jerking his chain, my sergeant is here to look at who it might be; with the help of your constable Busion if you don't mind".

"No problem, I'll call her".

"I think he is with her already".

"I'll leave them to it then. There must be more to this for you to come down here as well as sergeant Bonington. How can I help, you said you have a problem"?

"If we are to prevent a cover up we must make this public, which is something I cannot do. If I leak to the press it will come straight back to me, I will be removed and some puppet put in my place; these two bastards will get off with a slapped wrist and retire on full fucking pensions".

"What do you expect me to do; if you want me to phone the papers, instead of you, the result will be the same you will be blamed and removed".

"No that is not the way. I'm aware you have connections in France; their investigation is against French suspects which I believe has led to several arrests. What I want is for the names of Vale and Branch to be revealed by one of their suspects. One of them is bound to know who they are after all they paid Vale thousands for the kids; trading the names for a consideration on their sentences I'm sure is done there the same as here. French police have no axe to grind, as far as police corruption is concerned, so naming them in the French papers would not be a problem for them".

"I like the idea, once the French press have a story about corrupt London police being involved, the British press will be all over it like a rash. No way a cover up will be possible then".

"There you have it, do you think you can help"?

"I'm going to France tomorrow; it was to be just a personal visit. I am seeing an old friend who is influential but has nothing to do with the case. I will explain what is happening he may help I don't know. He will not allow anyone inject false testimony concerning the names but if one of the suspects gives them up during interrogation I believe he will help. I will have a problem, if the French papers run the story my timely visit will appear to be more than just a coincidence. Don't worry I have broad shoulders; I don't care what they do to me as long as they are put away".

"I knew I could count on you, thanks DCI Webb".

"Now we are 'partners in crime' Vernon, please call me Toni".

"Yes, okay. Thank you Toni".

"Now let's go down to Compton's den and see how Simon is getting on".

"This guy knows a lot of people; I am making a list of those in Government and in the police at the rank of Chief Superintendent and above. I will put them in order of number of times contact has been made, by phone or known face to face. I can't know if we have all his contacts or the numbers of meetings; not without the chance of being detected".

"Sounds good Compton, how long will it take"?

"Not long, I am using the same programme when searching for the cars; half an hour or so".

Waiting was obviously not one of Smith's strong points so Toni suggested a coffee in the canteen; he accepted.

"Simon look at this our Commander Blakewood seems to have a most friendly relationship with our Assistant Chief Constable. Several official phone calls not unusual but a few private calls on mobiles too. The dates are significant with these private calls as they are the same as the abduction dates and one just before the raid on Reynolds farm".

"It must be a coincidence. The ACC would not have access to the daily events at Basingstoke his office is in Winchester. Let's see who else is talking to your ACC."

"Well what do you know, Superintendent Munroe speaks to him regularly".

"This is not unusual after all he is the boss".

"I suppose you're right Simon; we are seeing gremlins everywhere. We will let Toni and Smith see our research results they will know what to do".

"Come on Compy let's keep looking what else can we find out about Blakewood; on a more personal level this time".

Compton smiled; this was the bit she liked best.

Chapter 46

Today was the first time Toni had used the tunnel; on the few occasions she had visited the near continent the ferry had been her crossing of choice. The speed and efficiency of the 'Chunnel' set up impressed her. It took longer to drive from Basingstoke to the terminal than it took to be well on the road to Rouen. She had set the address Jules had sent her into the satnav, it gave her a projected journey time from the Calais terminal to the house of just under two hours. Her call to him, the night before, confirmed he was eagerly waiting to see her again. Toni was a conservative driver keeping well below the more than eighty miles an hour speed limit of the French motorways; she also stopped in an 'Aire' for a coffee and the loo about halfway so her journey took a little longer than the electronic prediction. Early afternoon saw her pull up outside a modest and very old house set in its own grounds. Two similar houses were on one side about fifty yards distance. They were resting in a short lane halfway down one of the steep hills of Rouen overlooking the river Sein. Many colourful trees and shrubs abounded in front and to the side; the yellow, red and dark brown leaves of Autumn were scattered everywhere; a few flowers hanging on from Summer dotted the bushes here and there. A silver Citroen was parked in the long drive to one side leaving plenty of space for Toni to park her modest Ford. She was turning into the space behind the Citroen when the front door opened revealing a face aged but well remembered. Jules moved over to the door as Toni eased herself from her seat. As she stood he took her shoulders in both hands and kissed her twice on each cheek.

"Welcome old friend come to inside".

Toni kicked the door of her car closed with her heel allowing herself to be led through the front door straight into a living room of a size that belied the small exterior facade. A short grey haired woman moved from the window towards her and completed the welcome with a single kiss on each cheek.

"Bienvenu Toni, a chez nous".

"This is my wife Monique she speaks only a little English, from school days a long time before".

Toni took her hand and smiled; eye contact between them lingered, sending a message of a warm welcome far more sincere than words.

"Merci madam".

"Please say me, Monique".

"Yes, Monique I will".

"Please have a seat a coffee a glass of wine"?

"A coffee will be good black no sugar".

After a long hour of reminiscing with a glass of red wine following her coffee; Toni was shown to her room by Monique whilst Jules, as instructed, fetched her small case from the car. A rest before dinner was the order of the day. She lay on the bed not intending to sleep but succumbed in a few moments.

A tapping on the door and a call of her name to get ready found her floating like a feather in the breeze, adrift looking down on her body, prone in a steel box, her torso had been opened and her insides laid bare, an empty carcase for all to see, there were no eyes, they had taken her to pieces and given her life to someone else.

Jules called again when there was no response.

"Toni wake up, is time soon, dinner one half hour".

Toni woke with a start, feeling shaken, sweat on her brow, she looked down to see she was still dressed laying on top of the quilted bed. Jules voice calling her name finally registered on her conscious mind.

"I'll be down soon Jules thank you".

The image of her nightmare still fresh in her mind she raised herself from the bed. She would ask the favour of her friend today and lay this devil to rest.

The dinner prepared by Monique was like nothing she had ever had before. A simple soup that tasted of everything she liked but had no idea what. Prawns, the size of which she did not believe existed, cooked in butter and wine. A salad with a variety of unidentified meats mixed with leaves fresh from somewhere also unknown, and chips. A crème desert made from cheese to finish. A white Sancerre like nectar smoothed the way to a sleepy feeling.

"Monique, Jules that was magic, a meal to remember merci".

Monique left the table clearing the plates, Toni stood preparing to help with the washing up when Jules shook his head indicating she remain seated.

"I know you have something on mind speak me now".

"I am sorry to bring you in to my problem but you are the only one I know who can help. We have two police officers who are very corrupt we have good evidence but the power they have is strong. Their names must appear in the news or they will win. They organised the transport of our children to that house and have killed for money. I cannot go to the press in England direct it will damage the case and they go free".

"Ah I see you want me to leak names".

"Oh no not you, one of your suspects must tell the names to Detective Hergeot, he can then have official press conference, you know what I am saying"?

"I do, I do. You send email to Maurice on private number I give you with names, nothing more, I will speak and he will do rest".

"I wanted to visit the sites of where children died but it is best I stay away until this is all finished".

"That is good then you stay your time now with us; we take you for tour of our Belle Ville Rouen, oui"?

"Oui Jules I like".

Chapter 47

Commander Newton Blakewood sat with Montague Brown, the Assistant Chief Constable of Kent looking at the headlines of the Daily papers in dismay.

"How the hell did they get hold of this, that bloody Smith must have opened his big mouth; you can kick his arse out of there right now".

Newton thought he knew different.

"I don't think so, he was quite cooperative when I spoke with him, he will prove useful in the future. Have you read the article"?

"I don't have to it is blown wide open look at the bloody headlines will you".

'SENIOR LONDON POLICE IN CHILD ABDUCTION AND MURDER SCANDAL'

"If you read more you will find the French police have made arrests, it was they who came up with the names of Vale and Branch not Smith, it is all over the French press, that is how our papers got hold of it nothing to do with IOPC".

"Well the result is the fucking same; we have to go all out now and tell Smith to bring them to trial asap. We must appear proactive and show we were well ahead of the French in dealing with this terrible corruption".

"You don't have to pretend with me, save it for your press conference; remember it was your officers in Basingstoke who broke this case, you may as well go and extract your piece of glory if nothing else".

Brown didn't get much chance to enjoy the limelight, his Chief Constable conducted the press conferences himself, relegating Monty to dealing with the multitude of phone calls directed at the Chief Constable's office from all quarters.

Commander Blakewood's struggle with numerous claims for release from those wrongfully imprisoned were only outweighed by the many demands for his resignation. He did not resign; he was not sanctioned in any way. Smith knew then this man was all powerful, untouchable and confident. Vernon would bide his time.

Following a call from Toni, Smith did arrange for Mrs. Duden's brother John to be released on parole pending a hearing of a claim for a mistrial.

Henry Giles had been put away for life the first week in February. Frank Branch had received his multiple life sentences two weeks earlier. John Digby was found well along with eleven other children from all over Europe, discovered safe at various locations in France and returned to their homes.

The downsides were the six families suffering at the funerals of their young loved ones and the second defiled body in the garden having been identified as Sean Brightwell.

The French police had made multiple arrests, trials pending for many who had committed these acts of evil.

Jake Snell remained at large; investigations were underway to trace his whereabouts; DI Fortune was confident of a result soon.

This journey for justice was as complete as it could be from Toni's standpoint; another journey would no doubt be undertaken soon.

Chapter 48

The Four Horseshoes was brimming with many of the station officers from Basingstoke. Hot chicken wings and copious amounts of beer were being consumed. Colin and Simon had driven down for the occasion. Compton's thirtieth birthday just happened to coincide with a guilty verdict at the trial of Mitchell Vale. Jonny had called from the court with the news; he and Toni were on their way from the court in London and would be with them soon to join in the double celebration.

§

Text received by Toni Webb.
'I think Commander N.B'.
Text reply to Vernon Smith.
'I know; I can wait'.

The End

Printed in Poland
by Amazon Fulfillment
Poland Sp. z o.o., Wrocław

62706976R00211